The Black Maria

R.P.G. Colley

Novels by R.P.G. Colley:

Love and War Series:
The Lost Daughter
The White Venus
Song of Sorrow
The Woman on the Train
The Black Maria
My Brother the Enemy
Anastasia
Elena
The Mist Before Our Eyes
The Darkness We Leave Behind

The Searight Saga:
This Time Tomorrow
The Unforgiving Sea
The Red Oak

The Tales of Little Leaf
Eleven Days in June
Winter in July
Departure in September

**The DI Benedict Paige Crime Series
by JOSHUA BLACK**
And Then She Came Back
The Poison in His Veins
Requiem for a Whistleblower
The Forget-Me-Not Killer
The Canal Boat Killer
A Senseless Killing

https://rupertcolley.com

Prologue

Moscow, 28 February 1992

Stepping out of the taxi into the weak February sun, I felt as though I'd been smacked in the face by the intensity of the cold.

'So, this is where she lives,' I said, as the battered Trabant sped away through the snow.

Caroline, wrapped in fake fur, pulled her hat down over her ears. She turned and smiled at me. 'Poor Richard, your nose is red,' she said, laughing. Around us, the snow fell, its flakes caught by the sun, glittering like gold dust.

It took some fifteen minutes before we were able to find the right entrance to the apartment block, by which time, my feet were becoming uncomfortably cold. Relieved to enter the warmth of the large lobby, we approached the concierge; a squared-jawed man sitting behind a desk, reading a newspaper, a damp cigarette clamped on his bottom lip. Caroline showed him the piece of paper that had the address written on it, and spoke to him in what sounded, to my ignorant ears, like fluent Russian. The man eyed us suspiciously and responded in a dulled tone, the cigarette moving where the lips did not.

'Fourth floor,' said Caroline.

'*Spaseeba*,' I said enthusiastically, feeling slightly foolish by his lack of response.

In the lift, Caroline uncoiled her scarf. 'Are you ready for this?' she asked, as she removed her hat and shook her mane of bleached hair.

'No, it's going to be grim.'

'Oh come on, Richard, don't start that again. We're here now and there's nothing to worry about.'

'But what happens if I find out something I don't want to know?'

She sighed; we'd had this conversation before. 'Like what exactly?'

'I don't know – something about my father.'

'What, like he was a KGB agent? Look, all we're going to find is some old lady wanting to reminisce about her life and put in place the missing pieces of her jigsaw. It'll be fine.'

'Thanks for coming, Caroline.'

'Don't be silly, I wouldn't have missed it for the world.' She leant forward and planted a kiss on my lips leaving behind the lingering taste of her lipstick. The lift doors opened and moments later, we were outside the apartment door. 'Go on then, knock,' whispered Caroline.

I held my breath – I was about to meet my only living relative and it was too late to turn around. My Russian ancestry was not something to which I'd ever given any thought. I'd been born thirty years ago in Russia but I was English, brought up in London and, as far as I was concerned, that was that. But now, I was about to come face to face with the Russian grandmother I had never known. Would she see her son in me? Would I see myself in her? Would she approve of me? Did it matter? No, not on the face of it – she hadn't been part of my life. But having no parents now, I felt as if approval was the one thing I craved in my life.

The apartment door opened and there, in front of us, was a plump middle-aged woman with butcher-like arms. Caroline opened her mouth to speak but the woman, clearly expecting us, beckoned us in. She pointed to a coat-rack and, three short steps later, we found ourselves in the living room. Sitting in a red leather armchair, flanked by a large yucca plant, was my grandmother.

'Come in, come in,' she said in a heavy Russian accent, holding out her hand.

'Hello…' I hesitated, not sure how to address her. Her first name, I knew, was Maria, but that seemed too familiar and *grandmother* didn't seem right somehow.

'Maria, call me Maria. Please, sit down, sit down.' I liked the way she sensed my dilemma and felt slightly more at ease. She was small and frail, as one might expect an 87-year-old woman to be, but her eyes were bright, her smile broad and her skin surprisingly smooth. The room, stiflingly hot and claustrophobic, smelt of cleaning polish. A large number of paintings adorned the walls, shelves stacked with paperbacks. Caroline and I sat down together on the settee and smiled inanely, wondering what to say.

Maria had a brief conversation with the woman who showed us in, who then vanished into another room. 'My housekeeper Irina,' said Maria by way of explanation. 'She is half my age but oh, how she complains. Like an old hag. Not like me! But she will make us tea.'

Caroline and I laughed, and I felt an immediate warmth for this spirited old woman.

'So, you found me all right, yes?'

She asked after our hotel, our flight, how we liked Moscow and how we were coping with the cold. She spoke quickly, finishing her sentences with a slight chortle. She seemed nervous, but then, so was I. She was dressed differently from what I'd seen of other old Russian women, wearing elegant clothes of vigorous colours and sporting a kingfisher brooch. She'd applied a hint of make-up and one could see the beauty of the woman beneath the years. I wondered how much the make-up and the elegant clothes were for our benefit.

After a while, she stopped talking, perhaps conscious of how much small talk she'd made in so little time. She stared at me with a slight inquisitiveness, taking in the image of her grandson, the lost piece of her jigsaw. I tried to hold her gaze, tried to smile, and found myself feeling awkward under her scrutiny and increasingly aware of how hot it was in her apartment.

'We've brought you some souvenirs from England,' I said, fishing around in my satchel. I passed her a heavy plastic bag full of things I'd bought in the supermarket – English tea, English mustard, golden syrup, chutney, marmalade, and other delicacies of the English palate. She looked at each one in turn, trying to read the labels and making appropriate noises of approval. Placing all the tins, jars and packets on the occasional table in front of her, she smiled, and tilting her head to one side, thanked Caroline and me for our generosity. That, I concluded with quiet satisfaction, was money well spent.

'Richard, I must tell you now, your father – he die last year.'

'Oh.' I thought of my stepfather, dead at fifty, but of course, she meant the Russian father I never knew.

'Yes, last year. A cancer. He was not old.'

'Oh. I see.' I felt my cheeks redden as I desperately searched for something appropriate to say. Who, I wondered, was meant to be consoling whom? Should I appear upset? I never knew the man, and news of his death registered nothing but an awkward awareness that perhaps I should be consoling my own grandmother on the death of her son. I glanced up at Caroline, hoping for a lifeline, some form of intervention.

'He was not a good man.'

Maria's stark verdict was the lifeline I was looking for and I smiled in relief. But then, realising that my grinning face was perhaps not the most fitting response, I tried to look grave and concerned. But my efforts were obvious and Caroline giggled.

'I – I'm sorry,' she blurted.

Maria snorted. 'Poor boy, he doesn't know how to think. But I can tell you, because I can see you are not like your father.' Well, that was something, I thought. 'You have a kind face, a kind heart. This I know. Your father, he was not kind. He could not travel across the city to come see me, but you – you come from England, and with all these lovely things to eat.'

'I wanted to… to….' What had I wanted, what had made me come, almost on a whim? Was it to find a direction in my life? God, I needed one. I was thirty and still had no grounding. I'd spent years floating from place to place, from one job to another, and all my relationships seemed to have lasted less time than the lifecycle of a dragonfly. Caroline, I hoped, was different. I wanted stability; I needed a foundation. Is this why I'd come to Russia with Caroline, to find something that was missing from my life? Part of it, I think, was to find my father. Well, that was one avenue closed already but it hardly seemed to matter. What would I have said to him, what was I hoping to find? Somehow, with this old lady, it was different; here was a buffer zone, an extra generation between us.

'Your father, he thinks he is Casanova, he thinks he can make things into gold,' said Maria, slipping into the present tense. 'Always looking ahead, never looking back. Some people might say that is a good thing, but each time he forgets his mistakes. He tries too hard, always too hard.' I found her words strangely familiar, perhaps that was my problem – never assessing, never learning, always too eager to jump in feet first. There was a silence and I followed Maria's gaze to a photograph on the sideboard. It was a coloured portrait of my father, wearing collar and tie in an official head-and-shoulders shot, with his long thin nose, his dark wavy hair carefully brushed and a slightly self-conscious smile. He was my father, all right – a neater version of myself.

Bursting in with a tray of tea and biscuits, Irina broke the uneasy silence. 'Here we are,' declared Maria. 'Put it on the table here,' she instructed Irina in English, gently pushing my gifts to one side of the table. Irina glared at her and said something in Russian, which, by its tone, sounded like, *Where else would you have me put it?* before disappearing again.

'Karen, you pour,' said Maria.

Caroline looked awkward but obliged.

'Richard, please, take a look at my photographs and the pictures.' I smiled and rose, self-consciously, to my feet. 'Don't be shy,' she said with a hint of a laugh.

On the sideboard, next to the portrait of my father, was a photograph of a soldier, tall with jet black hair, his arms folded, grinning at the camera. Framed pictures of Maria caught her at various stages of her life; her eyes always sparkling, her pose natural. Sometimes, by herself, sometimes with children and family. Sitting among the photos was a small golden bust of Lenin, with that permanent scowl etched on his face, and a curious little wooden bear, its paws clawing the air; quite fierce looking. The paintings on the walls were also framed – mostly small landscapes and churches. At the far end of the room, opposite the window, was a large painting, a proper work of art and, to my untrained eye, an original. It was a country scene, a small gathering of peasants crowding around a wooden table. The men all looked strong, their sleeves rolled up, the sweat glistening on their collective brow. The women poured and handed around pitchers of drink, their faces smiling, their cheeks full of country air. It was an impressive piece of work but let down by its ham-fisted propagandist message, its overt triumphalism. I was about to turn away when my attention was caught by the woman dominating the far right of the painting; holding a jug, wearing blue overalls, her hair tied back – I recognised the sparkling eyes.

Caroline handed Maria her cup of tea. 'Thank you, Karen; you make a good Russian wife. So, Richard, you like the big painting?'

'Yes,' I said, noticing the flush in Caroline's cheeks. 'I was just admiring it. It's good, very good.'

Her face froze for a few seconds and I feared I'd said the wrong thing. 'Yes,' she said slowly, 'those were the very words my Petrov used.'

'Petrov?'

'Sit down, Richard, sit down.' I liked the way she pronounced Richard, each syllable stretched so that it sounded like *Reech-hard* with a double 'h' in the middle. 'Tell me now, you are an English boy, yes?'

'Well, technically, I am partly Russian,' I ventured nervously.

'And what do you know of your Russian history?'

'I… er, well, not that much really.'

'I want to tell you a story, my story, and then you will know your Russian history.' She paused and watched for my expression. Perhaps, I looked doubtful, for she seemed intent on justifying her claim, 'Yes, you will know the history of Soviet Russia, for I have lived it. I was born before the Revolution and now it has gone – but I, I am still here. I think maybe I am the last. Not many can survive my life and live to my age. My story will tell you all you need to know about the Soviet Union. And then, you will know more about yourself. You understand?'

'Yes, I think I do.'

Irina re-appeared with her coat on. The two women exchanged a few harsh-sounding words and then, without acknowledging us, Irina picked up a set of keys from the sideboard and left abruptly, slamming the front door behind her.

'What age are you, Richard?'

'Thirty.'

She sipped her tea. 'Thirty, hmm. I was here in Moscow when I was your age in nineteen thirty-five. I was married, for my second time. I am suppose to envy your age, to be so young, to have one's life before one. But I do not. My heart beats with fear when I think of myself as a young woman in those days. It was the year I fell in love. That should make me happy, no? But love in those days brought danger. Do you want me to tell you?'

Caroline and I exchanged glances. We knew we were in for a long haul but, at that moment, despite the overbearing warmth of the room, I knew there was nowhere else I could be. This was a story that preceded my own existence, a tale that might show the twists and turns that would, ultimately, lead to my own beginning. How could I not listen, how could I not know?

'You must understand,' said Maria, 'never before have I told my story. You are my grandson but you know nothing of me or my country. It is not your fault, of course. But for you, Richard, and Karen, I will tell this story, and then you will know.'

'OK, that sounds…'

'Many times, I have remembered this story. Some facts, I do not know. But I imagine them so well, and so many times, they are as good as true to me. My story begins with a secret. But this is too terrible to tell. I know I will be damned when soon my time comes. This is the part I have not rehearsed – you must understand, it is too difficult for me. Perhaps, I tell you – another day, I do not know. I came to Moscow, with this secret inside of me. If anyone knows, I will be arrested and sent away to the prison camps, I cannot say a word. No one knows. In nineteen-thirty, I come to Moscow and meet a man, Petrov. We marry but I was not in love. No, that came later when I met Dmitry – such a handsome man. I was friends with his sister, Anna. I remember so well, I was with Anna in my apartment and she was telling me about her brother. She makes me a cup of tea, like this, and I remember her words exactly. She says to me – "I suppose he is quite good-looking. But as his sister, it is not something I think about"…'

Part One

Moscow, 1935

Chapter 1: The Invitation

'I suppose he is quite good-looking. But as his sister, it's not something I think about.' I was polishing a small golden bust of Tchaikovsky while Anna was trying to describe her brother Dmitry. 'I've always found it rather strange he's never married. Too busy painting, I expect.'

'Good looking, you say?' I asked pointedly.

Anna's nose wrinkled as she grinned at me. 'You're a married woman, Maria Radekovna.'

'Hmm.'

Anna was the only person I could consider a friend. A good ten years older than me, she looked younger by wearing her hair in a bob. She glanced over at my brother. Viktor sat in an armchair in the corner of the room. The chair, now mottled and pink, had once been red and the odd spot of its former colourful glory still showed. A pile of books substituted a missing leg. Viktor's sunken eyes were closed; his head slouched against the stained blanket on his chest. I went to him and placed the Tchaikovsky bust between his hands, and pulled the blanket up beneath his chin and around his shoulders. His breathing seemed so loud in the smallness of the room.

'He likes his Tchaikovsky; it reminds him of better times.' I smiled at him as a mother would to her child. 'He has his good days,' I said almost apologetically. 'Days when he can wander around the apartment and talk a little. He'd be dead by now if they hadn't let him out. At least, here, he can have the dignity of dying at home.'

I knew Anna felt sorry for me – where once I'd tried to maintain a clean home, everything had gone to seed since Viktor's return. The whole place smelt of boiled cabbage, and the feel and smell of damp hung in the air. Piles of clothes and old crumpled newspapers littered the linoleum floor. Kitchen utensils were heaped in a dish for fear of them being stolen by my neighbours in the shared kitchen. A Primus stove stood in the corner, towels drying over the clothes horse, and the only window was covered by a torn curtain that hung precariously on a sagging wire. To anyone who didn't know it was as if I didn't care any more.

Petrov had not always approved of my friendship with Anna. He felt she wasn't quite the right type to be associated with, lacking the true credentials of a proletariat. But Anna and I continued to meet once or twice a month while Petrov was out at work and gradually he became more tolerant of my older friend.

'So, tell me, does your Dmitry live comfortably?'

'Of course, he's an artist; he lives like a king. They gave him a furnished apartment *and* his own telephone. They even gave him a dacha. He gets what they call an artists' ration as one of the "creative intelligentsia". So, he has access, you know, to the special stores and he helps me out. I could never invite you to dinner at my apartment.'

Viktor coughed – a tortuous, rasping cough that woke him up and made Anna jump. He glanced around the room and his eyes settled on her for a few seconds but he made no attempt to acknowledge her or show any sign of surprise that she should be there. After a few moments, his eyes closed again and his head lolled back down against his chest.

'He'll be OK for one evening,' I said. She was offering to cook for Petrov and me at her brother's apartment; a rare night out for us.

'Rosa's welcome to come to dinner as well, if she wishes.'

'Anna, it's very kind of you, but she always has her own plans. You know what eighteen-year-olds are like. But thank you, I'm looking forward to it.'

'Is eight o'clock OK? You've got the details?'

I fumbled in my pocket for the piece of paper on which she'd written Dmitry's address and read it out aloud.

'That's the one,' she said.

I stared at the scrap of paper and re-read it to myself a couple of times. It would soon become an address that would be forever etched on my memory.

*

Why had I known that that evening would change my life? What inner voice had forewarned me? Perhaps because I was willing it to happen, for *something* to happen because I knew that my future lay not with Petrov. I owed Petrov my survival, my existence, but where once he was my protector, he had become my warder. Where once he had given me the chance to breathe, he was now suffocating me. I was only thirty and still had hope for something better. But there was one thing I knew I couldn't escape from – and that was my past. It lay within me, an unspoken tale that would haunt me forever more. It was inescapable. Sometimes I longed to tell someone, to allow the unspeakable to be spoken. But what choice did I have? My own existence was at stake.

Every day in Moscow one sees beggars; it's a common sight. These are the disenfranchised, the "former people" whom the State has thrown aside as outcasts. One ignores them; for to sympathise, to make any form of social contact, is to tar oneself with the same brush. But I feel for them because, for our first few months in Moscow, Viktor and I counted among their number. Eventually, I found work as a maid for an accountant and lived in a crowded corridor outside his door, working long hours merely for the privilege of food. It was through the accountant that I met Petrov. Within three months, we were married. The ceremony was quick and without fuss, taking place in a small office on the fourth floor of a district police station. We waited in line behind a queue of others – people registering marriages, births, divorces and deaths. But whatever their reason for being there, everyone wore the same expression, one could not differentiate between the joyful and sorrowful. Having waited our turn, we leant against the high counter, signed various forms, paid our three roubles to the sullen, chain-smoking clerk, and left. The 'ceremony' took all of six minutes.

I now wore the mask of a respectable wife to a middling Party activist, but beneath the camouflage, the conscience remained indelibly plagued. I took his family name and Petrov obtained my papers and an internal passport – my new persona was complete. I invented for myself a new history – the daughter of a Leningrad watchmaker, I'd come to Moscow to further my education and to work closer to the heart of communism. Viktor too was able to obtain a new identity and before long his wife and daughter joined him in the city. We'd perfected our history and, it has to be said, it was all down to Petrov. But even Petrov only knows what I've told him and although he knows nothing of our real story, he knows enough to have us stripped of our internal passports and arrested. Without the passport, one is finished – you lose your right to work, your ration card, you are barred from State benefits and the whole Soviet system is closed to you – you wear the stigma like a badge, you are one of the disenfranchised, a former person. As the Party becomes more and more paranoid of alien elements infiltrating its ranks, people are more liable to arrest and deportation than ever before. Petrov knows this but never mentions it. It is enough that I know.

Petrov, I know, is also disillusioned. He's always wanted children, lots of them, and now feels betrayed because I haven't been able to satisfy him. I know his desire stems more from his sense of civic responsibility than any paternal longing; for the State makes it clear that it is our patriotic and social duty to bear future Soviets. Indeed, it pays families with seven children or more about 2,000 roubles a year in child support. Petrov, always fervently keen to fulfil his social obligations, sees it as a failing in both of us. My infertility has become the subject of silent reproach, a ritual of humiliation.

I also want a child; I simply don't want Petrov as its father. Perhaps God is aware of this, for after all this time I am still without child, despite Petrov's best efforts to the contrary. I'd hoped he would divorce me and find himself another, more productive wife. Divorce is so easy in the Soviet Union – you don't need the consent of the other and can be done in a matter of minutes. But despite his revolutionary leanings, Petrov is, in many ways, old-fashioned and won't contemplate divorce. Especially, as he thinks he loves me. Of course, he doesn't – he's never experienced real love to know the difference between love and habit. Sometimes, I visualise myself walking into a registration bureau and signing the declaration of divorce, freeing both me and Petrov from our mutual encumbrance. If only he knew it, he'd thank me. But I know that far from giving me a future, such an action would bring the past back to the present and my mask would slip and fall.

And so, for these last five years, I have lived as Maria, with my invented history and my assumed name as Petrov's attentive wife.

It was time to break free. It was time to live again.

Chapter 2: The Dinner Party

The following evening, a cold blustery night, Petrov and I arrived at the appointed hour of eight o'clock. The building, according to Anna, had until recently been a run-of-the-mill tenement block before being spruced up and renovated into an artist's co-operative consisting of over a hundred luxury-sized apartments. Petrov and I gave our name to the portly concierge who pointed us towards the lift.

As we walked down the echoing corridor, we exchanged glances, his eyes furtive behind his rimless glasses. It was almost as if we felt guilty to be in such surroundings. This corridor did not stink of cabbage, nor was it populated by ragged occupants, nor piled high with rubbish and decaying food. I think Petrov realised how far down he came in the Party's pecking order. We knocked and, as we waited, I quickly straightened Petrov's sombre blue tie. Petrov was nearer to Anna's age but, in appearance, seemed older. He was wearing his customary dark suit and polished black shoes, and, for the occasion, had specially trimmed his moustache and goatee. The door opened with a flourish and we were greeted by Anna.

'Welcome, comrades,' she said rather formally, 'come in.'

'Hello, Anna,' I said, planting a delicate kiss on each cheek. She took us through to the main room that was bathed in a warm welcoming light. The table was already laid for dinner. A large, patterned rug covered the expanse of floor; the walls of the room were painted a dark yellow and everything seemed so spacious compared to what we were used to. There hung, as usual, portraits of Stalin and Lenin, and another of Molotov. Among the photographs were a number of small landscape paintings. I wondered whether these were the work of our host. Standing in the corner, wearing a checked shirt and a brown corduroy jacket, opening a bottle of red wine was, I presumed, Anna's brother. He smiled at us as Anna showed us in, placed the bottle on the table and stepped towards us, hand outstretched.

'Hello, welcome. I'm *the* brother, Dmitry, how nice to meet you.' His voice was deep, each word carefully articulated. I felt myself blush as he shook my hand. His eyes were dark and had a slightly mischievous look about them, etched with prominent laughter lines; his hair, black but slightly greying, was longer than was customary and swept to one side. And, I couldn't help but notice, he smelt of aftershave, such a rarity in Moscow. He was tall – at over six feet, he towered above Petrov but his posture was slightly stooped. He looked strong; this, I thought, was not a man routinely bothered by food shortages.

'I hope you're both feeling hungry,' he said.

'Mmm.'

'If you'll excuse me,' said Anna, 'I need to check in the kitchen.'

'Do you need any help?' I asked, thinking how nice it must be to have a whole kitchen to herself. What a difference between this domestic splendour and my own sordid accommodation with its communal kitchen and shared utensils.

'No, no, it's all done, just the finishing touches, you know.'

Dmitry smiled and I couldn't help but feel a tingle of pleasure at the way he looked at me. 'Please, let me take your coats.'

We chatted about the weather and our journey there. Anna reappeared from the kitchen, wiping her hands on her apron. 'Dinner won't be long,' she said.

As Dmitry lit the candles, Petrov wandered around the room, picking up ornaments and books as if inspecting them for auction or perhaps for authors who had earned the Party's displeasure. In the corner of the room, on a small wooden table, sat a gramophone player and, next to it, a case full of records. I saw Petrov grimace; he evidently disapproved of such extravagance, forgetting how only a few days before, he had talked of buying one himself.

'Looking for evidence of counter-revolutionary objects?' asked Dmitry pointedly.

Petrov laughed with embarrassment. 'No, of course not,' he said. But I feared that Dmitry had already got the measure of my husband.

*

Half an hour later, we were coming to the end of the first course – mushroom and paprika salad. I couldn't remember the last time I had had mushrooms. 'This is truly delicious, Anna. I didn't realise you were such a good cook.'

'It's not so much the cooking; it's having the right ingredients in the first place. I could never have done this without Dmitry's culinary contacts.'

Dmitry laughed. 'It's all a matter of where to go.'

I glanced at Petrov. I could tell he felt uneasy; he liked his food simple and this dinner was bound to give him indigestion. 'So then,' he said, helping himself to a second glass of wine, 'I never knew the Party looked upon the artist with such high esteem. I always thought of art as a bourgeois pastime but you seem to be doing well for yourself, if I may say so, Dmitry.' I knew that this was a political rebuke framed as a rhetorical question. Fortunately, Dmitry rose above the implied criticism.

'Well, it's like Stalin says, the artist is the engineer of the soul–'

'A toast to Comrade Stalin,' said Petrov gushingly.

'Comrade Stalin,' we all said in hearty unison.

'Dmitry's been nominated for an Order of Lenin, haven't you Dmitry?' said Anna. 'For his "contribution to socialist art".'

'Well, yes…'

'If he's awarded it, he'll receive it on Labour Day at the Gorky Park celebrations.'

'Congratulations,' I said.

'Thank you, but I haven't won it yet. Although it's what I *do* that's important, you know. Art has a vital role in society. I have a job to do and fortunately for me, the State considers my job as pivotal in expressing socialist realism as it is, or at least as it should be.'

'As it should be?' Petrov was still trying to score political points of his host and we were entering delicate ground. One dared not criticise the State, however obliquely, unless one was totally sure of one's company. But Dmitry was not likely to have his comments misconstrued by a rank-and-file Party activist like my husband.

'Yes, as it should be and as it *will* be when we achieve true socialism. The road is a long, arduous one, my friend, and it may take generations to fulfil Lenin's vision. And anyway, everything you see around you – it's not mine, not in the true sense of possession, all this belongs to the State, I'm just looking after it on a sort of permanent loan, if you like.'

Petrov was getting agitated. He was a man of contradiction. He either fell prey to envy and quickly criticised those who were better off than him, believing them to be contrary to the spirit of true socialism; or he looked disdainfully down on those who struggled, believing that they hadn't done enough for the Revolution to reap its rewards. He was often quoting Marx's edict: *He who does not work, does not eat.* But what really got his goat was when others used Lenin's name as a means of justification. 'But have you no pity for our fellow countrymen out there who go short, who queue for hours–'

'Do you? I don't suppose for a moment, comrade, you have to queue...'

Petrov took a quick slurp of wine to cover his embarrassment. 'No, but–'

'But perhaps you're right, sometimes I do feel oppressed by a sense of guilt. But look at it this way: what I have here is evidence that scarcity is waning. For every citizen who is privileged, there's one less in the bread queue. Soon privilege will be so widespread it won't be considered a privilege any more. *That's* when we'll know we've got there.'

'It's bourgeois decadence if you ask me,' said Petrov quietly.

'No. No, it's not. It's cultural betterment.'

'"Life has become better, comrades",' said Anna quoting Stalin's edict from a few months previously.

'Yes and "life has become more cheerful",' said Dmitry, finishing the quote.

Anna laughed and Dmitry pulled a face. I glanced again at Petrov. He was watching them and something in his eye made me most uneasy. He was trying to work out whether they were sincerely quoting Stalin or, as I feared, mocking him. If they were, they were being unbelievably careless. To deride Stalin or the Party in company, however gently, could mean denunciation and arrest. Anna knew she could trust me but equally, she knew that even I wouldn't trust Petrov. He had never, as far as I knew, denounced anyone socially, but at his work, many had suffered at his hands for their careless banter. Petrov was a staunch supporter of the Party that had promoted him well beyond his ability. His success had depended on their favour and the downfall of his more able predecessors, but with promotion came responsibility and with responsibility came risk. The further you went up, the more likely and the more devastating the fall. He paid the Party his dues with an intense devotion to the cause by uprooting wreckers and exposing enemies of the people wherever he thought he saw them.

Generally, people were more careful now. If you knew what was good for you, you simply avoided conversation of any substance and stuck to the banalities of everyday life. Even a whispered criticism ten years ago could land you in trouble. And I knew of parents who kept their guard in front of their children – especially their children – for it only took an innocent repetition of what Mama or Papa had said to see Mama or Papa whisked off by the secret police, the NKVD.

Needing to divert the conversation, I asked Petrov to regale us with the story he told me about bumping into an old Party friend who had "disappeared" for making a joke about the first Five-Year-Plan. Petrov gulped his wine and told his tale adding unnecessary embellishments and digressions. I pretended to listen and made appropriate clucking noises to show my approval while subtly looking at Dmitry. It was rare to meet someone so full of confidence, so relaxed, so sure of his place in the world. I'd known Anna for about five years and she'd occasionally mention her brother with almost reverent respect. I had built up a picture in my mind of a handsome, self-assured man, but usually, when one has an image of someone, the reality differs vastly from one's preconceptions. In this case, the mental image was unerringly correct – he was indeed self-assured, and he was most certainly handsome.

The main course was something to behold – roasted duck cooked in a black cherry sauce with rice; I hadn't eaten such delicious food for a long time. Even Petrov began to relax, dominating the conversation as he tackled his third and then fourth glass of wine. Dmitry and Anna smiled politely as he talked about his work and shared his fictitious reminisces of his revolutionary childhood on the streets of Moscow. I hated it whenever conversation turned to one's social origins; it was the subject where I felt most vulnerable. I'd become adept over the years at immediately steering the topic to less controversial territory. Accordingly, I asked Dmitry about his painting.

'I have a patron,' he said. 'He finds me work, gets me commissions, that sort of thing. He's the sub-regional chairman of our local division of RAPA.'

'RAPA?'

'Russian Association of Proletariat Artists, of which I'm a member. Moscow East division. In fact, right now, I'm working on a commission – a piece for the director of a locomotive factory.'

'How interesting, what sort of painting is it?'

'Usual thing, a healthy slab of social realism, the nobility of the peasant, that sort of thing. I've almost finished. Maybe if Anna doesn't mind, I'll show you it before our dessert.'

Anna waved her hand. 'No, no, you go ahead, I'll clear up the dishes.'

Dmitry took us to another room and turned on a light, which seemed unnecessarily bright for such a small space. Inside, was a large table pushed to one side, covered with tubes of paint, and palettes, sheets of paper, brushes and various other tools of the trade. The smell of paint and turpentine hung in the air. In the middle of the room was a large canvas perched on an easel. 'It's far from finished yet,' said Dmitry by way of explanation.

'It's good, very good,' said Petrov. I couldn't help but raise an eyebrow; it was so unusual for Petrov to voice a spontaneous opinion, let alone a complimentary one. But he was right; it was good, more than good. It was a bright, autumnal countryside scene, although in an overly idealised style. Of course, in Dmitry's position, he could hardly depict anything different. A table dominated the viewer's eye, and gathered around it were a number of healthy-looking peasants sharing what looked like a well-earned drink. Some of the figures were already well-defined with careful and realistic attention to their weather-beaten but content features. Others were sketchy in their execution, awaiting their characteristics, their proper place in the painting. The men wore overalls, mainly dark blue, some still clutching their pitchforks or hoes. Fussing around them, pouring drinks, were a couple of plump older women with black dresses and practical shawls around their hefty shoulders. Running around beneath the table, a couple of dogs and, playing in the dirt to the left, a small group of children. In the background, a field in the process of harvesting, the straw bathed in golden sunshine, and further beyond, a cluster of trees. Every detail was precisely rendered, every nuance of expression carefully represented. This was what collectivisation was meant to look like, the idealised peasantry, the countryside at its harmonious best.

For a moment, I remembered with a shiver my own experiences of collectivisation, but then the warmth of the painting quickly eclipsed my reservations. This was the work of one man's imagination, the toil of a creative force. I felt privileged to be standing next to its creator, an artist capable of giving life to an abstract, glorified vision in his head.

'Yes, very good,' repeated Petrov.

'Art has to appeal,' said Dmitry, 'and its appeal has to be immediate.'

'It's magnificent,' I purred.

He smiled at me with almost childlike gratitude for my genuine enthusiasm. We looked at each other, longer than was strictly necessary, each trying to read the other's thoughts. It was, I think, the moment I fell in love with him.

*

We were eating Anna's meringue pie and Petrov once again held forth, singing the praises of the Party, proposing frequent toasts to various Politburo dignitaries and, as was often the case, exaggerating his role at work and his responsibility as an unofficial and unpaid informer for the secret police. The slightest digression at his work or the hint of a wrongly placed word, and the NKVD came to hear about it. It was something Petrov was proud of but rarely talked about unless stripped of his modesty by the influence of alcohol. I smiled weakly; Dmitry and Anna seemed on edge.

Interrupting Petrov's flow, Dmitry turned to me and said, 'So, are the two of you planning on children?' Petrov's eyes flared up and I fumbled with my napkin. Dmitry realised his mistake. 'I – I'm sorry, I didn't mean to pry,' he said awkwardly, exchanging a brief glance with his sister.

I looked into my glass and swilled its contents. 'It doesn't matter,' I said quietly.

'Doesn't matter?' growled Petrov. 'Of course it bloody matters. Five years, that's how long we've been married, five years. You'd think in that time, we'd have half a dozen babies, but oh no, not one, not a bloody thing.'

Anna coughed delicately and Dmitry played with the stem of his wine glass, neither of them able to look us in the eye. Petrov, oblivious to the tension he'd caused, finished his glass of wine. Reaching for the empty bottle, he held it up and peered into it inquisitively. Fortunately, Dmitry didn't take the unsubtle hint.

Petrov belched. 'It's all I've ever asked of you,' he mumbled into his glass. 'All I've ever asked and you can't even do that, can you?' I tried to ignore him. 'Five years,' he said, raising his voice. 'I wouldn't even mind that much if it was a girl, I just want a child. But no, my wife here, she can't or *won't* do it. God, it's not as if you have anything else in your boring life, I mean–'

'Stop it, Petrov,' I said, trying to contain the irritation in my voice.

Dmitry and Anna looked shocked by Petrov's outburst. Somehow, I'd been expecting it, but not at this point, not in front of company. Petrov was usually most careful about these things, never one to wash his dirty linen in public. Dmitry twiddled with his dessert spoon. 'Comrade,' he said, 'I know you're upset but I think perhaps we've heard enough.'

'Enough? You haven't heard the half of it.'

I swallowed; desperately trying to check the tears I could feel building up inside me.

Dmitry tried again, 'Yes but perhaps–'

'It's unnatural, that's what it is, and unpatriotic. Every night she uses every excuse under the sun. Christ's sake, she only has to lie there–'

'Enough!' shouted Dmitry, slamming his spoon on the table. Petrov glared at him incredulously, his mouth gaping open. 'Have you no manners, man? How dare you talk of your wife like this in front of others.'

I held my head in my hands, 'It's OK, Dmitry, really–'

'No, it's not OK, he talks only of himself as if you don't exist; and treats you like a second-class citizen…'

Petrov continued staring at his host. 'How dare you speak to me like that–'

'Consider your own behaviour before you pass judgement. You come in here, get drunk and then proceed to abuse your wife.'

'She's *my* wife.'

'And what sort of man do you think that makes you?'

'Not the sort of man so far removed from reality, he lives like a bourgeois nobleman.'

I saw Dmitry take a deep breath as if consciously deciding to resist Petrov's taunt. He turned to face him again. 'I think you should leave now.'

*

An hour later, I was in bed, Petrov next to me, dead to the world, impervious to the discomfort of the mattress, impervious, as usual, to my distress. I stared into the darkness, the tears rolling down my cheeks, and contemplated the gulf that divided Petrov and me, the gulf of empty space between us. It'd been an awful evening for him, an ordeal. He felt intimidated by men of standing, overwhelmed by intelligence, painfully conscious of his own shortcomings. And I can't say I blamed him, for few men could match the charm and splendour of a man like Dmitry. Poor Petrov, always eager to do the correct thing, to think the right thoughts. Deep down he was a good man but I was having to dig deeper and deeper to find the good within the increasingly boorish exterior. And for that, I was frightened.

Chapter 3: The Appointment

At this time of night, the streetcar was almost empty. I sat down near the back and stared idly out of the smudged window. How ugly most of Moscow was – a continual construction site with buildings torn down here and replaced there; old and new side by side, the new Soviet skyscrapers and the old buildings of Imperialist Moscow; the quaint and the ugly juxtaposed in a seemingly haphazard fashion but all uniformly grey and in a constant state of change. But everything looks ugly when one's nervous; when one's stomach is constantly churning over. However many times I made this fortnightly trip, familiarity never took away the dread. Every other Tuesday at ten at night, I crossed half of Moscow to keep my appointment. To keep my side of the bargain, I surmounted whatever obstacles were placed in my way – illness, the weather, transport difficulties – none of it could excuse me from my twice-monthly humiliation. I'd happily forgo the small amount of income this unpleasant duty affords me not to have to continue my sordid work. The headlamps of passing cars illuminated the steady drizzle. The streetcar trailed through the long, straight streets, passing the old squat houses, the uniform apartment blocks, the featureless offices, the occasional church. The time of night and the drizzle had emptied the streets save for the groups of beggars or "former people" heaped in doorways waiting to be evicted and moved on.

I opened my copy of *Pravda*. My eye was caught by an article about the arrest of an internationally renowned chess player for anti-Soviet agitation who, only the month before, had been glorified for his triumphs against foreign opposition. Otherwise, the news consisted of the usual exalted statistics of fantastic production rates, quotas exceeded, of technological advances – a new hydroelectric power station, the "biggest in the world!" Hail the Soviet experiment and let us compare and contrast with the evil capitalist empires and the plight of the working masses under the yoke of scheming exploiters. Here and there, mention was made of Comrade So-and-So arrested for bourgeois sympathy or for lacking vigilance against the enemies of the state. Another article glorified the extension of collectivisation – so many hundred kulaks exposed for lording it over the peasants and transported to some godforsaken place in the dustbin of Russia. It was all familiar fare but I tried to concentrate. Digesting *Pravda* on a regular basis was an important part of one's routine, for one didn't dare express an opinion until one knew where the newspaper stood on it. Whether it concerned foreign affairs, economic policy, or a review of the latest film, play or exhibition, it was essential to echo the newspaper's sentiments. If *Pravda* criticised, you criticised; and if *Pravda* approved, you followed suit. And if *Pravda* hadn't yet voiced an opinion, you kept quiet. People were too frightened to offer their own point of view for fear it didn't correspond with the official line.

I alighted near Gorky Park, from where I walked the rest of the way. Wrapping a scarf over my head, I crossed the road and made my way down a darkened narrow side street, turning left and right into various other alleys, a maze of twisting streets hidden within the main boulevards, punctuated by the occasional square, many decorated with a fountain. The dimmed lights from the small windows provided the only source of light, the sporadic barking of a dog the only sound in an otherwise silent city. I looked at my watch – it was almost ten; my heart fluttered. As I strode on, my shoes echoing on the wet cobbled stones, I tried to rehearse my words, the text of my weekly report. I turned into a short alleyway and slowed down as I approached the house. From the outside, it seemed like any other private dwelling, four storeys high with numerous windows, mostly dark. I approached the front door and pressed twice on one of the many bells. The door swung open almost immediately. A tall, uniformed young man with shrewd, unblinking eyes glared at me for a second before stepping silently to one side to allow me in. The man then leant outside and peered up and down the street. Satisfied that I hadn't been followed, he closed the door.

'Go up, Comrade Rykov's waiting for you,' he said mechanically.

Without acknowledging him, I made my way up the stairs to the top floor and crossed the hallway, where I paused outside a door to catch my breath. I knocked and, upon hearing the tediously familiar voice from within, entered. The room, which I was so accustomed to, had obviously been a bedroom once but had since been transformed into an office. A lamp shone brightly on the imposing mahogany desk, a desk incongruously large for such a limited space. Seated behind it was a clean-shaven, neat man in his late forties, his fair hair thinning almost out of existence exposing a heavily lined forehead. A small pair of glasses magnified his eyes, giving them an owl-like appearance.

'Maria Radekovna, how pleasant,' he said, as if my appearance had been unexpected. He waved his hand by way of offering a seat. I sat down in the hard chair in front of his desk and glanced up at the framed portrait of Stalin on the sidewall. 'How quickly two weeks come around. Drink?' I shook my head. 'Be spring before we know it.' He poured himself a vodka, his teeth bared under his curling smile. Despite his apparent neatness, his fingernails, I noticed, were dirty. His cordial greeting, the offer of a drink and a passing comment on the weather were all part of the routine. I waited for him to ask after Viktor. He took a swig of his drink and, leaning forward, looked at me earnestly. 'So, how's your brother?'

I thought of Viktor sitting limply all day in the armchair in the corner of their apartment, his eyes only occasionally registering my presence, uttering the sporadic half-sentence.

'No better,' I replied tonelessly.

'Oh now, that is a shame.'

My answer and his response were always the same. It was as if the two of us were actors who met once a fortnight to perform lines in our very own play, a play without an audience and without an end.

Rosa had come to terms with her father's dilapidated appearance but in a way, I found rather callous. Rosa's acceptance was borne out of avoidance. Instead, she busied herself with her studies and her new boyfriend, Vladimir. Within the walls of this very office, I had met Vladimir on numerous occasions but Rosa had no idea of my acquaintance with him. And for the sake of Rosa's security, it had to remain a secret.

Rykov picked up a piece of paper. 'Well I must say, Maria Radekovna, your report on the misgivings of the chap from the Technological Institute bore some fruit...'

I felt the tension in my head. I knew this meant that, on my say-so, some poor unsuspecting person had fallen victim to Rykov and his henchmen and had probably suffered dire consequences for uttering an unguarded word to me. Rykov continued, 'Turned out to be a right deviationist. Of course, he denied it, but eventually, he came around.' He stopped and smiled. 'They all do in the end,' he added. 'So good work, thanks to you we've all been spared another bastard of the counter-revolution.' I rubbed my eyes. Rykov smiled again. 'Come, come, don't look so perturbed, there's no point getting all sentimental about it. It's unpleasant work for a woman like you; I appreciate that, but think of what you're doing. We are fighting a war, and our enemy is an internal one, one that doesn't wear a uniform. We must always be vigilant; we can't afford to spare the rod, not until our work is done.'

The words were depressingly familiar, more lines acted out in our personal piece of theatre. I couldn't bear to look him in the eye and instead stared nonchalantly at the small bust of Lenin on his desk, which he used as a paperweight.

'So then,' said Rykov, 'how are things, what sort of fortnight have you had?'

'Usual.'

'Anything new to report?'

It was the question I dreaded, especially when I felt that I did have something to report. Normally, I picked my victim carefully – someone I'd just met, people I didn't really know. What I didn't know about the person, I made up. At least that way, I was spared the crushing knowledge of the repercussions. The more distant the victim, the less the effect on my conscience – that was the theory. However, it rarely seemed to work. For if I didn't know them, I knew someone who did. And then, sooner or later, I'd find out. I imagined the poor sap being woken up in the middle of the night by the dreaded knock on the door and hauled away in a Black Maria. I imagined the hysterical wife or the panicked husband, the bewildered children, the shattering of a family, of a life. But this week I had no casual acquaintance on whom I could report, no life to ruin.

'Well?'

'I'm sorry, Comrade Rykov, this week I have nothing to report.'

Rykov's eyes narrowed. An eyebrow rose. He spoke quietly, menacingly. 'I think perhaps, Comrade Radekovna, you should try to rack your brain – surely there must be something.'

In the six months we'd been acting out this ritual, I had never dared come empty-handed. But surely, I thought, after over a dozen reports, twelve or more lives destroyed, he'd allow me the odd blank. I shook my head.

'Did you not talk to *anyone?*' Rykov was speaking quickly. 'Did you not go out? Were you living the life of a hermit?' He rose from his chair and came to stand next to me, hovering menacingly. 'Yours is not a passive role, comrade,' he said, now speaking slowly, quietly. 'I don't expect you to lie back and wait for things to happen.' He ran his finger down the side of my face. The cold sensation of his touch caused me to shiver. 'I need you to be active, Maria; to mingle, make new friends, find out where their loyalties lie. I thought you understood that?'

'Oh but I do, Comrade Rykov, it's just that—'

'So where's your *fucking* report?' he screamed, his fingers gripping tightly my cheeks, forcing my mouth open.

'Please…' I managed to say, panting from the shock as his fingers tightened.

'What?' His fingers fell away.

'Please. I – I'm sorry, Comrade Rykov, I did s-speak to people but… but no one said anything incriminating. P-people are more enthusiastic these days, they have nothing bad to say.'

'Don't give me that bullshit,' he shouted, spinning away from me. Pacing across his room, he continued. 'More guarded perhaps, but nothing more than that. It's not good enough, do you hear?'

'Yes, yes, Comrade Rykov. I'm sorry, it won't happen again.'

'You assume I'm giving you a second chance?' he shouted.

Of course, I'd assumed. 'Well, I…' I didn't know what to say, conscious only of the tightening knot in my stomach as he stood next to his desk, glaring down at me.

He sat back down with the expression of an exasperated parent. 'You have failed me, Maria Radekovna. So what's to stop me from sending your brother back? Hmm? Answer me that.'

'But please, comrade,' I said, catching my breath. 'You know what state he's in. He'd die if he merely stepped outside; he's still suffering awfully. Please, I beg you… have a heart.'

'Heart? Ha, bourgeois sentimentality. I have no heart when it comes to the enemy. Your brother was a wrecker.' He slapped his hand against the desk. 'A saboteur of the Five-Year-Plan. If it wasn't for me, he'd still be languishing in Hell.'

I shook my head; I'd had this conversation too many times before. 'He was innocent,' I dared to mutter.

'Innocent? That's neither here nor there. Now, unless you want poor Viktor sent back, I'd suggest– '

A knock on the door interrupted Rykov's flow and a tall uniformed youth clutching a file stepped in, his height accentuated by the length of his leather coat. Barely a man but his blond hair was already receding, exposing large ears and a shiny expanse of forehead – a younger version of his boss, another Rykov in the making. On seeing me, he hesitated and then stopped. 'Maria Radekovna,' he said politely.

'Vladimir,' I said, trying to force a smile but pleased to see him.

His eyes, though bright blue, had already lost the radiance of youth, tinged as they were with a streak of ruthlessness that came with his job. He placed the file on Rykov's desk. 'The Technology Institute report you asked for, comrade sir.'

Rykov nodded without looking at his young assistant. He took the file, opened it, and scanned his eyes down the top page.

Vladimir shuffled from one foot to another, waiting for an instruction. He caught my eye and smiled weakly. I couldn't reconcile the two faces of Rosa's boyfriend. On the rare occasions we met, he behaved like any boy in front of his girlfriend's aunt – courteous, shy and slightly awkward. But, according to Rykov, Vladimir was set for a meteoric rise through the ranks of the Secret Police – and surely, that could only mean one thing.

Rykov closed the file and placed it to one side. 'Tell me, Vladimir Petrovich, are you still seeing something of the lovely Rosa?'

Vladimir blushed, his ears turning red. 'Yes, comrade sir.'

'And, Maria, surely, as a good aunt, it must bother you that your niece is seeing an employee of the NKVD. How much simpler it would be for you if your niece's boyfriend was the librarian he tells her he is.' He laughed. 'A librarian! I take my hat off to you, Comrade Vladimir.'

Of course, it bothered me; I hated it. And no matter how much Vladimir spoiled Rosa with trips to the theatre, the ballet or restaurants, I couldn't disguise my distaste for my niece's choice of boyfriend. I couldn't even find solace in the thought that he was safe from arrest. Employees of the NKVD were as liable to be arrested as any other citizen.

Rykov continued. 'You should see him at work. Unmerciful he is. Look at him, the long streak of piss – you wouldn't credit it, would you?' He looked up at the awkward youngster and winked at him. 'So tell us then, have you fucked her yet?'

I gasped for breath, my fingers gripping my thighs. Vladimir shot me a mortified look. 'This is my niece you're talking about,' I said.

Rykov's mocking expression turned instantly grave, his nostrils twitching like a bull's. Immediately I regretted my outburst. 'And it's your brother whose liberty is at stake here.' He kept his glare fixed on me while addressing his assistant, 'OK, Vladimir Petrovich, leave us now.'

'Sir.' Vladimir raised his eyebrows at me by means of apology and hurriedly left, closing the door gently behind him.

I trembled. 'I'm sorry, Comrade Rykov. Please, I beg of you, don't send Viktor back. Give me another chance.' I'd have gladly fallen at his feet, licked his shoes, lifted my skirt, anything. Anything. And it wasn't my sense of dignity that held me back – I'd lost that long ago – but the knowledge that Rykov must have seen it a hundred times before.

Rykov leant back in his chair, his fingers forming a steeple, and looked at me as if making up his mind. 'Well, Maria

Radekovna, I see our relationship as a contract based on a two-way dialogue. Come empty-handed again and I will have no option but to consider our contract finished, do you understand?'

I nodded enthusiastically, he was giving me another chance, and I was experiencing an unexpected warmth for the man. Rykov continued. 'You can have your second chance but don't fail me again. It's up to you, Maria – your home and your brother's freedom lie entirely in your hands.'

I thanked him profusely. Moments later, I was back outside with no remembrance of leaving the office, descending the stairs or being shown out. Outside, I shivered against the cold air while grimacing at the sticky feeling of sweat pressing on my back. How I wished to be home, in bed, asleep, away from Rykov. Walking quickly down the cobbled backstreet, I realised the enormity of what I still had to do.

Chapter 4: The School

'I don't believe it, the bloody water's frozen again.' Rosa stood shivering in her pyjamas and jumper, and stared at the dry washbasin, willing the water to appear. She turned and looked at her two friends: Claudia was sitting on the edge of her bed, her pink cheeks stretched in a yawn, while Ella sat in front of the mirror, combing her hair, concentrating on producing the perfect parting in her strawberry blonde locks. Rosa had always been jealous of Ella's hair, her petite nose, her pure blue eyes. She was by far the most attractive girl in the university. She placed her hand on the metal of the zigzagged flu. 'God, it's cold, can't we get the stove hotter?'

Claudia tutted. 'There's no more wood and we used up the last of the newspaper last night, remember?'

Rosa rattled the taps in the forlorn hope of making a difference. Everything felt so damn cold. She pulled back the grubby lace curtains and scraped her fingernails against the glass. 'Even the window's frosted over.' She climbed back into the warmth of her bed and pulled the covers over her. The dormitory room was small with a bunk bed, a second bed, the sink and a dressing table. The walls were decorated with pink and white-stripped wallpaper, the floor covered in dark blue linoleum.

'I can't concentrate when it's this cold,' said Claudia.

'Don't complain, it could be worse,' said Ella. 'Anyway, I don't know what you're moaning about.'

'What's that meant to mean?'

'Well… you know, you probably don't feel the cold as much,' said Ella, pulling the comb down the length of her hair.

Claudia stood up and hovered behind Ella, catching her friend's eye in the mirror's reflection. 'Are you saying I'm fat?'

Ella laughed. 'As if I would, I'm just saying–'

'I know what you're saying.'

'Stop it, you two,' said Rosa through a yawn. She watched Ella as her friend attacked the lipstick. 'Heck, Ella, how long does it take?'

'Long enough.'

'I hope he appreciates the effort?'

'Oh, he appreciates it all right,' she said, pouting her lips.

Claudia started getting dressed, pulling on a thick cotton dress. She prodded Rosa's bed. 'Come on,' she said, 'get up or you'll miss breakfast.' Rosa groaned. Claudia sneaked her hand beneath the covers and tickled her friend. Rosa squealed and before she had a chance to react Claudia was tickling her mercilessly.

The three friends had shared their dormitory room at the institute for almost a year. They'd become used to each other's habits and foibles, had become dependent on one another, and had become firm friends. Claudia was the youngest and despite the institute's inadequate diet, had maintained a healthy layer of puppy fat. Both her parents worked in a steel factory. Ella was the daughter of a technical engineer and lived with her vanity and an unswerving adoration of a chemistry student called Gregory. These were the children of the proletariat, the new class of students, where one's social origins counted for more than intelligence or standing; where their political credentials were held in greater esteem than their educational attainments.

Half an hour later, the three girls were in the packed canteen, a large wooden-floored hall that smelt of porridge and reverberated with the sounds of dozens of students on long wooden benches at linoleum-covered tables. A large banner draped on the wall proclaimed, *'Food Co-Operation Opens The Way To A New Life'*. On the far white-washed wall, above the main entrance, hung a huge portrait of Stalin in semi-profile, wearing his ubiquitous military jacket. Beneath the painting, stood an old brazier, the only source of warmth in the huge hall. Breakfast consisted of a small bowl of porridge, a piece of black bread and a lukewarm cup of black tea.

'So, what happened to you last night then, eh?' asked Ella, grinning at Rosa.

'What d'you mean?' said Rosa, catching the accusatory tone in her friend's voice.

'A little bird told me they saw you last night,' she said, with a mouthful of black bread. 'You were with your boyfriend. You were coming out of the Hotel Prague. Now, that's posh. So come on, who is he?'

Rosa sighed. It was impossible to keep a secret in Moscow. She was about to attempt an evasive answer when, from behind her, she heard a familiar voice. 'May I join you?' She raised her eyebrows in acknowledgement as the young student sat down next to her. He was a Jewish boy, his black hair swept to one side, his tortoise-shell glasses exaggerating the size of his eyes.

'Hello, Boris,' said Rosa, relieved at her friend's timely intervention. She noticed that he was still wearing the same jacket he wore every day, with its worn elbows and missing middle button. He smiled weakly and rubbed his hands against the cold. Rosa liked Boris; he was a loyal friend and she'd known him from school, but she couldn't help feeling slightly embarrassed in his company because of his undisguised fondness for her.

'Hello, Rosa,' he said with a smile. 'Claudia, Ella.'

'Rosa's about to tell us about this mysterious man she's been seeing,' said Claudia, gleefully.

Rosa felt her cheeks burn. Claudia could be so damn tactless sometimes. She shot her friend a scornful look but if Claudia noticed, she made no show of it.

'Go on then, Rosa, do tell.'

Rosa sighed and noticed Boris shuffling uncomfortably in his seat. 'If you must know,' she said, 'his name is Vladimir but he's not my boyfriend, he's just a friend.'

Ella grinned. 'Hmm, done well for yourself there, haven't you?'

'He's OK.'

She nudged Rosa with her elbow. 'Have you, er, you know…'

Boris interrupted. 'Please, do we have to?'

'I'm just interested, y'know. Well?' she asked, with a wink.

'Ella, it's none of your business, but as it happens, no we haven't. Like I said, he's just a friend, that's all.'

'What else did you do; last night I mean?'

Rosa blushed. 'He, erm, took me out for a meal.'

'Bloody hell, what does he do?'

Boris looked forlorn. 'I wish I had the means to take you out like that,' he said.

'Shut up, Boris,' said Ella. 'So go on, what does he do?'

'He works for the Moscow Public Library.'

Ella and Claudia scoffed and even Boris raised his eyebrows. 'Moscow Public Library, my arse,' said Claudia. 'Unless he's Mister Supremo, he'll be getting almost as paltry an amount as our grants. How could he afford to take you out to the Hotel Prague on what they earn?'

'I don't know. Maybe he saved up.'

'Wise up,' said Ella. 'He doesn't work for the library. He's got an important job somewhere.'

'Yeah, something that comes with privileges,' added Claudia.

Rosa felt herself blush again, this time because of her naivety. The thought had already occurred to her but she had pushed it to one side, preferring not to know. But did it matter what he did? She tried to tell herself that no, it didn't matter. But somehow, she'd failed to convince herself as much as she'd failed to convince her friends – because it did matter, it mattered very much. Vladimir was holding something back and how can you give yourself to a man who doesn't fully give himself to you?

*

'And so, in conclusion, comrades, we are left with Comrade Stalin. And only Stalin can truly be considered Lenin's natural successor, his one and only disciple. In a truly Marxist tradition, only Stalin is capable of carrying Lenin's teachings forward and interpreting them in a manner that Lenin would have approved of and been proud of. We live in a glorious time. When the world finally catches up with us, when the masses dominate throughout the globe, when the capitalist empires are revealed for what they are, we will be the envy of nations, the forefathers of class revolution. And Comrade Stalin will be at its pinnacle, standing as no leader has stood before...'

Rosa listened eagerly. She'd heard it a hundred times before over the years, from when she first started school, when it was drummed into her with constant regularity. And although she was still listening to it now, at university, it was something she never tired of. Her country was leading the way, and for that she felt immense pride. Almost half her curriculum consisted of politically-orientated subjects – the history of the Revolution and the Party, socialist economics, Marxist theory and so on. Yes, sometimes it could be dull but she didn't mind, education was the passport to a good life. She hoped, one day, to become a teacher, to contribute to the liquidation of illiteracy.

The lecturer, Comrade Kalinikov, was a thin tall balding man who wore red braces and the same suit every day and Rosa reckoned, by its condition, he had worn it daily for years. He wore a pair of metal-rimmed spectacles which he fiddled with continuously, as if perpetually nervous. The classroom itself was a shabby affair. The peeling white paint had taken on a yellowy tinge and everything was filthy. The floors were covered in dust, cobwebs stretched across the ceilings and the windows had ceased to allow light through their blackened panes.

'Of course, artistic fashions change, often dictated by the political climate of the time – there is no contradiction in that. The abstract art of the early years following the revolution is now, quite rightly, frowned upon, but it served a purpose that was right for the time. Politically, the country had just gone through radical changes and art reflected that. These were progressive men who sought to rid themselves of the yoke of the bourgeois tradition and we can understand that. But the revolution is almost twenty years old now, and we live in more stable times. Yes, things are still changing and improving apace, but we can allow ourselves the luxury of looking back and embracing our rich artistic heritage…'

She loved her country, loved Stalin and read Lenin voraciously. She felt nothing but pity for the rest of the world and the wretched conditions in which the workers laboured. But the USSR was there to show the way. There wasn't enough paper in the world to describe the joys of being a citizen of the Soviet Union. She'd been born in 1917 – the year of the Revolution! That made her special. She thanked God for having given her the privilege of being alive during such wondrous times. Could any other country provide its workers with theatres and clubs, and education for themselves and their children; free medical facilities, crèches, kindergartens and so on? Yes, OK, she'd heard vaguely of the famines, of the mass liquidizations, the forced exiles, but that all harped back years. Now surely, things were different. And yes, she'd also heard of the purges, the arrests, the deportations. But things were only that bad if you paid any attention to the scaremongers and the gossips. Anyway, no one ever said the road to the socialist utopia was easy. The Soviet citizen was one who lived in the house at the same time as building it. The ends justified the means, as far as she was concerned, and if it meant a few dubious elements were rooted out, then so be it. It just so happened that one of the victims had been her father. He was her one secret. But that was just a mistake – after all, they sent him back, didn't they? But somehow, it was still a secret. She visualised his drawn face with those deep, shallow eyes devoid of any perceivable emotion. Sometimes she found herself wondering whether it had been a mistake. What if he had deviated from the path? Well, if that was the case, then it served him right. Father or no father, Stalin always came first.

And then there was Ella. That was someone else's secret but did her knowledge of it make it her secret as well? Poor Ella, desperate to use her looks to advance in life, to become an actress. But then, recently, she became pregnant. A baby was the last thing she needed, so she had an abortion. Had she had it only a few months before, it would have been permissible. After the revolution, women were allowed to do to their bodies as they saw fit and abortion was perfectly permissible. But with the new emphasis on the family, the Party introduced harsh new measures against it. You were no longer allowed to have an abortion for personal, economic or social reasons. Ella had taken a risk and now she had to live with the knowledge of what she had done.

Comrade Kalinikov was finishing off. 'OK, we meet again tomorrow, when we'll be discussing historic materialism.' Now that, thought Rosa, was something she wasn't so keen on. 'Thank you, you may proceed to the canteen for lunch now.' Lunch – what a euphemism that was. The students were perpetually hungry, but we suffer today, she said to herself, so we may reap the benefits tomorrow. With tomorrow, would come abundance. It was just that sometimes, tomorrow seemed a long way off.

*

Carrying her tray, Rosa queued at the canteen's long counter. A kitchen operative, wearing white overalls, passed her a bowl of cabbage soup, a plate of gruel and a cutlet of some indeterminable meat, together with a slice of black bread. The queue for cutlery at the end of the counter took even longer; such was the shortage of knives and forks. Eventually, a clean batch of cutlery was thrown into the large wooden box. Rosa helped herself and then looked around for someone to sit with. She found Claudia, Ella and Boris sitting together in the corner of the canteen under Stalin's scrutinising gaze. 'Hello everyone,' she said cheerfully, sitting down. 'We're casting this afternoon, aren't we?'

'Hmm,' muttered Claudia, through a mouthful of black bread.

'Chekhov is so boring,' yawned Ella.

Claudia thrust her elbow into Ella's ribs. 'Shut up, you fool,' she said quietly, glancing around her. 'That mouth will get you in trouble one of these days.'

Ella smiled sarcastically.

Rosa slurped at her soup, which was already cold. 'If we're lucky we might all get to play the three sisters.'

'Three witches, more like,' said Claudia, mashing the cutlet into the greyish gruel.

'Speak for yourself.'

Rosa eyed Boris who was busying himself by cutting his meat into small pieces. 'Are you hoping for a part, Boris?'

Boris looked up. 'A part?'

'You know, the play.'

'*The Three Sisters*,' added Claudia by way of clarification.

Ella winked at Rosa. 'Boris will be wanting to play the charming Andrey Sergeyevitch, won't you, Boris?'

'If you say so.'

'Come on, Boris,' said Rosa. 'Out with it, what's the matter?'

Boris carefully laid his knife and fork on the table and adjusted his glasses. He looked pointedly from Claudia to Ella and back to Rosa. 'You haven't heard, have you?'

'Heard what?' said the girls in unison.

'We're going to be purged,' he said in a whisper.

The expressions on Rosa and Ella's face froze.

'What'd you say?' said Claudia as she scooped up another spoonful of gruel.

Ella leant towards her. 'They're purging us.'

Claudia's hand stopped halfway between the plate and her mouth. 'What, *us*?' Boris nodded solemnly.

The word *purge* echoed through Rosa's mind. Purges were what happened in offices or factories, she thought, surely they wouldn't purge a bunch of young, fervent students such as themselves. Boris stood up to leave, his lunch barely touched. Perhaps, she thought, Boris was simply passing on a rumour; but, given rumourmongers were harshly dealt with, that in itself was a dangerous thing to do.

'Boris, how do you know?'

He paused. 'I heard a couple of the lecturers in the toilets. They sounded terrified; they'll be as vulnerable as us. I heard them say it though, they're sending a Purge Commission.'

'When?' asked Ella.

'Next week,' he said, before disappearing into the throng of students.

The three girls glanced nervously at each other. Rosa knew how indiscriminate the purges could be – however loyal one was to the Party, however idealistic one's revolutionary zeal, no one was immune, no one safe. A false word last week, an unguarded comment last year, was all that they needed. She looked at her two friends and tried to smile. Friendship was no safeguard against incrimination when people were placed in front of a Purge Commission and subjected to their ritual of confession and humiliation. But Ella and Claudia were different. Together, the three of them had become like sisters; trust and loyalty bound them together – the three sisters, the three witches. She believed she could trust them, but now that their loyalty to each other was about to be put through the sternest of tests, could she trust herself? She had nothing to fear, she told herself – after all, she loved her country. But nonetheless, her blood ran cold at the thought of it.

Chapter 5: The Proposal

The morning after our meal with Dmitry, Petrov woke up feeling terrible, not that I was in the least bit surprised, the way he had guzzled Dmitry's wine. For some reason, I had woken early and found my mind full of thoughts about Dmitry. I remembered the way he looked at me and I felt touched by the way he'd tried to rescue me once Petrov had started his tirade. I thought of his painting and his artistic and emotional sensitivity. He seemed altogether the antithesis of the man now groaning and clutching his forehead in the bed. It was as if Dmitry represented man on a further stage on the road of evolution while Petrov languished in some dark age. *Homo Sovieticus*. I needed to do something and, without thinking, found myself dusting the dressing table in semi-darkness at six-thirty in the morning.

'What are you doing?' said the hoarse voice from the bed.

'And a good morning to you, Petrov.'

'What time is it?'

'Time you got up. You don't want to be late.' Being more than twenty minutes late for work could have serious consequences.

Petrov sat up in the bed, grunting with the effort. 'Was I really rude last night?' he asked.

'Yes, you were abominable.'

'Uhh, I thought so.' He rubbed his eyes. 'I said some fairly horrible things, didn't I? I'm sorry, you know I get like that when I drink. Why didn't you stop me?' Petrov had the knack of making his misdeeds my fault. 'Don't expect we'll get invited around there again. Perhaps I should phone Dmitry and apologise.'

'No, leave it for now.'

'I'm sorry,' he said again, climbing out of bed.

'You'd better hurry. You don't want to be late for work.'

'Damn, is that the time, couldn't you have called me earlier?' He always had to have the last word, but there was nothing like the threat of ten years of hard labour to ensure people got to work on time.

*

About a week after our meal with Dmitry, he rang me. Like our bathroom and kitchen, we shared the telephone with all the other occupants on the floor. It was situated down the corridor and it seemed to ring continuously day and night, but only rarely was it for us. This time, however, it was. A neighbour of ours had knocked on our door. Petrov was out at work. I opened the door a fraction, fearful, as always, of the ruffians who shared our living space. 'Telephone – it's for you.'

The sound of Dmitry's voice made my heart leap. But our conversation wasn't easy – I felt awkward and he sounded embarrassed. He asked whether Petrov and I had arrived home safely after our visit. Then, to my surprise, he asked whether I could spare the time to call on him at two o'clock the following day. He had a proposal I might be interested in, if it wasn't inconvenient. Yes, I said, desperately trying to disguise the delight in my voice, I think I would be available – let me just check – yes, as it happened, it would be convenient.

A proposal? What, I wondered, did he have in mind? It all seemed somewhat officious and I found myself conjuring up all sorts of possibilities. Indeed, all week I had thought of little but Dmitry. My mind invented dozens of little scenarios where we would accidentally bump into each other and he would invite me back to his apartment for a cup of tea. But I hadn't thought of a phone call and a proposal.

My duty as a housewife was to provide a cultured and welcoming environment to which my husband could come home to and enjoy after a strenuous day at work. And to be fair to Petrov, he did work hard – usually an eleven-hour day, often more. I used to keep our two-room apartment "Snow White clean", as Petrov demanded but since Viktor's return, I've not kept to my old standards. Otherwise, I spent much of my time on my sewing machine, sewing table napkins, curtains and suchlike, which would eventually find their way into the local Party offices or the barracks of the Red Army. Occasionally, I worked in the offices of the Komsomol, the organisation of the Communist Youth, as an English translator. I had spent my first few years of marriage learning to speak English, hoping it would, one day, provide me with the means of escaping my daytime tedium. I also read as much as I could. As the wife of a Party bureaucrat, I was expected to be cultured in Russia's literature. It was all part of the camouflage. I was currently ploughing through *War and Peace* but during the week after meeting Dmitry, I found I could hardly concentrate for more than a page before my mind wandered off into another daydream. And the day following his phone call, I could barely assemble my thoughts in a coherent pattern. Had he been thinking of me as much as I of him? Should I wear my best skirt or my other one? Should I wear my hair up or leave it down?

In the end, I wore my ordinary skirt and kept my hair as normal. This was, as I reminded myself many times, an afternoon visit to discuss some proposal with my friend's brother – no more than that.

*

Upon arriving at Dmitry's, I was disappointed to see he had a visitor – a stout middle-aged man dressed in a brown suit, broad in the lapel, long in the pocket. 'Come in, Maria,' said Dmitry. 'Let me introduce you – this is Mikhail, my patron.' His thinning hair was greased back and shone under the harsh light of Dmitry's living room. With his small rounded glasses and portly stature, I couldn't help but think he resembled a tax collector.

'Hello, my dear,' he said, offering his hand. 'How delightful to meet you. I've just popped in to disturb Dmitry from his important work. So, old man, how is it going?'

I sat down on the settee.

'It's almost finished,' said Dmitry. 'Can I get either of you a drink?'

'No, no, thank you, I won't take up too much of your time,' said Mikhail.

'Just as well really. The kettle's broken and it takes ages on the stove.'

'Can't you fix it?'

'No one to do so.' He was right, of course, it was hopeless trying to get anything fixed. Artisans and craftsmen no longer existed, eliminated as profiteers, and it was nigh on impossible to find the raw materials to do it oneself. When was it ever going to get easier?

Dmitry opened the door of his studio and stepped to one side to allow his portly patron through. He beckoned me to follow. I noticed again the scent of his aftershave. Mikhail had stopped a few yards short of the painting mounted on its easel and was adjusting his glasses, pushing them further up his nose. I watched for his expression, a spontaneous reaction. The painting seemed even more impressive in the light of the day. Each blade of grass carefully represented, the fur on the dogs finely executed, the slight tear in the boy's trousers, the reflection of the sun in the straw field. All I remembered of the reality was the dirt, the mud, the unending days of grey, the hunger. Mikhail nodded slowly to himself and a small grin spread across his lips. 'Marvellous,' he said. 'Marvellous. I knew you wouldn't let me down.'

'Do you think it'll do then?'

'Do? Of course, my dear boy, it'll more than do, it's perfect. The director will love it. I told him you were the man for the job and he'll see that I was right.'

'Good. So when's the big day?'

'The director reckons it'll be in about a month's time. I must say, it's a fine piece of work; you've surpassed yourself. It'll take pride of place in the director's office for a year or so and then probably be transferred to some gallery where he'll take great delight in telling all his Party colleagues that he commissioned it. He'll take more credit for it than you will; you know what they're like. They like to show they're in with the creative intelligentsia. And I won't deny it, it will further my cause too, you know. Discoverer of hitherto unknown genius, you know how it works. The director and I gain political capital and you'll get the sort of elite access that'll make middle-ranking Party workers green with envy. You could get a car out of this and a bigger dacha too.'

Dmitry laughed. 'Yes and if either of you fall, then we're all in the stink.'

'Oh come now, let's not be so fatalistic. We don't have any skeletons in the cupboard; we keep our noses clean, we toe the Party line, so where's the problem?'

'We're like a row of dominoes, you need only to–'

'Yes, yes, let's not go into that now. Tell me, young lady, have you heard our Dmitry here is up for an Order of Lenin?'

'Yes, I'd–'

'He's a clever chap.'

'In some ways,' said Dmitry, 'it's nothing more than the Party's way of saying I'm doing the right thing. As an artist constrained by the State, it was not the kind of endorsement I necessarily need.'

'Oh, come on, Dmitry.'

'But you're right. Despite myself, I can't help but feel flattered. I suppose, if I'm honest, it matters more to me than I care to admit. The award has prestige – it will, undoubtedly, open doors for me and spread my reputation.'

'Absolutely. So tell me, can I fix a time for someone to come and pick this up?'

'I'm not sure it's finished yet.'

'Looks finished to me. That's the problem with you artists – you never know when to let go. It's perfect, leave it as it is, man.'

'It's the old women, I was thinking of replacing one with a young woman.'

Mikhail's eyes flashed. 'Ah, now you're talking, you mean put in a buxom young wrench. Oh, I beg your pardon, young lady. What must you think of me? I do apologise.'

I smiled weakly. 'It's fine.'

'I just think a younger woman would broaden the appeal,' said Dmitry.

Mikhail pulled at his jacket as if trying to stretch out the creases. 'You won't have long though, ten days at the most, can you do it?'

'Oh yes, I'll start straight away.'

'Well, my dear boy, I'll leave you to it.' Dmitry escorted his patron to the door. 'Don't forget,' said Mikhail, 'last Tuesday this month,' he said, shaking Dmitry's hand vigorously.

'Last Tuesday?'

'RAPA meeting, seven o'clock. I'll see myself out. Delighted to have met you,' he said, addressing me as he left.

*

Dmitry's apartment looked different during the daytime – more disorganised, bits of paper and books strewn around his living room, a newspaper lying on the floor, a half-full cup of cold tea, the previously ordered coat rack now laden with numerous coats, hats and scarves. I wondered how a man could afford so many coats. Dmitry himself was wearing paint-splattered dark blue overalls, his sweeping hair was dishevelled and he seemed on edge. Having invited me to sit down, he started to pace up and down in front of me. Something was bothering him and I feared he was about to bring up the subject of Petrov's behaviour and I wondered whether to pre-empt him by offering an apology.

'I'll get straight to the point,' said Dmitry. 'It's about my painting and what I was saying to Mikhail just now–'

'Oh, Petrov and I were very impressed by it.'

'Thank you, it's very nice of you to say so, but the fact is the female figure I was thinking of–'

'The buxom young wench?'

'Yes, I'm sorry about that. He's a good man, Mikhail, but sometimes he speaks before he thinks. Anyway, leaving aside his unfortunate turn of phrase, I wondered whether I could use you as a model, so to speak.'

'Me?' I was flattered but I wasn't sure. 'Why me?'

'It's been troubling me. The women are all so damn *maternal*. Perhaps that isn't such a bad thing. After all, the State likes to be seen in a paternalistic manner, the old women could be seen to represent the Motherland, heartily providing for their menfolk, the toilers of the countryside, the workers of the Revolution. I want the painting to appeal to all age groups. I've got the men – young and old, and I've got the children, but no young women. So, what if I make this figure a young woman? Should she be wearing a dress or overalls; should she be fair or dark? Or perhaps a brunette? Ideally, I wanted to paint her as a gypsy but that didn't seem a good idea, politically. Then I remembered you and thought you would be perfect as a woman of the country. I wouldn't want to demean you; I'd depict you as a cultivated citizen of the land.'

'A what?'

'OK, that sounds rather pompous, but you get the gist. The more I tried to see her, the more I thought about you. I think your features would fit perfectly. It needn't take up too much of your time but, of course, if you–'

'I don't know.' The idea that Dmitry had been thinking about me in such a manner, I found strangely pleasing. And I couldn't deny there was something rather thrilling about it – for my face to be captured by the artistic hand and represented

in a painting for all to see, forever. But there was more to it
than that. I tried to explain. 'Dmitry, your painting is lovely,
really, but…' I hesitated. He looked at me carefully, his head
tilted slightly to one side. Could I trust him? I'd only met him
the once but something between us made me feel as if we'd
known each other for so much longer. And his sister was the
only person I could truly call a friend. Was that enough? Trust
was a rare commodity. When you place your trust in someone,
you are putting your very existence at their mercy. The fewer
people one trusts, the less you tell people, the safer one is.

'Yes? Go on.'

No. I could not tell him. Mine was a secret I would take
to the grave. I had no choice. 'Can I see it again?'

'Of course.'

I stared at the outlined female figure, stripped of her
features, of her characteristics, her existence. I tried to imagine
myself in her place dominating the right side of the painting
but peripheral in the action. I could smell the straw; I could
feel the breeze on my face.

'Something's bothering you.'

'No, it's just… it's so prominent.'

'Yes. Here, let me show you some drawings I did of you,
I hope you don't mind.'

I was intrigued; the idea of Dmitry drawing me after only
one meeting was incredibly exciting. He rummaged through a
pile of papers and handed me a few sheets. I looked at them
and was astonished. It was as if he'd known me all my life.
There I was in a series of pencil drawings, depicted as I once
used to be – a girl of the country. The detail to my clothing
was sparse but my hair, my face, and my expression were
alarmingly accurate. Had he stared at me so intently over the
dinner table without my noticing; had he secretly taken a

photograph of me? Was it *me* or was every person he met a potential source of material? I couldn't help but take Dmitry's interest in me as complimentary even if it was purely in an artistic sense. Petrov, in comparison, was so unobservant, so uninterested.

'OK, I'll do it.'

Dmitry smiled broadly, his whole face beaming like a child presented with the biggest present. For a moment, I thought he would hug me, he seemed so delighted. His pleasure in my acceptance was heart-warming and I felt a little shiver run down my spine.

*

To my surprise, we set to work straight away. It was still only mid-afternoon; it would be hours before Petrov returned home. Dmitry pulled the easel back to one corner of his studio and placed me diagonally opposite. He disappeared for a few moments, only to reappear with dark blue overalls which he asked me to put on. While Dmitry made a discreet exit, I took off my cardigan and skirt and slipped on the overalls. They were slightly too small for me and were spotlessly clean – hardly the case, I thought, for a peasant girl. Dmitry came back carrying a tray loaded with a pitcher and four or so empty glasses. He made me stand in various poses and with different variations of a smile – from a subtle grin to an outright laugh.

He began by making more sketches of me on scrap pieces of paper. After perhaps half an hour, during which time he didn't say a word, he seemed satisfied with a pose so subtly different from all the others, I could barely tell the difference. He then picked up his palette and squeezed various tubes of paint on it, and began gleefully mixing the colours, adding

63

minuscule amounts of this colour and that. I could tell that this was part of the process he enjoyed.

Finally, he spoke. 'I think we're ready,' he declared.

He painted as if the devil possessed him, his eyes focused in intense concentration, glancing from me to the canvas and back to me in rapid succession. It was, I have to admit, fascinating to watch the artist at work. I could see from the movement of his hand that he began with broad strokes, applying fresh layers of paint at regular intervals. And again, he worked silently, his thoughts and efforts engrossed in the work at hand. I, as a person, had ceased to be important; I'd become an object of artistic intent, of creative application.

After a while, my arms began to ache. The effort of keeping unnaturally still was tiring. I needed to move, to stretch. But the merest hint of movement was met with disapproval. He urged me to remain still. 'Not much longer,' he muttered after another five minutes had passed, then ten, fifteen minutes. And just as I thought I was going to drop the tray out of pure exhaustion, he unexpectedly threw his hands triumphantly in the air and declared that we had done enough. I dropped the tray onto the table and sat down on a small stool with utter relief. He laughed and apologised. Dmitry the artist had gone and in his place was Dmitry the man.

'Can I have a look?' I asked him.

'No, not yet, we haven't finished. It would be bad luck. Can you return tomorrow?'

'No, not tomorrow; I have to go to the kindergarten. I could come back the day after.'

'Yes, yes, excellent.'

I was thrilled, I hadn't envisaged more than the one sitting, hadn't realised the commitment of the task. Yes, of course, I could come back, and willingly – my life as a Soviet housewife was not exactly demanding. I was an artist's model now, someone needed me, I was important, I had a role to play. It was tiring work but I had to do it because he *needed* me.

'Come, let's have a glass of wine,' said Dmitry. He too was happy; his work had obviously gone well, perhaps better than he'd imagined. Maybe I had inspired him, chased out the artistic demons that troubled his thoughts. For the first time since coming to Moscow, my spirit was soaring. I knew I was getting carried away, but Dmitry had unexpectedly and unintentionally given me a purpose.

We clinked our glasses in mutual gratitude and enthusiasm. The red wine was thick, like sweet syrup. We stood only a few feet apart, our eyes burning into each other, the saccharine taste on our lips, the warmth inside our bellies. His bottom lip shone red with the concentrated thickness of the wine. I watched as he swallowed, the movement of his Adam's apple, the dark stubble on his throat.

'Is this the sort of work you enjoy?' I asked.

'Yes, it pays my way. But sometimes I wish I could break loose the chains of socialist realism and paint something truly extravagant.'

'Such as?'

'The nude.'

'Why don't you?'

'Come off it, it'd be too dangerous. You know what the Party thinks of anything it deems pornographic.'

'Yes.' But the mere notion of it was strangely exciting. 'I'd pose for you.'

He laughed. 'No, I'm not asking you to.'

'Really, I want to.'

He shook his head. 'No, Maria. I'm not sure if I want to paint the female figure and even if I did, it couldn't be you;

you have too much sadness in your eyes. I fear you would lack the confidence to give yourself fully to me. I would demand your unquestioned trust and I don't think you're ready to give me that. Forgive me, but I believe life has been too cruel to you.'

His words, so softly spoken, pained me as surely as if he'd hit me.

'I'm sorry, you look hurt, I don't mean to offend you but I have to be brutally honest for your sake as well as mine. And anyway, you know how risky it would be. Any art expressed in classical terms is viewed as nothing short of depravity. I'm sorry.'

He was right of course, but I never realised I wore my heart so clearly on my sleeve. Too much sadness in my eyes? I left Dmitry's apartment slightly deflated.

*

An hour later, as I began preparing Petrov's dinner, I heard the apartment door open and the familiar footsteps. I went through to the living room. Rosa was slumped on the settee, her college bag dumped on the floor. She looked pale and exhausted. 'Rosa love, is anything wrong?' She closed her eyes and shook her head. 'Come on, what's the matter?'

She sighed and rubbed her eyes. 'Have you ever been through a purge?

'No, why do you ask?'

'They're sending a purge commission to the institute.'

'Oh.'

'What do you mean by "oh"? I've got nothing to be worried about.'

I tried to smile. 'I know that, I know–'

'I do my work, I don't get in trouble, I read my books…'

'But…?'

Rosa's eyes wandered around the room. Finally, she said in a whisper, 'I'm frightened.'

The poor girl. I sat down on the settee next to her. 'You'll be all right. They might not even choose you.'

'Do you know what really happened to my father?'

'No, I don't. No one ever knows.' This wasn't exactly true.

'But he must have done something wrong. They wouldn't arrest anyone for no reason, would they?'

'I suppose not.'

'Well, there you are then. I'll be OK.' She looked at me carefully for a few moments and then turned away and closed her eyes again. I noticed a slight smile on her lips but it soon faded.

Chapter 6: The Rehearsal

"'I heard yesterday that she is going to be married to Protopopov, the chairman of our Rural Board…'"

'Stop, stop, stop.'

Rosa's mouth hung open, on the verge of delivering the next line. She was standing on the stage, playing her part, her Masha talking to Ella's Olga in Chekhov's *The Three Sisters*. The interruptions came at regular intervals. What now, she wondered. She turned and gazed at Comrade Ramzin, the drama teacher, who was sitting in the middle of the second row of haphazardly lined chairs. Various other students sat near her, all with copies of the script on their laps.

'Rosa,' said Ramzin, 'you sound like a parrot perched on a pirate's shoulder in some infantile nursery performance.' Ella grinned smugly at Rosa. Comrade Ramzin was a large woman, her long mousy hair pleated down her back, her cheeks flushed with circles of red. 'Try to give it some… some meaning,' she continued. 'Don't finish your sentences on the up, it sounds too optimistic. The intended emotion of Masha's words is not conveyed in the sound of your voice. Right, shall we try it again?'

Rosa cleared her throat and tried to ignore the asinine expression on Ella's mocking face. Think sad, she thought, think sad. She thought of the day they came for her father.

'Well, what are you waiting for?' yelled Comrade Ramzin, impatiently.

'"*Andrey, come here, dear, for a minute.*"'

'"*This is my brother, Andrey Sergeyevitch.*"'

Ella waited for the appearance of Boris as Andrey Sergeyevitch but was greeted only with silence. She repeated the last line. This time Boris took his cue and stumbled onto the stage from behind her.

'"*What do you want? I can't make it out?*"'

'No, no, no,' cried Ramzin. 'For goodness sake, Boris, that is your entrance from Act Three, *not* Act One. OK, OK, that's enough, I can't take much more of this. Now, Rosa, you still look so limp. Use your arms more, move your head, don't just stand there like a wooden soldier. Ella, perfect as usual, well done. All right, we'll call it a day. We meet again at two tomorrow. And perhaps we could have more of a concerted effort. I know you're amateurs but do you have to wear it so proudly on your sleeves? OK, class dismissed.'

Rosa and Ella jumped off the low stage, Ella wearing a satisfied grin that stretched right across her face, dimpling her cheeks. Boris took the more sedate route of the stage steps.

'Your big day tomorrow, eh, Boris? Got your speech ready?' asked Ella as Boris met them in front of the stage.

'I don't know what she expects from us, we're not the bloody Moscow School of Drama, it's only a college play.'

'Quite,' said Rosa. 'It's not even as if anyone important is going to be there, I don't see what the fuss is about.'

'Listen to you two,' said Ella. 'If it's worth doing, it's worth doing properly. Where's your pride?'

'We don't all want to be film stars,' said Boris.

'So, where are you off to tonight, Rosa? Home to practise your lines, I hope. Or have you got another date with your *librarian* friend?'

'He *is* a librarian. And as it happens, yes, I am meeting him tonight.' She shot Boris a sideways glance, but Boris, flipping through his Chekhov script, avoided her eyes.

'Where's he taking you tonight then?' asked Ella. 'What wonders await you from the toil and wages of a librarian? Another romantic meal at the Hotel Prague?'

'Come on, let's go to lunch,' said Rosa to Boris.

'Don't worry, I take the hint. Find out what he does,' said Ella, as Rosa and Boris walked away.

Sitting down at one of the long wooden benches with their plates of black bread and cups of tea, Boris talked about the play. 'I remember my father reading it to me when I was a child,' he said. 'He liked Chekhov, he often used to quote him, especially *The Cherry Orchard*. To him, it summed up the indestructible path of change. We call it progress but he hated it.'

'I've never heard you mention your father—'

'When will we ever get proper food?'

'Perhaps when they've rooted out all the wreckers.'

'Rosa, are you really seeing this man tonight?' Rosa turned away and toyed with her bread, crumbling it between her fingers, not wanting to answer. Boris continued: 'Forgive me, Rosa, but I need to speak my mind. Knowing that you're seeing this… this librarian is… well, I think you know how I feel about you, it's just that… I'm not saying this very well.'

Rosa's cheeks flushed. 'I know. Look, I do like you but…' she waved her hands about, trying to find the appropriate word. 'But…'

'I know, you like me as a friend.'

'Is that so bad?'

'From where I'm sitting – yes. I, I think of you all the time, Rosa. I hate this boy for being able to take you out and spoil you and–'

'Boris, no. You make me sound shallow. Do you really think I see him just because of that?'

'No, I'm sorry, I didn't mean to imply that.'

'You're a good friend. I know it's not enough for you but if we started seeing each other in that way, it would spoil everything. Anyway, what would your parents say, you a Jew seeing a gentile, and an atheist at that.'

'Mother just wants me to find a pretty girl, fall in love and settle down. She'd like you.'

Rosa smiled at the compliment. 'And your father?'

'My father's dead. He was a rabbi so I admit that would've been a harder nut to crack. Are your parents still alive?'

'No. Both died.' Her mother had indeed died but why lie about her father? She knew why. 'Don't let us fall out over this, Boris.'

'No.' He forced a smile. 'No, of course not.'

*

Rosa tried to visit her father at least once a week. She never wanted to, but somehow she felt obligated and it always cheered up Maria. She'd become used to living at the institute, it was so much more fun. She hated her aunt's apartment – two tiny rooms in a communal house with a couple across the corridor who spent half the day yelling at each other and at their baby. And next door to them, four generations of the same family living on top of each other, without breathing space and in utter squalor. And these families, along with half a dozen others, all shared the same kitchen. The massive kitchen stove was heated only twice a week when all the women fought for space and cooked their meals for the coming three or four days, to be heated later on their own Primus stoves. It was so depressing; there just weren't enough houses to go around. But, as she frequently reminded herself, it was their duty to suffer today to reap the benefits tomorrow.

'Rosa, love,' said her aunt as she walked in. The only armchair, which was usually occupied by her father, was empty.

'Where's father?' she asked, as she sat down.

'He's not feeling too well today, he hasn't got up.'

Rosa picked up a year-old magazine she could almost recite word for word and idly flipped through the pages.

Maria coughed delicately. 'Are you going out tonight?'

Rosa was looking at the photograph of the famous polar explorer, the huge man-mountain of Otto Schmidt with his long wild beard, staring maniacally into the lens.

'Rosa?'

'Hmm? Yes.'

According to the song, Schmidt's beard ran down to his knees. 'With Vladimir?'

Rosa closed the magazine. 'Yes, with Vladimir.'

'So, er, what's he like, this Vladimir?'

'He's nice.'

'Nice? Should you be spending so much time with a boy who's just *nice*? Can't you find someone nearer your own age?'

'How do you know how old he is?'

'Well, I can't imagine a boy of your age being able to afford to take you out like this Vladimir does. I mean, restaurants, cinemas, the theatre, what next? Surely, there must be someone at college you could go out with?'

'Sorry, Maria, but I don't know what this has to do with you. I'm eighteen now; who I wish to see is my business. If you'll excuse me, I'd better go see Father; see if he's awake.'

Rosa opened the bedroom door and was struck by the stale, musty odour. The smell was familiar yet it never ceased to take her by surprise whenever she was confronted by it. It was dark inside the room, what little light there was came through the thin curtain with its frayed edge.

Her father was lying on his bed, his blanket thrown back, covering only his legs. His eyes were closed, his breathing slow and silent. There was a chair next to the bed where her aunt sat for hours talking or reading to him, rarely receiving a response, never expecting one. Rosa sat down and stared at him. 'Hello, father,' she said, speaking as normally as possible. He looked hot, his forehead glistened with perspiration. She felt as if she should reach over with a handkerchief and wipe his brow but she couldn't face it – the idea, she realised with a pang of remorse, repulsed her. She opened her mouth to speak but then closed it again. Her aunt could do it, but she couldn't, it seemed too unnatural. She wanted to tell him about her day – the rehearsals, Ella's irritating smugness, Boris's forlornness, her pending date with Vladimir, her suspicions about his job. Damn Ella, Rosa thought. But instead, she said nothing and felt the awkwardness of the silence as acutely as if she was trying to make conversation with someone who could actually talk back.

He was twenty-six when she was born. She was eighteen now, that made him forty-four. Was this how a forty-four-year-old man was meant to look like? She was fifteen when they came to arrest him. Three years ago.

November 1932. There had been nothing to warn them, at least nothing that she knew of. One night, in the early hours of the morning, there was a knock at the door. An urgent, horrible knock. It must have continued for some time because by the time she peered through the crack of her bedroom door into the main room, her mother and father were already up, still in their pyjamas. Her father's pyjamas were red and white stripes; the same pair he wore now, lying in his bed, oblivious to his daughter's presence. But now, they were far too big for him and the red had faded into a murky pink. She remembered standing anxiously just inside the bedroom, hiding within the darkness of the room, her eyes blinking from the light of the main room. Her parents hadn't seen her…

'We give you five seconds to open this door,' said the aggressive voice from outside. 'One… two…' Her parents, Nadya and Viktor, exchanged terrified glances. 'Three…'

'All right, all right, I'm coming,' said Viktor. He unbolted the bolt at the top of the door and turned the key. Just before the lock clicked open, he paused and glanced back at his wife, as if to say, *here goes…* He turned the key through its last turn and reached for the doorknob but before he had a chance to open it, the door burst open and a flurry of black uniforms suddenly filled the space of the apartment. Nadya clasped her hands over her cheeks, Viktor looked older already, his face drained of colour.

The first uniform introduced himself and his two colleagues in a quick staccato voice, the names disappearing in a haze of fear. To the fifteen-year-old Rosa, they all looked threateningly the same with their long black, shiny mackintoshes and peaked caps. 'Citizen Tomsky, you are under arrest.'

Rosa's mother let out a shrill shriek and clamped her hand over her mouth, her eyes wide as spectacles. Her father's legs seemed to buckle from underneath him. He gripped the back of a chair, his mouth gaping open like a fish on dry land, trying to absorb the words, grappling for a response. 'W-what for?' he spluttered.

'I am not at liberty to say.' The first uniform clicked his fingers at his colleagues. The two men responded immediately and started pulling out drawers and tipping their contents on the floor, searching underneath the cushions of the armchair, under the carpets, on top of cupboards. Rosa withdrew behind the door and bit furiously at her nails. For so long, she pretended to be older than she was, but now, her fear stripped away the years and she felt unbearably vulnerable. She wanted to go to her mother, to disappear within her warmth but she couldn't face stepping out of the protecting darkness of the bedroom. She saw them go into the kitchen and heard them rummaging around.

'But – but can't you tell me what I'm supposed to have done?' she heard her father ask.

'No. Against regulations. You'll know soon enough.'

'But my husband hasn't done anything, have you, Viktor? We're loyal citizens, firm believers, my husband fought in the revolution–'

'Look, I couldn't give a shit; I've got my orders. Now go and get dressed. And you...,' he said addressing Nadya, 'pack him a bag, a few clothes, nothing more.'

One of the assistant officers barged into the bedroom and turned on the light. Rosa's unexpected presence made him jump. 'What the...' Rosa backed away from him, trying to squeeze herself into the wall. The man grabbed her hand from behind her back and dragged her into the main room. 'Boss, look what we've got here,' he said, pushing Rosa into the light.

Everyone turned around and looked at her. Her mother held her arm out for her. Rosa darted across the room, the veneer of maturity vanishing in an instant, and fell into the warmth of her mother's clasp. Nadya turned to the officer. 'Please, comrade, think of my daughter—'

He ignored her and, turning to Viktor, said, 'If you don't want to go out in your night clothes, I'd get changed right now, if I was you.'

'But I don't understand…'

'For Christ's sake, stop pissing me around. You're under arrest and you're coming with us, that much I would have thought was obvious. I'll give you two minutes, now go and get dressed.'

Viktor turned and went to the bedroom. Nadya and Rosa followed him. They found the room a mess of clothes as one of the men opened the drawers and scattered various objects across the floor.

Nadya began to crumple under the duress of violation. 'What, what are you looking for?' she asked the man. He didn't answer her, didn't look at her. Nadya busied herself by stuffing a few clothes for her husband into a small bag. Rosa sat on the floor in the corner of the room and drew her arms around her knees, desperate to make herself seem as small as possible. From the corner of her eye, she watched her father get dressed. Somehow she knew she'd never see him again, she knew that life as she knew it was coming to an end – right there, right at that moment. No sooner had Viktor finished changing, the uniform in charge declared that it was time to go. The assistants had searched the whole apartment, ripped everything apart in the process and had found nothing to incriminate their victim. But it made little difference, he was still under arrest.

The four men stood at the door of the apartment, Viktor surrounded by the three black mackintoshes, his vulnerability dwarfed by the menacing representatives of the State – man crushed by the machine. Nadya's face seemed to be covered by a blanket of pain; Rosa could see the fear in her eyes. Rosa stood as close as possible to her mother. She knew what was happening, but it didn't explain her incomprehension.

Viktor looked at them, looked at his wife and daughter, and said, in a quivering voice, 'It's just a mistake, you'll see, I'll be back in no time.' Nadya nodded, her hands gripping her daughter's arms.

Seconds later, Viktor was gone. Nadya and Rosa stared at the door, at the empty space where a few seconds before Viktor delivered his hollow reassurance. Then Nadya sat down at the table, her mouth gaping open, fighting for air. From the silent street, they heard the sound of a car start up. Rosa went to the window and drew back the curtain. She saw the black van draw away, the trail of exhaust fumes dissipating behind the rear lights.

'Black Maria,' she said quietly to herself. Walking through to the kitchen, she viewed the mess – the upturned packets of cereals and flour, the pots and pans lying scattered on the work surface, the shattered teapot and bits of crockery on the kitchen floor.

A moment later, the main room was filled with the sound of wailing, her mother's terrifying squeal – bitter and anguished. She looked at her mother, watched the unnatural contortions of her mouth, her body convulsed, her sobs reverberating. Her mother's heart was breaking right there in

front of her. Rosa felt a tremor of annoyance within her –
annoyed that she wasn't the centre of concern.

That was three years ago. Amazingly, Viktor was
eventually returned to them, but her mother did not live long
enough to see the day. She died within the year, her heart
broken, her spirit crushed.

But the man lying asleep in front of her wasn't her father.
Whatever the NKVD had done to him had killed him as
effectively as a bullet through the back of the head. She felt no
love for him now, just a faint longing for the man that used to
be, the man she could barely remember. However hard she
tried, she simply couldn't reconcile the two faces of the same
man.

After his arrest, neighbours pointedly turned their backs;
acquaintances shunned them, friends stopped calling. They
were no longer safe to know, they'd become pariahs. At the
time they had most needed friends, they found themselves
with none. Even at school, Rosa was avoided. Everyone knew
that her father had "disappeared". Soon afterwards, they were
evicted and all their furniture and belongings confiscated.
Uncle Petrov managed to use his influence and save them
from the streets. They were given a tiny, one-room apartment
– it was squalid and claustrophobic, but when she considered
what might have been...

Meanwhile, Rosa's mother, accompanied by Aunt Maria,
went out every day, trying to find her husband, to discover
what crime he'd been arrested for, where they had taken him.
Rosa grieved for him. She knew him to be dead. Where her
mother fought for a scrap of hope, she wallowed in grief. She
pitied her mother's pointless pursuit for some strand of news,
her need to find a lifeline to cling onto. Her mother's refusal
to give in and her own pragmatic acceptance of the worst

proved to be awkward bedfellows. Rather than offering comfort to each other, each found the other's reaction to Viktor's arrest aggravating. They fought and took out their frustrations on each other. Their shared suffering only served to sever their relationship. With time and the resilience of youth, Rosa survived her grief. It started the day she stood up at school and denounced her father. She'd been forced into it, and she had never told her mother, but from that moment on, her life began to change. With her uncle's help, she managed to get into the Komsomol, the Communist Youth League, and learnt the meaning of what it was to be a true proletariat. Her membership of the Komsomol guaranteed her a place at college – her life was falling into place after all. Her father's crime was a thing of the past, an aberration, for now, she had a new love – Stalin.

Her mother continued to talk of her husband in the present tense while Rosa referred to him in the past. Each year, on 28 February, Nadya bought Viktor a present for his birthday. Each year, on 6 November, Rosa mourned for the day her father was arrested. She'd come to see the date as the anniversary of his 'death'.

And then one day, Nadya died. The doctors said she'd suffered a stroke brought on by worry. Rosa hardly grieved. Her mother was not the mother she'd once been. Instead, that role was increasingly filled by Maria. Her aunt and Petrov gave her a room.

Then came the news that Viktor was coming home. They were told to expect him in two weeks' time. Rosa burst into tears; it was too unnatural to be true – the dead didn't come back to life. She'd buried him in her mind years ago and now she was to be confronted with his ghost. But what really hurt was the realisation that her mother had been right after all.

There had been a purpose for her hope, and Rosa hated herself for refusing so resolutely to share her mother's faith. She felt humbled, humiliated even. She'd let her father down, as well as her mother. And now, the opportunity to apologise to her mother had gone, although she doubted she would ever have found the strength to say sorry.

Those two weeks became unbearable for Rosa, heightened by her aunt's agitated nervousness. She could tell that Petrov didn't want anything to do with his brother-in-law. Maria had warned her not to expect the father she'd known and Rosa didn't know what she meant by that. When she thought of her father, there was only one way of visualising him, she couldn't contemplate an alternative. The anticipation of Viktor's return filled her with dread and tormented her thoughts.

There was no joy in Viktor's homecoming; no celebration, no bunting, no fanfare. Just an old man who looked close to death. 'Give him a hug, Rosa,' Maria had said. Rosa obliged but the bodily contact repulsed her. This wasn't her father, she'd been right all along.

Over the weeks, Viktor's sceptre-like presence filled the apartment. He rarely moved, spoke only occasionally and even then, very briefly, but his presence dominated the limited space, his shadow seemed to encroach over Rosa's domestic life. She never complained, didn't dare to, and merely tolerated his overbearing presence. She felt no love for him, just a resentment that the father of now wasn't the father of before. It wasn't his fault, she knew that, but she couldn't help but blame him for it. It was a huge relief when she secured a place at college, a lifeline to sanity, which she grabbed with indecent haste.

Rosa glanced at her watch. Vladimir didn't like it when she was late. It wasn't a woman's prerogative; it was merely bad organisation and lack of self-discipline. He was a librarian, after all, everything in his life was neatly compartmentalised. At least, she hoped he was. She took another look at her sleeping father and rose from the chair. As she turned to leave, she stopped. Then, turning around, she approached him, leaned down and kissed his forehead. For a moment, she thought she saw a faint flicker of a smile on the old man's lips.

*

'Tonight, Rosa, you're in for a very special treat.' Vladimir's grin spread broadly across his face, like a boy with a secret he can't wait to reveal. His eyes positively twinkled with anticipation.

'What on earth do you mean?'

'Wait and see.'

Rosa was used to being spoiled by her new boyfriend – each trip out seemed to reveal an even greater surprise. She wished sometimes that she had the appropriate clothes for these glamorous places. Each time she had to wear the same drab outfit, so poorly made and carelessly sewn. Occasionally, he managed to commandeer a car, but tonight they caught the streetcar to a destination unknown. And yet, he did all this and asked for nothing in return. At 25, she'd expected him to be more demanding, but no, his manners were exemplary, his conduct chivalrous. Frankly, it was disappointing. Sometimes, she wondered what Vladimir wanted from her. However much she dolled herself up, however much she lingered at the college gates when he dropped her off, he never made an inappropriate pass. What did it take? she asked herself.

Vladimir was wearing his usual cream mackintosh, tied tightly by a belt, his black shoes carefully polished, his fair hair neatly combed with a perfect parting to the left. But tonight he was also wearing a dark blue, silken scarf that Rosa hadn't seen before. She'd been tempted to ask him where he got it from but decided against it.

'Were you at college today?' he asked.

'Yes, we were rehearsing the play.'

'And how are your friends, Boris and Ella, isn't it?'

Rosa thought of Ella and her excessive make-up, her perfect hair and the abortion so carefully filed away in the depths of her consciousness. 'Yes, and Claudia. Ella's the pretty one, though, very pretty – you'd like her.' She hoped for a reaction but Vladimir's expression gave nothing away.

'And how about this Boris, you said he's a Jew?'

'Yes, I found out today his father was a rabbi. And he, er, also declared his undying love for me today.'

She watched him carefully. 'Did he indeed,' he said with a muffled laugh, gazing out of the window at the passing pedestrians. 'Can't say I blame him.'

'Oh, really? Why do you say that?'

'A rabbi, you say?'

She sighed. 'Yes, Vladimir, a rabbi.'

They rode in silence for a few stops down Tverskaya Street, or, to use its new name, Gorky Street. The street was being widened and consequently, it was like travelling through a continuous building site. Rosa looked sideways at Vladimir. Perhaps, her aunt was right. She liked Vladimir, she liked him a lot but she needed something more. His mystery had been part of the charm but now the novelty was wearing off. She desired trust, not secrets. After a while, he asked her about the Chekhov rehearsals and she replied in detail and wondered whether he was listening. 'So how's life at the library?' she asked nonchalantly.

'Quiet,' he said, abruptly. 'Here we are.'

As they jumped off the streetcar, Rosa noticed a row of large black cars parked along the street and wondered what they were doing there. The sight of them made her shudder, they all looked so shiny and officious, with their spoked wheels and running boards. Near the cars, a small huddle of ragged people had gathered, looking through a shop window. Vladimir walked towards them and silently but brusquely pushed his way through. People stepped back to let him through, and Rosa saw they were eyeing a shop display and the goods no one but the people in the black cars could afford. To Rosa's surprise, Vladimir walked directly up to a door where a militiaman stood, flashed a card which he produced from his pocket, and then said something to the soldier in a hushed tone. The soldier nodded and stood aside for Vladimir to pass.

'Come,' he said.

'Are we going in?'

'Yes, come.'

'But this is Gastronom Number One, isn't it?'

'Nothing but the best, Rosa, nothing but the best.'

Rosa stepped in and was surprised at how big and extravagant the hallway seemed. From outside, it seemed like an ordinary dwelling but it was obviously something a bit special. A colourful red patterned carpet lined the corridor, chandeliers hung from the ceiling and portraits of Party officials adorned the walls. 'What is this?'

'You'll see in a minute. You have to sign here,' he said, pointing to an open visitor's book resting on a table covered in a bright, white tablecloth. Vladimir led her down the corridor and knocked on the large imposing door at the end of the hallway. The door swung open and Vladimir walked through taking Rosa by the hand. Another uniformed man approached Vladimir with a polite smile and took his coat. The man turned to Rosa.

'Rosa, your coat?' said Vladimir.

But Rosa was standing next to the door; her mouth had dropped open in awe of what was laid out in front of her. From outside, no one would have suspected, but inside was a lavish store of such grandiose means that it took her breath away. 'I never realised there were places like this,' she said to herself as Vladimir relieved her of her coat. Men in uniforms wandered around the room accompanied by extravagantly dressed women, inspecting what was on offer to them, making purchases, handing over ration cards, filling their shopping bags. The nearest table was laden with foodstuffs of the sort she didn't know existed in such abundance. She knew that there were shops for the privileged but she never imagined this. It wasn't so much the sight of all this food, but the assault on her sense of smell. Olfactory memories crowded in on her; smells she'd forgotten, aromas she didn't know. The pure perfume of dairy goods fought against the smell of freshly butchered meat, which finally succumbed to the dizzying smell of fish. Her stomach contracted as if rebelling against the saliva forming on her tongue. She approached the table and avoided the assistant's helpful smile as if her eyes would give away that she didn't belong, that she was only here under false pretences. She cast her eye over the glorious bounty of foodstuffs. There were a dozen varieties of cheese; yellow, white and blue, cheeses with fancy French names. There was butter as yellow as gold, and eggs – huge shiny eggs. She'd forgotten that food could smell so strongly. Next to the dairy products was a table of fruit. Rosa picked up an orange and tried to remember the last time she'd eaten a piece of fruit. She wandered to the next table and stood awestruck by the sight and smell of sausages in numerous shapes and sizes, of freshly-cut bacon, of recently-plucked fowl.

Rosa wandered in a daze, aware that Vladimir was hovering behind her. 'I have my uses, don't you think?' he said gleefully. 'Have you ever come across this?'

He was holding up a blood-red bottle with a bright label on it, written, she thought, in English. 'What is it?'

'It's American. It's called ketchup.'

'Catch up?'

Vladimir laughed. 'Ketchup. It's a sauce.'

A few paces further along, Rosa came across a fish tank full of *live* fish. 'What would you like, comrade?' asked the plump male assistant, wearing white overalls, poised with a small fish net, at the ready. 'We have pike, trout, carp, bream, whatever you like.'

Rosa smiled weakly.

She presumed that the prices would be astronomical, she imagined a month's salary for a few sausages, but no, she was wrong. The cost for the most gorgeous, mouth-watering food was so much less than the most basic, unappetising food available to them as ordinary citizens.

'But I don't understand, how do you...' She couldn't finish the sentence, unsure how to frame a dozen questions into one.

'Let's just say, I know a few people,' he said, with a wink. 'But even I'm rationed, there's only so much I'm permitted per week, but I want you to enjoy yourself, whatever is mine is yours, Rosa.' He handed her his ration card. She studied it for a few seconds and realised that in one week, Vladimir could purchase what Maria could afford in perhaps three months or more. She thought of her poor aunt and her *just-in-case* bag.

Rosa stared at him, still in a state of disbelief. His gleeful grin had changed into a smile of sincerity, of a man who wanted to make a difference in her life, if only briefly, and to show her that another, better world existed under the very noses of those who daily survived without. But Rosa's disbelief was not joyous. She realised she knew little about her boyfriend but not until this moment had she realised quite how deep her ignorance was. She knew nothing about him and even less about the world he occupied. Ella was right, this man was not a librarian and she had every right to ask for the truth but something held her back; the truth frightened her. Instead, she merely shook her head.

Vladimir looked concerned. 'You don't seem happy?'

'But why, Vladimir? How?'

Vladimir shuffled from one foot to the other; his usual confidence had ebbed away. Perhaps he recognised that he'd taken her too far, too quickly. 'Because I... I like you.' His gaze fell to his polished shoes, the chandelier lights reflecting in the shiny blackness of the leather. 'Because I like you very much,' he said, almost apologetically.

Rosa's bewilderment at her surroundings disappeared in an instant. For the first time, Vladimir had stripped himself of his exterior and had allowed her a glimpse of the person within. She knew it'd taken all his strength to humble himself in front of her, and for that, she cherished the moment.

'Yes,' she said. 'And I like you too, Vladimir. I like you very much.'

Chapter 7: The Unveiling

The more important factory workers had crowded into the workers' restaurant. I stood with my back pressed against the wall, watching their blank faces. Rows of mostly men, their overalls grimy, traces of dirt on their faces, their eyes fixed on the table at the far end of the large, over-lit room. One could tell that, given a choice, they'd all prefer not to be here; it was obvious they had been press-ganged into attending. Behind the table sat Comrade Trifonov, the prestigious factory director, a couple of his deputies, then Dmitry and, next to him, his patron, Mikhail. Trifonov was a man in his late fifties, a small, rounded man with dark, thinning hair and a long, thin nose and a lugubrious expression. Dmitry seemed uncomfortable and kept shooting me glances as if seeking reassurance by my presence. Along the sidewall hung the usual portraits of Stalin, Lenin, and the NKVD boss, Yagoda. On the back wall hung a large banner, proclaiming *Work productively, rest culturally*. And behind the main table, covered by a dark green piece of cloth, hung Dmitry's painting.

I couldn't help but feel disappointed for Dmitry. His carefully crafted work was to be unveiled in this nondescript hall in a routine factory, no different to the hundreds of others dotted around Moscow. It deserved better – a wider, more appreciative audience than the bedraggled unenthusiastic workers currently present. But Trifonov was an influential man and a painting by someone such as Dmitry provided a degree of prestige to his establishment. It would show him as a man of taste, a patron of the arts. The agreement was that after spending a year in the factory, Dmitry's painting would be transferred to one of the smaller art galleries. If Dmitry received his Order of Lenin, then his reputation would spread. He could work for the art galleries and not bother with these commissions from men who knew nothing about art.

Nonetheless, I looked forward to the prospect of even a small gallery. The idea of my image being seen by hundreds of people was immensely thrilling. I had posed three times for him, each time longer than the previous. The middle session was particularly difficult. Dmitry knew his deadline was looming and the pressure did little for his output. Whatever he did, he immediately erased under a stream of muttered curses. He frequently paused and paced up and down his small studio or circled around me, eyeing me like a dress in a shop, rarely looking me in the eye. He talked constantly but only to himself. I soon realised that when he talked, things were going badly. After an hour or more, he finally gave up and seemed despondent. I changed back into my ordinary clothes and quickly left. Later that day, he phoned to apologise. But I understood, I had learnt to distinguish between the charm of Dmitry the man and Dmitry, the irascible artist at work.

Two days later, we had our third and final session. With the deadline forthcoming, I arrived with trepidation. As much as I looked forward to seeing him, the appeal of being an artist's model was already losing its gloss. This time, however, it was thankfully different. He seemed more relaxed; the paint went where he wanted it to go, the image in his head translated itself easily onto the canvas. He even addressed me directly on a couple of occasions and towards the end, he worked with a small smile on his lips. Eventually, he stepped back from the canvas and stared at his work, nodding his head with obvious satisfaction. He beckoned me to join him. I was impressed. There I was, my profile in a work of art. My image stood at the front and to the right of the painting, my left hand clasping a jug of water, the right hand passing a filled glass to the outstretched hand of one of the workers. My posture was one of a pride – pride in my fellow workers, pride in the process of collectivisation, pride in my country. The sun reflected off my gleaming blue overalls, my hair tied back. But despite the androgynous nature of the clothes, I was still very much a woman, the maternal future of the Motherland. The top of the overalls opened enough to reveal the roundness and texture of my bosom, too much I feared, and the elasticated waist exaggerated the shape of my hips.

'What do you think?' he asked.

'I think it's wonderful.' He looked at me as if seeking the truth in my eyes. 'Truly, I think it's really very good.'

He nodded. 'Yes, yes, yes.' He paced to the other side of the room and back again, grinning broadly, his eyes sparkling with pleasure, barely able to contain his glee. 'Yes, so do I,' he said.

'You don't think it's a little too…'

'Too what?'

'Daring? I mean, my…'

'Breasts?'

'Yes.'

He put his arm around my shoulder. 'It's beautiful, the whole thing is. Don't worry; it'll be fine.'

The touch and the weight of his arm around me made my insides tingle and a shiver of pleasure ran down my spine; I felt so comfortable and attached. I leaned into his embrace and breathed in his odour of paint and warmth.

'Yes, it'll be fine.'

'You know, it's such a joy finishing a work but sometimes it takes a day or two to fully sink in and when it does, it's… it's wonderful, I feel like punching the air and shouting out of the window. Do you know what I mean?'

'I… I don't know.' As much as I wanted to, I couldn't think of a time when I felt such spontaneous joy.

'Thank you, Maria, you made a good painting a perfect painting.'

'Pleased to have obliged.'

He laughed and pulled me closer. I looked up at him, his face hovering above me, and stared into the darkness of his eyes. The seconds lingered. Kiss me, I thought, just kiss me, just for a few moments, let me know what it is to be alive, to be kissed for a reason, kissed with a passion.

'Perhaps next time,' he said, 'I will paint you nude.'

'I thought it couldn't be me, I thought…'

He stepped away from me – the moment had passed. 'We could place you in a classical setting, the Soviet Olympus, with her mirror and her black cat or perhaps draped against a column of a Greek temple with cherubs at your feet, gazing up at you adoringly …' I stopped listening, aware only of the closeness that was no more. He was Dmitry the Artist again.

The recollection of that evening made me smile wistfully while Mikhail delivered his patriotic speech, his thumb hooked into the small pocket of his waistcoat, his greased hair shining under the hall lights. I tried to concentrate. He talked of Russia's expanding industrialisation within its second Five-Year Plan, of the need to maintain the momentum, the necessity to catch up and ultimately overtake the West. He talked of the wisdom of the Party and Stalin in particular. Occasionally, Comrade Trifonov would nod in agreement but his expression remained static, still lugubrious.

'A work of art has to depict a story as surely as a piece of fiction. And that story has to be Soviet, whether it's the miner, the soldier, a field of grain, a factory, or the worker on the collective farm. By the very nature of their ordinariness, they become heroic standard-bearers of the mundane. Art has to have immediate appeal, free of distraction or any form of disorder. Art for the sake of art is a bourgeois indulgence. The viewer must believe he is viewing a story not a piece of art. And the proletariat has to be seen as strong in mind and body, resolutely moral in character, and, even under capitalist oppression, they must be defiant and brave, unwilling to cede their higher moral ground. The artist, therefore, must surrender his individuality to the greater god of ideology. "The artist is the engineer of the soul" – we are all familiar with Comrade Stalin's–' An eruption of applause interrupted him. He waited for a few moments before being able to continue. 'Comrade Stalin's phrase. And few artists encapsulate our beloved leader's vision as Dmitry here. As a member of the Russian Association of Proletariat Artists and a leading light of the creative intelligentsia, his work is becoming widely acknowledged as perfect examples of our glorious past and shining future. His work here is an example of socialist realism at its best. It shows the harmonious working of the countryside, the collective pride of the noble peasant. Its place here, in one of Moscow's most productive factories, is particularly fitting.' He paused as if expecting a response and looked momentarily embarrassed by the silence. He stepped back from the table and moved to the cloth-covered painting. The moment had come. I noticed Dmitry clasp his hands and my stomach churned. Only I knew how important this moment was to him. No one, apart from myself, had yet set eyes on the completed painting – Mikhail had insisted on maintaining the surprise effect and Comrade Trifonov had shown no resistance. He reached for the cord attached to the cloth and held it gingerly. 'So,' he said, stretching the word, 'with no further ado…' Mikhail eyed his audience and I realised that he was as nervous as me. His reputation also depended on Dmitry and his other clients. 'I am d-deep…', he coughed. 'Deeply honoured to unveil Dmitry's latest work. Dedicated to the workers of this fine factory and to all glorious workers of the Soviet Union, comrades, I present to you… *The Workers' Rest*…'

The audience of factory workers began to applaud mechanically even before the cloth had fallen away. I hoped that as the painting was unveiled, the acclaim might become more spontaneous, more genuine. I was disappointed, the applause was only one step removed from a slow clap – steady, rhythmic and ponderous. I hated them for it. The only show of enthusiastic reaction came from Trifonov's deputies sitting behind the table. Comrade Trifonov himself was not clapping but had turned his chair around and was intently studying the painting. I tried to read the expression in Dmitry's eyes, but for one who usually wore his heart on his sleeve, it was difficult to tell what was going through his mind. But then the sight of Trifonov rising to his feet took my attention. He still wasn't clapping but I assumed he was taking the lead in providing a standing ovation, at least theoretically, as the audience had been on their feet throughout. His deputies jumped to the same conclusion and, as one, rose to their feet and began to clap with greater rigour. At least this provided the spur to the workers to show more enthusiasm for this piece of work produced for their benefit. I saw Trifonov's mouth open and what seemed like a single-syllable, rounded word was lost in the noise. But there was something in his eyes that frightened me. I stopped clapping, suddenly unable to carry on. I concentrated on his mouth, stretching my ears. He started shaking his head and the third or fourth time, I heard it; he was saying 'No.'

The deputies had heard it too. Instantly, they stopped clapping and glanced nervously at each other. Trifonov turned to face his workers. With his hands slicing the air horizontally, he yelled, 'Stop it, I say. I said *stop it*!' The workers at the front immediately stopped clapping and, like a wave, row upon row fell silent until the last echoes of applause died away. The hall reverberated with stunned silence, all eyes focused on Trifonov, the question burned on their faces. They weren't bored now. Trifonov, his face flushed, paced back to the painting. He glanced disparagingly at Mikhail and then spun around to face the wide-eyed Dmitry. The director pointed to the painting behind him, 'What's *this*?', he hissed.

Dmitry shook his head. 'I'm sorry, Comrade Trifonov, I don't follow.'

Trifonov glared at Mikhail. Mikhail shrugged his shoulders and asked, 'Is there anything wrong, Comrade Trifonov?'

'Wrong? I would say there's something "wrong".' He stepped back towards the table. 'Are you blind, am I the only one to see it?'

Mikhail's nonplussed expression summed up the question of everyone present but I had a feeling that I knew what was coming next, and somehow I knew my alter-ego was about to become the focus of everyone's acute attention. 'See what?' asked Mikhail.

'Why you – you… Can't you see the blatant pornography in this picture? Look,' he said, pointing back to the painting. 'Look at her, the blazoned shape of her – her…' He struggled to find the word.

'Breasts?' said Dmitry mockingly. 'Yes, women have breasts, I don't understand–'

'Don't come the innocent with me; that overall is so unbuttoned, it virtually exposes her.'

'It's a hot day,' protested Dmitry. I could tell that inside he was laughing at the absurdity of the situation.

'Well, why didn't you paint her naked and be done with it?' A ripple of laughter swam across the room and Dmitry suppressed an incredulous laugh. Trifonov scowled at his workers. 'Oh, so you think the depiction of pornography is funny, do you? Another peep out of you lot and I'll give you something to laugh about.'

Mikhail coughed. 'I do understand your concerns, Comrade Trifonov–'

'Do you? I have the distinct feeling I'm alone in my repugnance. You know how strongly the Party feels about this sort of thing–'

'Quite so, Comrade Trifonov, quite so. But come now, the artist is merely trying to show the honest sweat of the worker on a hot day in the country. In fact, we are privileged indeed to be in the company of the young lady who posed for this figure…' My heart leapt. A titter of interest rippled through the audience as I felt my cheeks burn. My discomfort was obvious and being the only non-factory female in the hall, eyes began to turn in my direction.

Dmitry tried to interrupt, 'I don't think it's necessary to—'

But it was already too late; every head was turned, every pair of eyes fixed on me. 'Oh, I'm sure Maria wouldn't mind…' said Mikhail, as his eyes came to rest on me. Comrade Trifonov was the last person to realise that I was the new point of interest. As his eyes focussed on me, I pressed myself against the wall and felt myself physically diminish in height.

Mikhail continued. 'Maria, would you mind stepping forward so that everyone can see you.'

I smiled weakly but I couldn't move, conscious of how hot I suddenly felt.

Comrade Trifonov glanced at the painting and then looked back at me as if comparing the girl in the painting with the physical embodiment in front of him. I swear he glanced down at my breasts for a fraction of a second before refocusing on my eyes. 'Did you pose for this?' he asked.

I tried to speak but the nerves in my stomach silenced my tongue. Instead, I merely nodded. For a moment, his expression softened as if he was impressed by Dmitry's skill. But perhaps remembering his indignation, the moment soon passed. 'What would your parents think?' he snarled. 'Well, what do you have to say for yourself, young lady, has the cat got your tongue?'

I opened my mouth but the words wouldn't come. To my relief, Dmitry sprung to my defence. 'This is ridiculous,' he snapped. 'This has nothing to do with her.' His outburst managed to deflect the attention of everyone's focus away from me. I felt myself slide down the wall, the sweat breaking out on my forehead. 'I'm sorry, Comrade Trifonov, but I find your comments unjustified. The pornography that only you can see is obviously the product of your mind–'

'No!' It was Mikhail's turn to panic; he knew Dmitry was skating on very thin ice. Dmitry held his tongue and watched his patron. 'What I think Dmitry means, is that there is clearly a misunderstanding here–'

'A "misunderstanding"?' bellowed Comrade Trifonov. 'There's no misunderstanding. *He's* the pornographer in this room and yet he has the gall to try and turn the tables. Well, we'll see who's the fornicator here when I take this to the proper authorities.'

Mikhail shot a nervous look at Dmitry. 'Really, comrade, I don't think we need to take it that far.'

'Well, I do,' said Trifonov. He took a final look at the painting and then suddenly turned on his heels and walked away from the table and out through the door at the side of the door.

The hall erupted into a burst of thrilled conversation. After a few moments, one of Trifonov's deputies decided to take charge of the situation. Rising to his feet, he ordered the workers to go home and not to mention to anyone the events of the evening. As the workers filed out, each stealing a last glimpse of me, I kept my attention focused on Dmitry. Mikhail sat wearily down next to him and I noticed him pat Dmitry's hand. It was a small gesture but I was relieved. It meant Dmitry still had his patron's support. He wouldn't have to fight this on his own – at least, in the officious sense, for Dmitry knew, he would always have my support.

After a while, Dmitry looked up and caught my eye. Still unable to move from the spot, I smiled at him above the heads of the passing workmen. He smiled back but even from across the hall, I could see his usual confidence had ebbed away.

Chapter 8: The Purge

The students had been told to take their places in the main lecturing theatre at the end of classes. Rosa, Ella and Claudia arrived early, determined to sit towards the back and melt into the anonymity of faces. The wooden floor echoed with the sound of slow footsteps as the students and lecturers came in silently to take their places. Extra chairs had been brought in and arranged in a huge square; in the centre of which stood the temporary platform: a large table covered in a white cloth, decked with a lamp, glasses and jugs of water, and behind which were three unoccupied chairs. And on the other side of the table, another chair, conspicuous by its solitary presence. On the table lay a large pile of folders, held together by a thick, red ribbon.

Rosa shivered. The main hall was always cold – it was too large and the ceiling too high to maintain any warmth. But, today, it was the foreboding pile of folders that had made her tremble. Each folder represented a student or lecturer, each one filled with testimonies, histories and written accusations against the name on the front cover. Was her name among them? It was rumoured that there were spies in every classroom, invisible informants at every turn. One's student life, and private, family and political lives, were held within those sheaves of paper; every aspect of one's existence. But, Rosa reminded herself, *she* had nothing to fear; after all, she loved her country, she loved her leader, she worked hard, and her lecturers thought highly of her. But was that enough? Rosa wasn't a spy; she had never denounced anyone. But perhaps she should have. Was it something they could use against her? Had her failure to denounce others implied complicity? The table also had upon it a bust of Stalin and a vase of flowers. Somehow, thought Rosa, the flowers looked out of place. Flowers signified hope, a new beginning. But the atmosphere was not of hope but of dread. One could see it in every single face – the silent dread of what lay ahead. The best one could hope for was survival. It was either survival or condemnation. And Rosa knew only too well the meaning of condemnation – she had seen it for herself when they came and took away her father in their Black Maria. Condemnation meant expulsion from the Party, arrest and incarceration – it didn't bear thinking about.

Rosa glanced at her two friends but they were both too focussed upon themselves. Rosa knew what was going through their minds. Could Ella be a spy? Claudia? It was too absurd to contemplate. She had already rehearsed her story numerous times but the fear was still a continual presence. However much she tried to remember her past, there was always a chance of a forgotten conversation, a misconstrued word, a false impression. She loved Stalin just as a priest loved his own God, but that in itself wasn't enough to ensure her survival. Had she caused anyone to bear a grudge against her; was there anything about her that might cause envy? She knew, they all knew, that they had as much to fear from their friends as from their enemies. In this oppressive environment, one was very much alone.

She scanned the students sitting around her. Two rows in front and to the left, sat Boris, wearing his customary jacket. She wondered whether he might have replaced the missing button in honour of the occasion. Perhaps he felt the intensity of her gaze, for he turned around and caught her eye. The size of his pupils seemed more exaggerated than ever behind his glasses. There was a brief acknowledgement in his expression before he returned his attention, like everyone else, to the platform at the centre of the hall.

The whole college seemed to be present, every chair was occupied. But amongst all these people, there was no sound, just a hushed silence, the shuffling of bottoms on chairs, the occasional cough. But, thought Rosa, one could also hear every heart beating, sense the churning stomachs, the wringing of hands. She could see it in all the faces – the etched expression of fear. And she knew that their faces merely reflected her own.

In the midst of the silence, came the sound of more footsteps. Immediately, Rosa knew it was them. Their footsteps were too self-assured to belong to one of the students or staff. Into the hall, came three sombre-looking men, the judge and jury. They took their places at the platform and sat down. Rosa watched the middle man as he adjusted the lamp and poured himself a glass of water. He didn't look particularly threatening – he was younger than she'd expected and seemed to lack the air of arrogance she normally associated with those in authority. He had a head of dark, curly hair and a small pencil-thin moustache. The men on either side of him were more of what she expected – older men with stern, determined expressions. The middle man shuffled a few leaves of paper, took a sip of water and finally, stood up. The time had come.

At first, he didn't say anything and simply stood still, staring down at a piece of paper on the table. For a moment, Rosa thought he looked ill at ease. But then he looked up, narrowed his eyes and scanned the rows of people in front of him, as if calculating the amount of time and the degree of work that lay ahead of him. Rosa realised that despite his youth, his face had the hardened look of determination. This was a man who had a job to do and do it he would.

'There are some among us who are enemies of the people,' he said without introduction, his voice surprisingly deep, slightly guttural. 'In our very midst, there are deviationists, spies, double-faced opportunists, class aliens. Look around you, do you know whether your neighbour is true to the cause of socialism or a state enemy?' He paused and the whole auditorium became shrouded in suspicion while everyone thought disparaging thoughts about their neighbours. 'It is our duty tonight and all this week to ferret out these people who hide behind their masks; to oust these plotters, these supporters of Trotsky and his rabble. If you have cancer, what do you do? Forgive it, try to convert it, give it a second chance?' He slammed his fist against the table, 'No,' he yelled. 'You cut it out. You cut-it-out!' A murmuring of approval echoed through the hall. Rosa nodded her head in agreement while trying to conjure up faces of potential plotters among the people she knew. But the only face that kept returning to her again and again was that of her father.

The Chairman continued. 'Our job here is to rid this college of unsuitable elements, to purge the cancer. We shall not hesitate, for our socialist future depends on it. We can never rest until the work is entirely done. This is war, and you would all do well to remember that. But in this war, the enemy doesn't come at you in convenient uniforms, there is no 'them and us'; no, for they are *among* us. The enemy is the man next to you on the bus, the woman at the head of the food queue, the person sitting right next to you at this very moment, your kindly neighbour, even the person you share your dinner with. *They* will not hesitate, and nor should you. We must protect our future and we have a duty to protect our glorious divine leader, Comrade Stalin…' The name was lost in the spontaneous applause that erupted throughout the hall. Every pair of hands clapped enthusiastically, feet stamped, faces grinned. After three minutes, Rosa realised her hands were tiring. They'd made their point, she thought, but she felt as though she couldn't be the first to stop, so she continued. Fortunately, the Chairman raised a hand and his audience was allowed, mercifully, to stop.

The Chairman introduced his two stern-faced colleagues and introduced himself as Comrade Pletnev of the Party's Central Purge Commission. He sat down and untied the ribbon from the pile of folders. Rosa glanced at Ella on her left and winked at her friend. She knew Ella was silently beseeching her not to mention her darkest secret, the abortion undertaken, not on medical grounds, but for the sake of self-advancement. Pletnev opened the top folder, scanned the pages within and called the name of Comrade Breshkovskaya. Rosa looked around and saw Breshkovskaya rise and make her way towards the platform. She was an older student, perhaps thirty, with a round face, bobbed hair and flushed cheeks. She must have been conscious of every pair of eyes on her, thought Rosa.

Breshkovskaya took her seat in front of the three men and handed her party card to the Chairman. When prompted, she recounted her personal history, while the two men, either side of the Chairman, wrote notes. She spoke in a flat tone and told the panel about her parents' occupations, her upbringing and her career to date. There was an error in her past, she admitted, for which she had already acknowledged and been forgiven. A little misdemeanour, the folly of youth and inexperience. It was a trifling of a thing, a mere nothing. Pletnev nodded in agreement. Breshkovskaya was doing fine; she had passed the awkward part. Rosa realised what Breshkovskaya was doing – far better to confess than try to hide and then be accused. She remembered only too well the day she decided to stand up at school and denounce her father as a class enemy. And she remembered also the feeling of relief afterwards.

The panel each asked Breshkovskaya a couple of questions and then invited questions or comments from the students. Someone spoke up for her, said what an unblemished life she had led and a second voice commented on what a fine example she was to the younger students. The Chairman, satisfied, thanked Breshkovskaya and handed her back her card. Rosa watched her as she returned to her seat, her cheeks now totally red but with an unbridled grin on her face. A couple of colleagues patted her on the back or shook her hand. She had survived.

Rosa watched and listened as three more students took their turn in front of the Commission, and returned to their seats, clutching their Party cards, their proof of allegiance still safely in their hands.

Chairman Pletnev picked up the next folder. 'Comrade Kalinikov,' he said. Rosa's lecturer took his place in front of the committee and ran his hand through his receding hairline.

'Tell us about yourself,' said Pletnev, without looking up from his papers.

Kalinikov cleared his throat and launched into his pre-prepared personal history. He had been a soldier and a revolutionary and had fought against the Whites during the Civil War earning a reputation for bravery and selflessness. A stomach wound ended his military career and that was when he began teaching, moving from one college to another, before settling in this college five years previously.

Pletnev nodded and scribbled a few notes. 'Hmm, interesting. Are you married, Comrade Kalinikov?'

'Yes, Comrade Chairman, three years.'

'Second marriage?'

'Yes, my first wife–'

'Happily married?'

'Oh yes.'

'Children?'

Rosa smiled, this was turning into a polite exchange of conversation, Kalinikov was safe, the audience was bored. Rosa was pleased for him, his lectures may have been dull, but she wouldn't want to see him come to any harm. 'A small boy, eighteen months,' replied Kalinikov.

'Are you a religious man, Comrade Kalinikov?'

Kalinikov shuffled in his seat. 'No, Comrade Chairman, I have no time for such comedy.'

The Chairman slammed his palms onto the table. 'Don't mess with me, Kalinikov, I ask you again, are you a religious man?' The audience waited for his answer. The Chairman knew something and Kalinikov had to be careful not to confess to something the Chairman didn't know.

Kalinikov's face flushed. 'N-no, but my wife, I mean, my parents are, I mean they used to be. They – they insisted.'

'Insisted? Insisted on what exactly?'

Kalinikov cast his eyes down. 'The – the christening.' Some of the audience laughed. 'I didn't want it, believe me, I argued long and hard against it, said there was no point, but old habits die hard, they insisted–'

'So you said. Anyone like to comment?' he asked addressing the auditorium.

'I was there!' said a voice from behind Rosa. She strained her neck to see Comrade Ossipovna, one of Kalinikov's fellow lecturers, rising to her feet. 'And he's lying. There was no hesitation, you never saw a prouder parent.'

'No! This is not true, I hated every minute of the ceremony,' screamed Kalinikov. 'It is she who is lying–'

'Chuck him out,' said an anonymous voice from the far side of the auditorium.

'Believer,' shouted another.

Comrade Ossipovna remained on her feet. 'He took his oaths with great seriousness. He's a believer, all right. And what's more, he still is, he just hides it well.'

The chairman spoke: 'And what, may I ask, madam, were you doing at this religious ceremony?'

She sat down as if the ground had suddenly given way under her feet. The hall roared with laughter, and Rosa also found herself laughing at the absurdity of the woman's self-implicating accusation.

The chairman continued. 'You are a believer, Kalinikov, a superstitious renegade. That in itself is bad enough but then you are naïve to believe you can cover your heinous claptrap. You cannot have two ideologies–'

'No,' cried Kalinikov. 'Stalin is my only ideology. I fought for the revolution. Is this how you treat old revolutionaries?'

'Old revolutionaries are not lackeys of the church.'

'Forgive me, Comrade Chairman, it was a mistake, my wife, my parents, they all made me go through with it. I'll do anything, just don't – don't expel me, I have a child–'

'A child baptised. You dare ask for forgiveness when you lie, cover the innocent under a cloak of superstition and then have the gall to try to blame your wife and your parents. What sort of man are you?'

The audience clapped and stamped their feet in slow rhythmic time. Rosa rubbed her eyes, Kalinikov didn't deserve this. But Ella nudged her in the ribs, Rosa had no choice, she had to join in or people would notice and remember. She started stamping the wooden floor with her flat heels but closed her eyes; she couldn't face watching the tears streaming down Kalinikov's cheeks. Above the dim, Pletnev continued, his voice raised, making no attempt to quieten the baying hordes. 'I'll tell you what sort of man you are – you're a snivelling, lying snake and the Party and our beloved Leader–' His audience erupted into rapturous applause and cheers, and Pletnev's words were lost.

Kalinikov rose wearily from his seat and looked resigned to his fate, but then he straightened his back, clenched his fist and spoke in such a loud, authoritative voice, the whole auditorium fell silent. 'I fought the Whites for the likes of you, I have the wounds to show it, wounds I carry with pride for what I did for my country, the country I love. My generation didn't shed their blood to be thrown to the wall by bureaucrats like you. And then fifteen years teaching, fighting the war against illiteracy, preparing the children of the revolution for their tomorrow. But there is no tomorrow when we live under a tyranny worse than ever before–'

'Enough!' bellowed Pletnev, clicking his fingers at a uniformed guard. 'Take him away, take him away, I can't bear to listen to this any more.'

The guard took Kalinikov's arm and pushed him forward. At one point, his legs gave way and the guard had to haul him up. There, thought Rosa, was the end of a career. Even if he survived arrest, he and his family would forever be labelled. Friends would avoid them, no one would risk offering him employment and he'd be thrown out of his lodgings. Rosa knew only too well. For some reason, she had Kalinikov's address written in her address book, not that she had ever used it, but, she thought, she'd better erase it. If anyone ever looked through it, it wouldn't look good to have his name among her personal effects.

With Kalinikov's exit, the hall took a few minutes to calm itself and settle back into obedient silence. Pletnev reached for the next folder and looked at the name on top. Rosa's heart fluttered; it could be anyone's turn next, it could be hers. The name, when it came, made her jump as surely as if it had been her own.

'Comrade Pavlovna.' In a single moment, Ella's face was void of colour. Instinctively, both Claudia and Rosa grasped her hands. She had her secret and, as her friends, they knew it. Ella looked at each of them, looking into their eyes for their support while knowing her friends were the very ones who could secure her downfall. What was friendship when measured against duty?

Rosa, at least, had remained faithful to her friend, but she knew that in her knowledge, she was as damnable as her. Would the Commission know about the abortion? If they didn't and Ella confessed it, would they condemn her or applaud her honesty? 'Comrade Pavlovna?' Ella rose to her feet, still gripping her friends' hands. As she embarked on the long walk to centre stage, Rosa noticed the imprint that Ella's fingers had made on her own. She's got to tell them, thought Rosa, they'll know, they always do.

'Party card,' snapped Pletnev. 'Confirm your name.'

'Ella Pavlovna.'

'Age?'

'Nineteen.'

'Tell us about yourself, Comrade Pavlovna.'

Ella swallowed. 'I was born on the outskirts of Moscow. My father was a technical engineer and–'

'Was?'

'I mean, he is. He now works at the Kharkov Technological Institute, as a deputy in the metallurgical division. He was a young man during the Great War and fought against the Germans but he deserted – he didn't want to fight any more for the Imperialists. During the revolution, he was with the Bolsheviks but I don't really know what he did. My mother worked in a shoe factory but they divorced two years ago.' She stopped. Go on, thought Rosa, tell him, you have to tell him.

'OK, that's fine. So, what, Comrade Pavlovna, is your view of collectivisation?'

'Well, I agree with it, of course – wholeheartedly.'

'Why?'

'Because, because otherwise there is exploitation of labour.'

'Is that it?'

'Well…'

'Is that all your education teaches you? We expect our students to be fully versed in their politics. Platitudes have no place in our society. It is your duty to know the great achievements made in the name of socialism.'

'Well, it's also because—'

'All right, let's move on,' said Pletnev. Rosa swallowed. 'Do you have children?' Oh God, thought Rosa, this is it. Ella knew it too; she slunk in her chair and looked sick.

'No, Comrade Chairman.'

Pletnev wrote a note on his paper. 'And what are your plans after college?' He hadn't pursued it, thought Rosa. Was it a ruse, would he come back to it? Maybe not, maybe he didn't know, perhaps no one had informed on her. She allowed herself a sideways look at Claudia and her friend caught her eye for a moment before turning away as if frightened that a mere glance might reveal their shared secret. Ella spoke but Rosa was unable to hear her words for the pounding of her heart. But Ella had survived. Pletnev stamped her Party card and held it out for Ella to retrieve. At least, thought Rosa, she won't have to scrub Ella's name from her address book.

Pletnev spoke. 'We'll call it a day for now but the session will reconvene at ten o'clock tomorrow morning.'

The audience fidgeted while Ella returned to her seat, her face shining with sweat and relief. She was still shaking as she sat down.

'Well done,' whispered Claudia as she leant over and kissed Ella on the cheek.

Ella tried to catch her breath. 'I feel sick,' she said.

'Don't worry,' said Claudia. 'It's over, you're still with us.'

Rosa noticed that Boris had turned around and was smiling at Ella. But his face was struck with terror at the sound of his name echoing across the hall. 'Boris Gershberg – you will be first in line tomorrow morning,' announced Pletnev.

Chapter 9: The Lion

'I don't believe it, I don't bloody believe it.' Dmitry threw himself into his armchair. 'I mean, how dare that old sod pronounce on things he has no idea about. Pornography? I'll give him pornography if that's what he wants.' He sprang up from the chair and paced up to the window and glanced out before turning back to face me. 'He wouldn't know a work of art if it bit him on the arse.'

'It's only his opinion.'

'Yes but that's quite an opinion, the man has influence, so no one's going to dare contradict him. I'm finished; I'm done for. I can expect a knock on the door any moment.'

'Not necessarily.'

'Or they'll bide their time and watch me.' He went back to the window and looked out. 'I'm surprised there's not someone out there already, lurking outside, ready to follow me wherever I go.'

'Surely not while you still have Mikhail's support.'

'Perhaps for now, but once Trifonov's slit-eyed prejudice is accepted then Mikhail will have to step down in order to save his own skin. I suppose you can't blame him for that, but – but where does it leave me?'

He was right of course and I couldn't find the words to comfort him. His initial contempt for Comrade Trifonov was replaced by a deep anxiety bordering on paranoia, a justified paranoia. If Trifonov decided to take it further, then, as Dmitry said, his artistic and political future was in jeopardy. I remembered how Dmitry had told Petrov that his apartment and material belongings were his in name only. If Dmitry fell foul of the authorities, everything would go. I wanted to say he could start again and come to me, but of course, I was still a married woman.

Without a word, Dmitry disappeared into the bedroom and I sat in his living room wondering whether to follow him. I realised at that moment how unsure I was of where I stood in his affections. From the evening of the dinner, I had felt a longing for him that had taken me unawares. But at times like this, I thought that perhaps I was simply being fanciful. Was I reading too much into it? Dmitry, I had learnt, could be annoyingly enigmatic. Sometimes, the way he looked at me, I believed he felt the same way and that the only thing that held us back was Petrov. And I believed that had we met at a different time, in different circumstances, things would have been so much clearer. But at other times, I doubted my own convictions. I'd come to accept that he was unreachable once he had a paintbrush in his hand and that the only important thing was what was on the easel in front of him. Was I simply an occasional model and a woman he felt sorry for, or did I mean something to him? I sat there listening to him rummaging around maniacally in the bedroom and I decided I needed to find out there and then.

'Dmitry,' I said, pushing open the bedroom door. 'What are you doing?' A wicker chair in the corner of the room was piled high with various clothes.

'I'm packing – just in case.'

'In case they come?'

He nodded, and with a folded shirt in his hand, sat down heavily on the edge of the bed. 'I had a friend once. He was also called Dmitry, a sculptor, and a fine one at that. He used to do sculptures of all the big men, past and present – Lenin, Marx, Stalin, Bukharin…'

'Bukharin?'

'Yes, before his downfall. And after Bukharin's arrest, they came for him. His work of Bukharin was enough to ensure his own downfall.'

'But he couldn't have known…'

'That's what one would have thought, but you can see the twisted logic in there, can't you?'

'But you can't compare his case to yours?'

'No? How can you tell? You might be right; it'll just be a fuss over nothing, but you *can't* be sure.' He played with a button on the folded shirt. 'I fear I may have compromised you as well, Maria.'

'It's a risk I'm prepared to take.'

'You should go,' he said, standing up. 'Go back to Petrov. If they come for me, it would look bad for you if they find you here.'

'That's another risk I'm prepared to take,' I said, looking into his dark, worried eyes.

'No, it's too risky. Go back to him. I'll say I forced you into it, that you had no idea I was painting you like that. You'll be safe with Petrov.'

'I don't want to go back to him. Who would want the deer when one can have the lion?'

He smiled. 'Even if the lion exposes you to the poacher?'

He placed his fingers against my cheek. He made to lean towards me, a tiny movement of his head. But then, he paused as if seeking my assurance. It was one of those moments when time seems to stand still, when, far away through the windows, you can hear life going on at its usual frantic pace, spinning around you at dizzying speed, but where you find yourself in the middle of the vortex where everything is totally still and deathly silent. The most minute of gestures could sweep away a mountain. I tried to speak but the words, soundless, caught in the tangles of my throat. He pulled me in and kissed me, a moment's hesitation, then with an urgency that was all-consuming. I closed my eyes and drifted away. I seemed to drift above the bedroom, the block of apartments, and beyond the city. In the darkness of my closed eyelids, I was aware of a new light pouring through my heart. His kiss seemed both conscious of its illegitimacy and aware that it was right. I tried to reassure him with my response, to let him know I wanted his kiss, his touch, his intimacy. My hands around him, pulled him tighter, my fingers bit into his back, down the length of his spine. I felt his hands clutching clumps of my hair, his fingernails catching on the ruffled strands. His hand grappled at my blouse, freeing it from my skirt, his cold hand against my shivering skin. I gripped his buttocks, my fingernails implanting themselves firmly into the seat of his pants. While his hand fumbled with my brassiere, I slipped my hand beneath his chemise and slid them up and down his ribcage, catching the hairs on his chest. Together, we eased ourselves down, our lips still firmly against one another's, as if our very lives depended on the continual contact, too frightened to let go. In a whisper so hoarse, I scarcely recognised my own voice, I uttered, 'Fuck me.'

*

Sometime later, maybe an hour, we were lying on his bed with the sheets and blankets wrapped over us. A single lamp shone dimly on the wooden table by his bed. Within the shadows, a small smile of contentment lay on his lips – I knew exactly how he felt. I was thirty years old and had never felt such a depth of passion, such an urgency of longing. Indeed, I doubted for years whether I was capable of passion. When one's whole life has been a matter of mere existence, when one's past consists of pain, then love is as inconsequential as a fistful of roubles to a rich man. But not now.

'Paint me,' I whispered.

'I will.'

'No, I mean now.'

'Now?'

'Yes, now. You said you wanted to paint the nude, so I'm offering myself to you. Paint me now.'

'Are you sure?'

'Don't you want to paint me?'

'Yes. Yes, I do.'

*

Dmitry worked quickly – this was a different process entirely from before. Once done, we returned to bed and made love again. Afterwards, as we lay there, he ran his fingers through his hair and I noticed the stains of paint on his skin – mixtures of yellow and pale red. The same paint-stained fingers that had explored my body, slid down my back, cupping my breasts, gripping me tightly and engulfing me in his warmth. I lifted the sheet and saw the same combinations of blotchy colours smeared on my skin.

In the corner, my clothes lay in a heap on the wicker chair, and in front of us lay my naked full-length portrait. Having previously watched Dmitry's methodical approach to his work, I was amazed he was able to conjure up a coherent form in such a short amount of time. But this was, after all, a doodle in comparison, with broad brushstrokes and crude mixtures of colours. And yet, it still seemed so real. My features, so haphazardly drawn, stared back at me like a reflection in a steamy mirror – blurred but still very much me. But it was the pose and the attitude that I didn't recognise. I was standing with my hands behind my head, purposely accentuating the curve of my hip. I wasn't sure if I felt proud or embarrassed by such a display of lustful arrogance. A few hours before, I would not have thought I had it in me. Was it sex that had made me stand like that? Or the sudden sense of freedom? I felt intoxicated as the layers of inhibition were stripped away in a flurry of excitement and empowerment. Dmitry the Artist had brought out Maria the Woman.

Dmitry reached over and kissed me. 'I've worked under various states of mind but that was a first.'

'What do you mean?'

'I've painted when so drunk I could hardly stand; I've painted after a three-day fast and even after a self-imposed period of sleep deprivation, but never under the influence of... of lust.'

'It's good, and it's certainly...'

'Provocative?'

I laughed. 'Yes, provocative.'

'What do you think old Comrade Trifonov would make of it?'

I looked at my image and felt those fleeting moments of empowerment and arrogance drain away. The thought of another set of eyes seeing my flesh made me shiver. 'I think you should tear it up.'

Dmitry propped himself up on his arm and looked at me. 'I thought you liked it?'

'I do, really. But it's not safe.'

'I've never destroyed any of my work, I don't think I could do it.'

I leaned against his chest and ran my finger across his jawline and down his neck. 'I don't think you have much choice. What do you think they'd say if they found it here?'

'Well, my reputation as a pornographer would be sealed.' He guffawed to himself.

'And so would be your fate,' I said, trying to be serious, but he merely laughed louder. I thumped him playfully on the chest. 'It's not funny, Dmitry.'

'I know, I know.'

My naked image stared at me from across the room and I tried to look back at her. But the harder I tried, the more she seemed to mock me. She was no longer me, no longer representational, and she knew it. Already, she belonged to an unreal moment of euphoria when everything seemed possible. *She* had a future; I merely had a past. 'What time is it?'

Dmitry leant over to the bedside table and picked up his watch. 'Just gone ten.'

'God, I should go,' I said, swinging my legs out from under the sheets.

He sat up. 'What, now?'

'Petrov will be furious with me.'

'You can't go now, how will you get back? Let him stew.'

'I can't.'

He placed his hand reassuringly against my back. 'It's too late to go back now; might as well be hung for a sheep as a lamb. Stay the night and tomorrow morning we'll think of something.'

'No, Dmitry, I have to get back, I can't stay – as much as I'd like to.'

'You don't have to do it, Maria, you don't have to go back to him.'

But I did. It wasn't Petrov's choice, nor Dmitry's; it was mine. And that left me with no choice at all.

*

I travelled home on the tram, my head in a daze - I had committed adultery. The law did not impose any legal obligation on conjugal faithfulness but the consequences of infidelity, I knew, were still potentially disastrous. I was convinced that nothing would be the same again – and the thought was not necessarily a welcome one.

It was approaching eleven at night by the time I got home. 'Where in the hell have you been?' said Petrov as soon as I stepped into the apartment. Rosa was there too, sitting in Viktor's chair. She looked embarrassed by Petrov's outburst.

'Out.'

'Where?' He was standing in the middle of our living room, a newspaper rolled up in his hand as if he'd been squatting flies.

'Just out; does it matter?'

'What's that smell?' He sniffed me. 'Oh, good God, you've been to see that brother of your friend, that Dmitry, I can smell that turpentine stuff. What the hell are you doing seeing him?'

'He wants to use me as a model – for his painting.'

'You? A model? Don't be ridiculous. You've got better things to do. I hope you said no.'

'I said yes.'

'Well, you can bloody well go down to the phone now and say you've changed your mind.'

'Don't you want to support your local artist?'

'My "local artist"? I think not. Not until he finds himself some proper work, man's work. I refuse to allow my wife to indulge in his little artistic fantasies.'

'Hello, Rosa, love. Have you had anything to eat?'

'Yes, I–'

'I hope that's all he's asked of you,' said Petrov, now pacing up and down, swinging his rolled-up newspaper.

'Is your father OK?'

'He's asleep – as usual.'

Petrov slammed the newspaper against the table edge. 'Why are you ignoring me? You're not to see him again. Is that understood?'

'You can't tell me who I can and cannot see.'

'Oh, but I can. You and I both know that, Maria. And don't you forget it.' With that, he stormed into our bedroom, slamming the door behind him.

Rosa looked sympathetically at me. I tried to smile. 'Are you all right, Rosa?' I said, remembering that the poor girl was having to run the gauntlet of a purge.

'Yes. Are *you* all right?'

'Don't worry; he'll get over it. How's it going at college? Have they started?'

'Yes.'

'And?'

'Oh, Maria, I don't know what to think any more.'

'What do you mean?'

'I always believed they were a necessity. But it was so frightening. Now I just don't know what to think.'

'You can't be too careful, Rosa, the hidden enemy is far more of a threat than the outside foe. They have to do these things. Vigilance is the watchword.'

'You sound like one of the purgers; it's exactly what they said and what I believe in but… You should have been there. There wasn't a person who was not petrified for their own skin. And they pounce as soon as they sense blood.'

'It's a way of protecting themselves. It's a matter of self-preservation.'

'I suppose.'

'You still believe, don't you, Rosa?'

'Yes, of course, but I wonder whether Comrade Stalin realises what these bureaucrats get away with under his name.'

Her faith in the apparatus of the Party machine was disintegrating before my eyes. Perhaps it was a good thing – everyone had to believe but it was safer if one only believed on the outside. That way, you knew how to look after yourself; you were more attuned to the danger signs. You knew what to say, how to think, how to laugh in the right places. Those who *really* believed had the furthest to fall; they were the ones who were unaware of the minefield that lay at every turn.

'Oh, I almost forgot,' said Rosa. 'You got a telephone call. I took a message for you.'

'Really? From whom?'

'He wouldn't say but the man said you've been given an extra appointment, at least I think that's what he said.'

My heartbeat quickened.

'He said you would know what he was talking about. You have to attend a meeting at the usual place tomorrow at midday. Does it make sense?'

A shiver ran down my spine. 'Yes,' I said, 'it makes sense.'

Chapter 10: The Purge, Day Two

Boris handed his internal passport to Comrade Pletnev and then gingerly sat down. The Chairman glanced at the card and placed it to his side. Boris stared at it and realised that never before had he wanted something back so dearly, for the card meant survival; without it he was finished. He waited while Pletnev scanned his eyes over the notes in Boris's file. It was strange, thought Boris, what large amounts of documentation existed of which one had no idea. The lamp on the table was tilted slightly at an angle giving Boris the sensation of being under a spotlight. He had never felt so frightened and was aware that his right eye was twitching ever so slightly. Around him were almost two hundred people, all of them pitying him for they knew it could be their turn next. But equally, he knew they were all eager to see him purged. The Commission couldn't purge everybody, so the more people purged at the beginning, the greater their own chances of survival. It was like being a gladiator – but worse, because here, everyone was a participant, each person, a potential victim. The Chairman, still studying Boris's file, was the emperor with the power to decide, the man with the thumb. Aware of the hot sweat trickling down his back, Boris wasn't sure how to sit – he crossed and uncrossed his legs. He rubbed his palms against his thighs and realised how wet they were.

He wanted to turn around to see Rosa – she was probably the only person willing him to survive, but he didn't dare move. He had prepared and rehearsed his life story, including the confession – he had been friends with a student whose father had signed a pro-Trotsky declaration. It wasn't much of a confession, at least he hoped it wasn't, but it was generally accepted that it was best to say something self-incriminating. As for his other secret, he was sure he was safe. Yes, his father had been a rabbi, but his father had died twenty years ago when he was still only five. Since then, his mother had remarried and moved to Moscow. His original birth certificate had been conveniently lost and replaced with another where his stepfather was declared his biological father. He had never told anyone, so unless there was someone who remembered him as a five-year-old, five hundred miles away in Kirov, or Vyatka as it was known until the year before, his secret was safe. Yet, his eye continued to twitch and the sweat on his back itched like a many-legged insect.

At long last, Pletnev was ready to start. 'Comrade Gershberg, thank you for your time. Be so good, if you would, to tell us something about yourself. Where you were born, what your parents did, and so forth. I'm sure you know the drill by now.'

Boris found his voice and started his tale, telling the Commission that he was the son of a tailor who had scraped a living for many years in a small village near Kirov. Then, when he was about eight, his family received permission to move to Moscow and start anew. Boris followed his father's example, and, as a sixteen-year-old, trained to become a tailor, but after a couple of years, decided he would better serve his country by getting an education. And what, asked Pletnev, did he hope to do on graduation? Boris replied, truthfully, that he wanted to work in a theatre, with the ultimate aim of becoming a director. So far, thought Boris, so good.

'Tell us about your friends, Comrade Gershberg.'

Boris listed a few male acquaintances, especially a boy he considered his best friend, a chap by the name of Shulman. For some reason, he decided against mentioning Rosa's name.

'Anyone else?' asked Pletnev.

This was his cue, thought Boris, this was the moment of confession; to try and ignore it would only spell trouble. He took a deep breath and ran his fingers over his eye, beneath his glasses. He knew his friend was in the audience and would be wetting himself by now. 'Well,' he said slowly, 'I was friends for a while – a short while – with a fellow student called Milyukov, but …' He imagined Milyukov's heart leaping on hearing his name. '…but we are no longer friends.'

'And why is that?'

'Well, it's not Milyukov's fault, he was only a child, but many years ago, his father was duped into signing a Trotskyite declaration. Apparently, he immediately retracted it and confessed, and the Party forgave him. But all that was years ago.' It seemed so far removed to be ridiculous.

'But presumably, you must feel as if Milyukov Junior is still tainted?'

'Oh no, Comrade Chairman, not at all.'

'So why did you break off your friendship?'

Boris was almost enjoying this; he had subtly manoeuvred the focus onto Milyukov. Milyukov wouldn't thank him for it but, as he'd said, the business with his father had been dealt with years ago and Milyukov had no reason to fear it. Boris was doing them both a favour. 'No reason, Comrade Chairman, he changed classes and we lost contact, that's all.'

'Very well.' Pletnev scribbled a few notes and Boris puffed his cheeks. He was almost there, he'd passed the difficult bit, the crowd was becoming fidgety with boredom – the gladiator was emerging unscathed. He looked at his passport longingly.

The Chairman looked up at him; was there a hint of a smile? 'Just one thing I'm a bit puzzled about, and maybe you can help me, Comrade Gershberg.' Boris nodded. 'Your father – you say he was a tailor?'

It was as if a thunderbolt had zapped across the sky and hit Boris directly in the stomach. Why was Pletnev questioning him about his father? 'Yes, Comrade Chairman.'

'Has he always been a tailor?'

'Y-yes, Comrade Chairman, sir.'

'*Comrade Chairman* is enough, no need for the sir, thank you.' He made a note in Boris's file and mouthed the words audibly as he wrote them, 'Always-been-a-tailor,' and then looked back up at Boris. 'Are you sure?' A rustle of expectation spread through the audience.

He knows, but perhaps he doesn't; perhaps it was just a bluff, to make him confess to something he needn't. But what if he *does* know, this was his last chance? And what if he did confess: yes, all right then, my father *was* a rabbi. What was the reason, Pletnev would ask, for not having said earlier? Boris knew his survival, his whole future depended on how he answered. He felt as if the whole audience had, as one, moved to the edge of their seats, anticipating his reply, the scent of blood in their noses.

'Well, Comrade Gershberg?' asked Pletnev, twisting his pen between his fingers.

He's bluffing, thought Boris, he could see it in his eyes; Pletnev was testing him. 'Yes, Comrade Chairman, my father has always been a tailor. He started in Vyatka—'

'Don't call it that – it's Kirov, and don't you forget it.'

'No, I'm sorry, Comrade Chairman.'

'Go on.'

'Yes, erm, my father was an apprentice under the stewardship of his own father. It takes a good two years to learn all the skills necessary to make every type of suit, and then...' Boris continued, without drawing breath, to describe his step-father's trade in unnecessary detail, anything to make it look more convincing, anything to keep talking, to delay whatever was coming next, to bore the Chairman into submission. Pletnev, watching him intently, listened patiently as Boris prattled on about the life of a tailor – the type of clothes he made, the sort of customers he served, the conditions he worked in, the skills he had picked up from his father.

A familiar voice echoed out from the audience: 'He's lying!' A ripple of laughter spread across the hall. Boris stopped in mid-sentence, unnerved by the sudden outburst.

Pletnev turned to the audience. 'Who said that?'

'Me, Comrade Chairman.' A young man stood up quickly, his back straight as a ramrod, his shoulders seemingly too big for his suede jacket. Boris groaned inwardly.

'Name?'

'Milyukov, Comrade Chairman.'

'Ah, the same Milyukov whose father signed the Trotskyite petition, I presume? Do you know for fact Comrade Gershberg is lying?'

'No, Comrade Chairman, but it's obvious, look at him.'

'You were his friend, did you know about his father?'

'Yes, he said his old man was a tailor but I never believed him.' Boris regretted bringing Milyukov into the equation; had he not named Milyukov, he might have been spared this battering. 'He was lying then as he's lying to us now, Comrade Chairman.'

Pletnev turned his attention back on Boris. 'It does seem strange that as an apprentice tailor and a son of a tailor, your jacket is missing a button.' Boris glanced down – he'd quite forgotten about it. Pletnev continued, 'But the point is, it says here, your father was a *rabbi*.' The audience exploded into laughter and wild whoops. Boris stared at Pletnev incredulously. It couldn't be possible, how could he know? 'Well, Comrade Gershberg…' Pletnev lowered his voice to a menacing sneer, 'What do you have to say about it?'

The audience quietened down, revelling in Boris's torment, waiting to see how he could squirm his way out. But Boris had no idea. His mind seemed incapable of forming a reply. It was already too late, he knew that the truth was now the only option. 'But he died when I was only five, surely I can't be held responsible for his beliefs.'

Pletnev snorted. '"An apple never falls far from the tree".' The proverb drew a roar of approval from the audience.

'No, I'm a Jew in name only but I don't believe in that rubbish; I'm a communist to my last drop of blood, I swear, Comrade Chairman.'

Someone shouted, 'Kick him out!'

'Jew boy!' People sniggered and a chant began, accompanied by a slow hand clap: 'Jew boy, Jew boy!' Pletnev rapped the table but failed to control the gleeful chant and the accompanying howls of derision. Boris was wounded and they were in for the kill. 'Jew boy, Jew boy!' The rhythmic noise pounded inside Boris's head as he felt all semblance of self-control ebb away. He felt dizzy and, clenching his eyes shut, felt the sweat seeping from every pore. He found himself shouting to make himself heard above the din. 'I beg you to believe me, comrades, I may be a Jew by descent, but not by faith, I have no religion, only my devoted allegiance to Comrade Stalin.'

'Enough!' Pletnev knocked again on the table. 'Enough, I say, this is becoming farcical,' he shouted. Slowly, the chant died down until, eventually, the hall was quiet again, save for the occasional muffled chortle. 'Comrade Gershberg...' Pletnev's voice, Boris noticed, had taken on a deeper, more ominous tone. 'It is one thing to have had a father as a rabbi, but another to lie about his occupation–'

'May I speak, Comrade Chairman?'

'If you must.'

'I have no recollection of my father, he is as dead in my mind as he is dead in the ground. My stepfather, my *real* father, the one who brought me up, he *was*, and still is, a tailor. Everything I said was true, it's just that I don't recognise my dead father as having any bearing on my life. My stepfather is the only father I've known–'

'You're rambling and I'm fast losing my patience. What you say has little relevance. The fact is, you are perfectly aware of having had a father who believed in superstition, the sort of claptrap that keeps our weaker comrades in a state of perpetual backwardness. You lied to us. And we have to ask ourselves, if you can conceal a part of yourself so effectively for so many years, what other skeletons lurk in your conscience? You have a rabbi's blood coursing through your veins, and that you try to deny it implies you have failed to confront your past. Comrade Stalin himself–' Pletnev was obliged to pause and wait for the enthusiastic applause to have its say. The two men stared at each other. For a moment, Boris thought he saw a flicker of empathy within the Chairman's eye, as if, he too, knew they were both pawns in this ridiculous theatre, that they were equally victims of the system that demanded its pound of flesh. But as the applause for Stalin dwindled away, Pletnev's outward dehumanising expression reasserted itself. Boris knew the emperor was ready to jerk his thumb downwards – his fate was sealed. But how did Pletnev know, who'd informed on him? Eventually, Pletnev was able to continue. 'In short, Gershberg, you are unreliable, and the country can do without your sort defiling its good name.' Yelps of agreement came from the audience. 'Comrade Gershberg, you are to be expelled from the college.' Boris felt himself melt into the chair. 'Dismissed.'

The audience erupted into a huge cheer, the gladiator was dead. He sat there for a few moments, his mind blank, his heart thundering, his glasses steaming up. Pletnev scribbled down more notes for Boris's file. Eventually, Boris felt a hand nudge him on the shoulder. He looked up and saw the uniformed guard standing above him, motioning him to follow. Boris rose unsteadily to his feet, conscious of his sweat-laden trousers pulling away from the wooden seat. As he followed the guard, he felt as if he was not himself, as if it was all happening to somebody else. He felt as if he could almost look down on himself, like a dying man, whose spirit has already fled from the departing body. He looked up towards where he had been sitting in the audience. The audience had already quietened down, no doubt, he thought, each worrying that they might be next. He saw no evidence of the people who, moments earlier, had bayed for his blood. Instead, he realised he was being watched by a sea of pitiful eyes but not one of them would risk talking to him again.

Except, perhaps, for Rosa. He noticed her, she was standing on her feet, trying to make herself visible to him. She smiled sympathetically and he was about to smile back when, suddenly, he remembered. His knees buckled and he almost fell. The guard, realising, stepped back and hauled him up from under his armpits. It had been the only time he'd ever mentioned it, the only time in his whole life, and only because he assumed that of all people, she was the only one he could trust – really trust. But he'd been wrong. The bitch. It was *she* who had betrayed him.

Chapter 11: Two Interviews

Rykov sat in his red leather chair, writing a few notes at his desk. A red lampshade threw a mysterious light on the desk, outshining the feeble ceiling bulb above. Lurking behind him, on his feet, was Vladimir. I sat with a small handbag on my lap and fidgeted with its clasp. I tried to catch Vladimir's eye, to seek his reassurance, but he studiously ignored me. Why was I here, I wondered; did Rykov want to tighten the screw; I hoped to God not.

'Well,' said Rykov finally, placing his pen down on the table. 'How pleasant to see you again so soon, Maria, sooner than normal. First of all, let me apologise for calling you in at such short notice, and thank you for being able to attend.' I tried to smile but managed only a nervous twitch at the corner of my mouth. Rykov continued, his palms opened wide. 'So, before we begin, tell me, how's your brother?'

'No better.'

'Oh, now that is a shame.' He pushed his small, rounded glasses further up his nose. 'Now, I shall try not to detain you longer than necessary. You're probably wondering why I've asked you to come in when our next appointment is scheduled for next week – it's a fair question and I can't pretend this is going to be easy.' My heartbeat quickened. 'You see, a rather unfortunate incident has come to our attention and, I'm sorry to say, it concerns a friend of yours. Please, don't overly concern yourself. It's just a triviality, you know how these things are, usually something of nothing. But we're obliged to investigate. I'm sure you understand.'

'What… what is he meant to have done, this friend?'

'Wouldn't you like to know who we're referring to first? His name is Dmitry Kalinin. I believe he is an associate of yours, if my sources inform me correctly. Is that right?'

'I've met him.'

'Can I ask how close a friend you are to Comrade Kalinin?'

'Erm, well, I wouldn't say we were that close.'

'Passing acquaintances?' I nodded. 'So how do you know each other?'

'His sister, I'm a friend of his sister.'

'Your performance at the unveiling of that painting certainly helped us join the dots. But like I say, it's a nothing. But the chap at the factory, some upstart bureaucrat called Trifonov, a man with too much time on his hands, has put in a complaint. Trifonov was, as I think you know, upset by your depiction in the painting. Now, I've not seen the painting, but I've been told there's nothing unduly wrong with it but still, it isn't the point. It has brought to the fore an interesting side issue that was already sitting in my in-tray. You've heard of the Russian Association of Proletariat Artists?'

'In passing.'

'And this Dmitry chap, I believe, is a member?'

'I – I wouldn't know.' I was sure he could see through me.

'You see, rumour has it that RAPA is fast falling from grace. They've become too big for their boots and the Politburo are losing patience. We also have our suspicions that there are unsuitable elements within RAPA–'

'No, not Dmitry–'

'Now, now, Maria Radekovna, not so hasty; I'm sure you're right. We don't know as yet how he stands but nonetheless, what about this association of which he is a member? Are they reliable servants of the State? Or do they harbour within their ranks a few rotten eggs? And…' Rykov leant forward and fixed his gaze into my eyes. 'This is where *you* come in. I need you to find out information about his colleagues and their beliefs. Are they firm believers in the art of social realism or are they merely paying lip service? Use your contact with this Dmitry fellow and get yourself invited to a meeting. See who's saying what.'

'But what if I can't?'

Rykov narrowed his eyes. 'Oh, but you can. All you have to do is sieve through the crap and see what scum floats to the top.' He paused to allow his instruction to filter through. 'I know what you're thinking – what if my new friend is implicated? Well, I would like to think that you wouldn't hesitate to denounce him. Remember, your ties to the Party are stronger than any ties of friendship. Stalin is your brother, your father, your benefactor, your guide. Your duty is to Stalin and your country, don't forget it. *Don't ever forget it.*' He scribbled a note on a piece of paper on his desk, before looking back at me. 'OK, you can go now. We'll call you when we need the information.'

Gripping my handbag, I rose unsteadily to my feet. As I turned to leave, Vladimir spoke, 'How's Rosa?' he asked.

'She – she's well, thank you.'

'Give her my… my regards.'

I tried to smile as I made quickly for the door.

*

Vladimir lounged in Rykov's chair, enjoying the sensation of sitting in the boss's place, wearing the blue, silken scarf that his mother had given him. This, he thought, was power, and this is where, eventually, he wanted to be. He cast his eye across the desk – the two Bakelite telephones, the bust of Marx, the Lenin paperweight. He pulled open the drawer to his left. Inside was a small pile of forms, which they were obliged to fill in after each interview. Beneath the papers, a couple of pamphlets – NKVD manuals and a book on Marxist-Leninist theory. And beneath that – a revolver, a Mauser 2.1, a beautiful piece of equipment. He closed the drawer.

He was tired. Hours spent lurking at the back of the school auditorium watching Pletnev at work had taken it out of him. He thought about Rosa and the expression on her face at seeing the rich offerings of produce in the closed store. The look on her face was a delight but he regretted his haste. If he was to have a future with this woman, then truth was of greater importance than dazzling her with access and privilege. But what could he tell her? As a young employee of the NKVD, his occupation had to remain a secret. If they became engaged, then that was okay, as long as future spouses could be relied upon. But would he be allowed to marry her? Her father had been arrested as a wrecker, a saboteur, and imprisoned. She was therefore, by default, a tainted being - and worse, her survival depended solely on her aunt's continued cooperation. So far, it was working out nicely.

But now, with Rykov tightening the screw, would Maria be able to cope? For her brother's sake, and Rosa's, she had little choice, but, nonetheless, Vladimir was worried. What if Rykov pushed her too far? The effect would be like a stack of dominoes – Viktor would fall first, followed by Maria, and then, very probably, Rosa, and, possibly, even himself. Common sense told him to rid himself of all contact with Rosa; his relationship with her could only spell trouble. But love, he realised, can sometimes override common sense.

At least, he had the satisfaction of seeing his rival removed out of Rosa's reach. He had enjoyed that, watching from the back of the auditorium. The look on his face, the way that smug certainty drained away as the realisation hit home. He so admired the way Comrade Pletnev had put the questions, slowly raising the pressure – the man was young, but what a professional. Vladimir could learn a lot from men like him. Poor Rosa, an unguarded word (*Yes, Vladimir, a rabbi*) and he had him where he wanted. The rest was simple. He wrote out a brief denunciation and posted it into one of the college's special boxes, erected specifically for the purpose. It'd amused him how he had to take his place in a queue of students and even a few lecturers – all eager to post their foul scribbled notes into the black metal box. It was incumbent on all to denounce each other – one was viewed suspiciously if one didn't. Whom, people might ask, were you trying to defend, why aren't you doing your duty and exposing these traitors, these spies and deviationists? And yet, putting one's name to paper still took some courage. What if the allegation backfired? And no one would dare add their name if the allegations were untruths or simply downright lies. So, although some may have been bold enough to have signed their damning indictments, most, like his, would have been written anonymously. What had he said? He tried to remember. Something, he thought, along the lines of:

'Dear Commissioners,
I can relate that the student, Comrade Boris Gershberg of the Institute's Arts Faculty, is the son of a Jewish rabbi, now deceased. My contacts affirm that his father never made any attempts to renounce his faith for the stupidity it is. I have this information on good authority and in good faith.
Yours, etc.,
A concerned senior lecturer of this college.

At first, he'd signed it as *"A concerned student..."*, but decided it would have more impact if delivered by a lecturer, a senior one at that. And that signalled the end of old Boris and his lovelorn ways. Vladimir looked at his watch – he and Boris were due their first meeting.

A knock on the door brought him back to the present. 'Enter.'

'Your interviewee, boss,' said the guard.

'Ah, I was just thinking of him. Bring him in.' He leant back in the chair and smiled as the young Jew with the tortoise-shell glasses entered the room and stood before him. The guard closed the door behind him. He looked at Boris, whose eyes darted from Vladimir to the divan behind him, the bookshelves and back to Vladimir. He was nervous all right, thought Vladimir with satisfaction as he stretched and clicked his fingers. 'Sit.'

'Tha-thanks.'

'So, why do you think you're here, Comrade Gershberg?'

'I don't know.'

'Sure?'

Boris nodded. Vladimir sighed, he was tired and didn't want to play games. 'Tell me what happened last night?'

'I got expelled from college. Am I under arrest?'

'And why were you expelled?'

Boris shrugged his shoulders, an action which, for some reason, Vladimir found deeply annoying. 'Am I under arrest?' he asked again.

'Now listen here, you yid, I was there, so I know, but I want to hear it in your own words.'

Boris swallowed, his brow wrinkled. 'Someone informed the Purge Commission that my father had been a rabbi.'

'And…? Go on.'

'But it's ludicrous. He died when I was five. Why should I be held responsible for that? My mother married again and together, with her new husband, they brought me up – *he's* my real father, not some man I barely remember.'

'An apple never–'

'"Falls far from the tree", so they said.'

'No, to answer your question, you're not under arrest – yet.'

'So, why am I here?'

'I just thought you and I should have a chat. Are you a practising Jew?'

'What d'you think? Of course not. Come to my house, you won't see anything.'

'So, what's your relationship with Rosa?'

'You know Rosa?' Boris raised an eyebrow.

'Yes, I know Rosa.'

'How do you know her?'

'*I'm* the one asking questions here. I ask you again, what's your relationship with Rosa?'

'She's someone I thought I could trust but apparently, I was wrong.'

'And why is that?'

But Boris didn't answer. Instead, he fixed his eyes on Vladimir as the wheels of his brain worked it out. His eyes widened as the realisation hit him. 'It's you, isn't it? *You're the librarian.*'

Vladimir sniggered. 'Well, it worked for a while but I don't think she thinks I'm a librarian any more.'

'So, she told you.'

'Yes, she told me; told me you're a yid.'

'I'm not a yid,' said Boris quietly. 'I'm a communist and you can't tell me otherwise.'

'Yes I can, as did the Purge Commission,' he said, rising to his feet. 'Your social origins are detestable.' He paced around the table and placed a hand on the back of Boris's chair. Boris instinctively leant away. 'Understand this, Gershberg, you are this far from arrest,' he indicated the narrowest of gaps between his finger and thumb. 'We have plenty to arrest you with already, but work is piling up at the moment, lots of purges to work on–'

'Oh, poor you–'

Vladimir's fist lashed out. He caught him in the jaw with a dull thud. Boris pitched back but managed to maintain his balance and remain on the chair. He rubbed his jaw when Vladimir struck him a second blow catching him on the side of his nose. This time he fell sideways off the chair and landed on his knees, his glasses falling to the floor. Vladimir darted around from the back of his chair. Boris cowered. Vladimir hovered above him, his fist ready to strike. 'Now hear this, you little shit, you speak to Rosa again, I'll pulp your balls, you understand?' His words came in short breaths as the sweat formed on his forehead. 'And… and if she finds out what I do, I'll hold you responsible, got it?'

Boris, still on his knees, his hands cupped around his head, looked nervously up at him.

Vladimir glared down at him, breathing through his teeth, and felt the hatred rising inside him like a torrent. With a grunt, he swung his boot, calf muscles clenched, and felt the surge of pleasure as the leather made a crunching contact with the ribs. This time, Boris bawled in pain as he fell back on the floor.

He whipped out his scarf and deftly wrapped it around Boris's neck. Tightening it, he growled, 'I said *got it?*'

'Yes,' spluttered Boris. 'OK.'

'Right, get out.' Boris peered up at him. 'Get out.' Vladimir watched him as Boris collected his glasses and staggered to his feet, wincing in pain and panting as he tried to straighten up. 'Don't forget, one word to Rosa and your balls are pulped,' he snarled. Boris took this as his cue and made for the door. As he opened it, a guard appeared from the hallway and blocked his path. 'Show him out,' muttered Vladimir, wiping his forehead with his handkerchief.

As the door closed, Vladimir puffed his cheeks and went to sit back in Rykov's chair, the big chair. Sitting down, he rested his head on his arm. He felt exhausted but at least, he thought, he'd made his point. Now it was down to him to take Rosa into his confidence and introduce her to the idea that this was a dirty but necessary job. The defence of the Motherland was paramount and no one ever said it was going to be easy.

Chapter 12: The Meeting

'Why are you doing this to me?'

I was running through a churchyard in my nightgown, darting in and out between the headstones in the warm moonlit night. 'Why are you doing this to me?' The question came again, this time louder and nearer, catching up. The whiteness of my night gown glowed under the light of the fluorescent moon, my hair loose, trailing behind me as I ran glancing back at my pursuer. But then I tripped over something in the dark and landed with a thud at the foot of a grave. 'Why are you doing this to me?' I still couldn't see him, but the voice was so near, I felt as if it was coming from within me. I opened my eyes, and there he was, looming above me, his eyes barely inches above mine.

'Petrov? Petrov, it's still dark. What… what time is it?'

'About five.'

I smelt his breath, the warm, musty smell of his sleepy breath. 'But what… I don't understand. Why are you awake?'

'Why are you doing this to me, Maria?'

'I don't know what you mean.'

'Don't you love me any more?'

Love? I'd never heard Petrov use the word. And yet he said it without any hint of self-consciousness as if it was part of his everyday vocabulary.

'Maria?'

What could I say? The question contained a presupposition – that I loved him in the first place. He saw love where I saw dependence. He held my life in his hands, but I held his love in mine. I needed to say something affirming but not promising. 'You know I'll always be indebted to you, Petrov.'

'So why then?'

'Because you think you love me but you don't; not truly—'

'No—'

'Please, let me finish. All you need from a woman is someone who stays at home, has little contact with the outside world and as few friends as possible. Perhaps, that's enough for some women, but… but not for me, not any more. I'm bored, Petrov, you must see that. I need to start living; I need to connect with the world. You can't imagine what it's like for me – I do virtually nothing. I keep the house tidy for you and what else? I have no friends, I spend hours queuing, a bit of translation and sewing, and that's about it. We hardly speak because I have nothing to say. I'm still young, you forget that sometimes. Oh, I've seen a lot, too much and yes, for a while, I needed to hide away, but now…'

'Now?'

'You don't love me. To you, I'm just another household object. Please, I'm asking you, no, I'm begging you… give me my freedom.'

He sat on the edge of the bed, his back to me, running his fingers through his air. He seemed to be contemplating it for a moment. Without turning, he said quietly, 'No, I shall not, I cannot. You are my wife, you will remain my wife.' Was that it, I thought? Was that the end of it, a stark declaration? But then he continued. 'Furthermore, you are not to see this artist *friend* of yours again. Is that understood?'

'No,' I snarled, 'it *isn't* understood. How… how dare you dictate.' Stop it, I thought, just stop it, my anger wouldn't change anything. I took a deep breath and decided to try a different tack. 'Petrov, what's the point? You're a man of position, you could find yourself someone else, someone who values you for what you are. Surely, you must realise it, I… I don't love you.' His shoulders moved as if my words had caused him physical pain. 'I don't think I ever have and I think you know that.'

'Love? You talk of love as if it's important.' He spun around to face me. 'It's not though, is it? If you think about it, love is merely a convenience. What's important is living. This obsession with the self, it's not right, it's not why we're here. Don't you see we're the lucky ones? We're building a future, we're part of the experiment, the great socialist experiment. And it sickens me to hear you carry on about yourself as if nothing else mattered. What we do for socialism, what we do for the Party – that's what's important. And do you know, sometimes I lie awake at night and worry. I worry because of whom and what I've married.'

'Well, let me go then.'

'In my position? I can't be seen as a divorcee. No, but if I denounce you, then yes, that's all right, one less enemy to worry about.'

'You wouldn't denounce me, Petrov.'

'No? You try to leave me and what choice would I have?'

'And if I told them the truth, that you knowingly married me despite knowing that I was an outcast on the streets?'

'I'd deny it. Who do you think they'd believe, eh? Answer me that.'

I fell back against the pillow. He was right, of course. They'd never believe me; whatever I said would account for nothing. Petrov returned to bed and wrapped himself in the warmth of the blankets. After a while, I realised he'd fallen asleep. But for me, sleep would not come. The years stretched before me: a life of servitude, servitude to Petrov, servitude to the Party and the mighty Socialist cause. I lay there, my eyes wide open and stared out of the window. As the sun rose, I felt a sheet of despondency drift over me. I was trapped and no number of new dawns was going to release me or offer me hope. I knew there and then, I had to do something. Desperation could only be remedied by drastic measures – that much I had learnt already. I'd hoped never to feel that desperate again but as the cold dawn rose, I could feel the surging in my heart. I had experienced it before and I knew where it had led me. But this time, at least, I had an ally.

*

I managed to persuade Dmitry to invite me to the RAPA meeting that Mikhail had mentioned. It was taking place in a large upstairs room above a café, just a couple of miles from where he lived. Dmitry had got there early in order to have a late breakfast with some of his old friends. I felt sick as I made my way, knowing what I had to do. I'd done this before – infiltrated a meeting, watched them at work, made mental notes and decided who I should choose to be the NKVD's next victim. It was a sickening chore, playing the role of the Devil, pointing my evil stick at some unsuspecting citizen.

I got there at ten thirty and the meeting had already started. The well-dressed manager of the café showed me up the stairs and knocked gently on the door for me before disappearing back down the stairs. I could hear voices from within but no one said *come in*. I waited for a few moments before opening the door a fraction and slipping in unobserved.

'Whether by accident or design, if the work is not worthy of socialism, it is our fundamental duty to point out the error of their ways.' Mikhail was at the far end of the room, standing behind a wooden-top table with iron legs, lecturing his select audience. 'The artist is an impulsive being, he doesn't always think before committing an idea to the canvas, the block of stone or whatever his medium…' I stood next to the door with my back pressed against the wall, and surveyed the scene: it was a large room with a high ceiling and long windows that flooded the space with cold sunlight. The smell of cigarette smoke hung in the air. There must have been twenty or so men in suits, men sitting in hard upright chairs in rows, their backs to me, listening to the animated Mikhail. I could see Dmitry among them, his black hair against the white collar of his shirt, sitting to the far right in the back row.

'You, as artists, know perfectly well,' continued Mikhail, 'that rational thought and inspiration are not always natural bedfellows. The artist gets carried away, his mind becomes single-tracked and nothing else matters but the work at hand.'

A hand shot up in the air, 'We don't all work like that,' said a bald-headed man in the second row. 'All my work is carefully worked out beforehand, I'm meticulous in my planning.'

'Here, here,' said another.

Mikhail turned to face the voice. 'Yes, yes, of course, I appreciate that, Comrade Mamontov, but what I'm saying is that *you* must also appreciate the impulsive tendencies of some of your fellow artists. We can't judge everyone by your own standards, old man. And we can't jump down their throats the moment they commit a creative *faux pas*. After all, we all deserve a second chance.'

Mikhail's comments drew a wave of muttering among his audience. As he waited, I crept across the back of the room to a chair in the far corner. Dmitry and the man immediately to his left noticed me. Dmitry smiled and winked at me. Eventually, the same hand shot up.

'Comrade Mamontov?'

'I'm sorry, Comrade Mikhail, we think you're speaking like a sentimentalist and, dare I say it, like a cultural kulak.'

'I would refute that.'

'No, no, I don't mean to be over-critical but…' Mamontov rose to his feet, his bald head shining in the light. 'Comrades, the role of the artist has changed; we all know that,' he said, waving his arms. 'We can no longer afford the luxury of committing to canvas whatever comes to us in a rush of so-called inspiration. We're no longer here to satisfy our own vanities and dreams; why, it reeks of self-satisfaction and petty indulgence. Are we going to allow such extravagance? I think not, because to do so undermines the importance of our role in Soviet society. We're not sixteen-year-olds writing pappy poetry or painting pretty pictures, we're the new frontline of the battle; we're the state's foot soldiers. There's an enemy out there and we have to maintain our vigilance at all times. We must reflect the glory of collectivisation, the triumph of industrialisation. I'm sure you'll agree with me when I say we owe it to the second Five-Year-Plan and to our leader.'

Mamontov sat down with a smug look on his face and the eyes of the gathering returned to Mikhail.

'Yes, yes, of course,' he said, his hands resting on the table. 'But I say the more artists we have on our side, the greater the chance of victory. I believe it's short-sighted of us to pounce on the young artist who sticks his leg out slightly to the side of what's right. Rather than castigate him publicly, thereby alienating him and losing a potential future general, if, Comrade Mamontov, you permit me to extend your metaphor, I think we should point out his errors and give him a second chance.'

'Is that because *you* were given a second chance?' asked Mamontov.

The atmosphere in the room tightened. Trying to maintain his composure, Mikhail coughed and straightened his tie. 'All I'm asking,' he continued, 'is should we make examples of these unfortunates when there are those in power who take advantage at our expense?'

'Meaning?'

'It's no secret, you know what I'm talking about – the privileges afforded to high-ranking officials, the misdirecting of funds by bourgeois degenerates, those who promise higher standards of living but only they achieve it. Of course, I refer not to the Politburo who, as we know, lead by example but to the army of bureaucrats below them. We all know it goes on but we, as a society, turn a blind eye while targeting those less able to defend themselves….'

Mikhail continued on his new line of attack but my attention was diverted by Dmitry who had swivelled around in his chair and was smiling at me, his eyes full of mischievous charm. He faked an exaggerated yawn and then crept towards me, his shoulders hunched as if hoping not to be noticed.

Sitting on the chair next to mine, he took my hand and squeezed it. 'Hello, my pretty, shall we go?' he whispered.

I could smell his aftershave. 'Can you leave?'

'God, yes, I've heard all this a hundred times before, it's always the same. I always try to leave before someone reminds us we're the engineers of the soul. No one will care. Come, let's go.'

I hadn't heard much but I'd heard enough. I knew the identity of my next victim. Rykov would be pleased with me.

*

'Interesting meeting,' I said as we walked back.

'Interesting?'

'Well, maybe not so interesting.'

Dmitry laughed. 'Yes, we go round in circles, always talking about the same thing, how to interpret social realism.'

We strode side-by-side through the packed snow, hands deep in pockets, the sky as grey as lead. 'I wouldn't mind attending again.'

'You surprise me. Oh, I forgot to tell you,' he said, slapping his forehead. 'My award's been confirmed: the Order of Lenin for my "Contribution to Socialist Art".'

'Wow!' I spun around and, hugging him, kissed him, our red noses touching. 'Congratulations, my super talented artist.'

'That I am! I get my moment of glory in a special presentation during the Labour Day celebrations. Gorky Park. And it gets better – it comes with twenty-five roubles a month and a small pension.'

'To add to all the other privileges they give you. How the State spoils you.'

'Ha! There's a fine line between honour and ruin.'

'I'm very proud of you, my Dmika.' I smiled at an elderly couple walking passed, featureless in their heavy coats and scarves.

'Thank you,' he said, taking my hand. 'But I'm no fool; I know it's more a political award than artistic. I play by the rules; I paint what I'm supposed to paint. The real artists of this world, the free spirits, they're the ones who suffer, just as Mikhail was alluding to. People like my old student friend, Busygin, believed that, as artists, they're entitled to paint as they see fit. He was a true artist, more than I'll ever be, but he's paying the price for his stubbornness and his integrity – arrested for daring to show the proletariat life as it really is. Once the word was out, he was roundly condemned, even by those who'd never heard of him. He ended up in hospital with the stress of it all but they soon kicked him out.'

'Why – because he was an enemy?'

'Of course, the silly bugger. It's strange when you think about it – when I was a kid growing up in Moscow, there were the writers and artists our teachers recommended and those we were warned against. Of course, we all sought out the ones we weren't meant to. But kids today, they intrinsically believe in the system and if the system tells them not to read Dostoevsky or listen to Tchaikovsky, then they say "all right, we won't read Dostoevsky and we won't listen to Tchaikovsky". It never occurs to them to do anything different. They are the children of revolutionaries but they themselves have not got a rebellious bone in their collective body.'

'Your patron Mikhail – he says things that perhaps he shouldn't.'

'He ought to be more careful, I agree. But he has a generous heart; he believes we all need a second chance when it comes to art. We don't necessarily agree with him, but he's among friends here, he'll be all right with us. Yes, there're informants at every turn, why should RAPA be different? We have to toe the line or expect the worst. We've led a charmed life up to now.'

'Yes, of course,' I said as my stomach tightened. 'And your Comrade Mamontov seemed antagonistic.'

'He and Mikhail go back a long way and they haven't always seen eye to eye, but Mamontov is all right; he wouldn't do anything to harm the reputation of the association, and he knows Mikhail is an influential supporter of ours.'

A car passed us at speed, splashing us with slush. 'Silly idiot,' muttered Dmitry.

'What did Mamontov mean when he said Mikhail had been given a second chance?'

'What? Oh, that. Mikhail once refused to sign a collective petition demanding Bukharin's execution. He publicly recanted and the Party forgave him but the stain will always be there. Anyway, what's gone is gone.'

'Oh dear.'

'You OK, Maria?'

'Yes,' I said with a sigh.

*

Half an hour later, Dmitry and I were back in his apartment. As soon as he closed the door, he pulled me towards him and wrapped his arms around me and kissed me. Oh, the smell of him, his touch. I felt myself melt in his all-embracing presence as his kiss became more urgent, his hand travelling up and down the undulating journey of my spine.

It was almost dark when I awoke in the warmth of Dmitry's bed. I was alone; the covers on his side of the bed pulled back, the sheet still warm. My picture was still there, in the corner of the bedroom, next to the wicker chair, taunting me with her smile, my smile. I wrapped the blankets tighter against me, pulling them up beneath my chin. My past, present and future seemed to be colliding into each other, each fighting for dominance, cancelling each other out. To escape my past, I came to the present; to escape the present, I needed a future, but however I looked at it, my past and present denied the future. However hard I tried to divide them like neat chapters in a book, the more they merged into one.

'Good evening,' said Dmitry softly, hovering over me, naked, holding two steaming cups in one hand, the other hand behind his back.

'What a sight!' I said, wiping my eyes with the back of my hand.

'I've bought you a present.'

'So I see.'

He placed the cups on the bedside table and his other hand came out from behind his back. He smiled as he held out something wrapped in a brown paper bag. 'A present for my love.'

'A present? I've never been given a present before.' I opened the bag and inside felt the texture of engraved wood. I pulled out a four-inch-high wooden carving of a bear. It was, I think, a grizzly bear, standing on its hind legs, its front legs pawing the air. Its eyes seemed ablaze with fury and his mouth was open, revealing small sharp teeth and a bright red tongue. 'It's lovely. What *is* it?'

'Flip open the head.'

Indeed, the head of the bear flipped open on a delicate hinge in the back of its neck. Inside was a small bottle, plugged with a tiny glass cork. I smiled, unplugged the cork and breathed in the lush fragrance. 'Oh, Dmitry, eau-du-cologne, how wonderful; thank you, thank you.' I dabbed some on my neck and he leant forward and smelt me.

'Hmm, very nice,' he declared.

'What a funny little bear.'

'Funny? Looks quite vicious to me. *Grrl!*'

'That sounds more like a lion.'

'Does it? I wouldn't know; you don't get many of either in these parts. Either way, the perfume is to remind you how much I love you.'

'And the bear…?'

'The bear? Well, he's there to protect you, of course. Forever.'

I laughed. 'I've always wanted eau-du-cologne, it's so divine. I'd better be careful when I wear it.'

'You won't have to soon.'

'What do you mean?'

'Leave him, Maria. I know what you're thinking, and the only answer is to leave him.' He handed me my cup of tea.

'I'm sorry?'

'Petrov. You know what I'm talking about.'

'Not long ago you were telling me to go back to him.'

Holding his cup, he sat on the bed and swung his legs up and covered them with the blanket. Sitting up in the bed, his naked torso against the pillow, he turned towards me. 'Not now. You could come here to begin with, and… and who knows, if you liked it, you could stay. And we could go out for trips to my dacha–'

'I forgot – you have your very own dacha.'

'Well, it's not really mine but it's on loan to me.'

'You're not going to start talking about privilege again, are you?'

'For every person that's—'

'No, please, no. Spare me!'

'Ha! Anyway, the dacha is my little perk for being a "valued" artist. It's only about an hour away by train. I'm going there next Wednesday, just to get away from the city for a while. You'd adore it. How about it?'

'Oh, Dmitry, you know I would love to, but…'

'But what? Come on, Maria, the man is stifling you; you have to make a stand. He's killing you slowly from inside, you must see that.'

'I know, I know. Don't you think I agonise about it every waking moment, but I'm frightened, Dmitry. I beg him to give me my freedom, but he's a proud man, he won't let me go.'

'You're worried he'll denounce you in some way?' I cupped my hands around the warm cup and gazed at the rising steam. 'Maria?'

I spoke softly, unable to meet his eyes. 'I have a lot to be ashamed of, Dmitry, I'm politically infected, and he knows that. If I left him, he could have me arrested within the day. And I'd be putting you at risk as well as myself. If he even knew I was here, I dread to think how he'd react. I don't know what to do.'

'We have to do something. I think of you all the time. I've never met a woman like you. It's strange, I feel as if I know you inside out already, but there's a part of you I know you can't share. I can't expect you to trust me fully yet, I understand that, but one day you'll realise you'll be able to tell me everything. Everything.'

'No, I can't ever, believe me, you should never know. At least…'

'At least?'

'Not while I remain tied to Petrov.' I took his hand and gripped it tightly and he leant towards me and kissed me on the forehead. 'What can we do?'

'We'll think of something, we have to. Whatever happens, we'll think of something.'

*

Half an hour later, I was washed and fully dressed, and wondering whether I should go, when there was a knock on the door of Dmitry's apartment. He glanced at me and at once we were both agitated, both immediately assuming the worst. He motioned that I should return to the bedroom. A second knock, louder, more urgent, startled us even further. Dmitry went to answer it and I, behind the door in the bedroom, found myself holding my breath.

'OK, where is she?' The voice, once the intruder had forced his way in, brought both relief and horror. It was my husband.

'Hello, Petrov, how nice to see you too. And so soon.'

'Don't give me that. I said, where is she?'

I listened to their exchange, my nude alter ego staring back at me. I hoped to God Dmitry would prevent Petrov from barging in. 'Who exactly are you talking about?'

'I think you know.'

'If you're referring to your wife, then I don't know. Now I'd offer you a cup of tea but the kettle's broken but if you're prepared to wait for a pan to boil...'

'So why's her coat here?'

I listened to the silence, pinned against the wall.

'Is that Maria's coat? Yes, I think you're right; so it is.'

'Well? Where is she?' I could hear him stamping around; he was looking for me.

'All right, I admit she was here but you've missed her. She–
'

'Stop lying to me! She wouldn't have gone out in this cold without her coat. What do you take me for? Is she in here...' I heard the door to Dmitry's studio open.

'Look, all right, I'll tell you.' Inside the other room, the voices were muffled but still loud enough for me to hear every word.

'Go on, I'm all ears.'

'I invited Maria over to pose for me – in the painting you saw the other week. It's gone now, hanging up in some factory. But look, here are some of the preliminary sketches I made. Don't you think she's perfect for the role?'

There was a pause. I knew what was going through my husband's mind – he was impressed but could hardly admit to the fact.

'Yes, it's all very well. She told me. And I forbade it.'

'Why would you do that?'

'Because I... it's none of your bloody business. You think you can have it all, don't you? First all of this... this luxury and now my wife. I despise your sort with a vengeance.' He'd come back into the living room. 'You smarmy your way around with your precious art; you live it up in this splendour like the high and mighty. You're no better than the bourgeois scum the revolution destroyed. You look at something and you think it's yours, that it's your goddamn right to take it.'

'And you think yourself different? You're telling me you don't spend your days like a puppy, trying to please your bosses, trying not to upset the apple cart?'

'I don't care what you think.' The bedroom door suddenly swung open, the door almost hitting me. I tried to disappear into the wall as I saw my husband's hands grip his hair as the vision of my naked self bored into his eyes. 'What the… what do you call this?' he bellowed, standing in front of the painting. He seemed to be gasping for air. 'I can't believe this.' Please, I thought, don't let him turn around.

'I'm an artist, Petrov, what can I say?' I could hear Dmitry's voice in the room but couldn't see him.

'This is not art; this is pornography. And Maria let you do this, to exploit her like a whore? You… you bastard.'

Talk to him, Dmitry, don't let him turn around.

'Oh, for the love of saints, shut up, man. Have you not been to the Tretyakov recently? Half the paintings are of the nude.'

'Painted by the great masters, not some lowlife bastard like you. This is not art, this is titillation.'

'Titillation is in the eye of the beholder. Let's go through, Petrov, you look like you need to sit down; you've had a jolt, dear man.' I held my breath, praying he wouldn't see me.

Petrov was still facing the painting but his shoulders had slumped, as if the shock had drained him. 'I don't mind if I do,' he said.

'This way,' said Dmitry, steering him out of the room. I pressed myself still further against the wall. But they'd gone, back to the safety of the living room. My knees trembled. I found myself panting with relief.

'Now, you sure you won't have that cup of tea?' Oh please, Dmitry, don't prolong it.

'No. No, I've got to go.' He sounded like a man defeated.

'Look, I know I'm not a great master deserving of a place in the Tretyakov, but I am still an artist; it's what I'm paid to do and, as I said when you came around for dinner, the State values what I do. Maria is not a whore, she is a good woman

152

and for me, a perfect model. Now, go home, Petrov, and think about it.'

I could tell from their voices that Dmitry had almost shoved Petrov out of the apartment. 'OK, you can paint,' he said, 'I'll give you that, and what you paint is your business. But please, have some respect, don't paint my wife again. In fact, I'd ask you not to see her again, you understand? And that painting in there, don't even think about putting it on display. I'm sure you can appreciate my wish not to have my wife paraded naked for all of Moscow to see.'

'Of course, I understand. Now, you mind how you go.'

I waited for the front door to shut but Petrov had not quite finished. 'What are you going to do with it then?'

'Maria's portrait? I shall destroy it.'

'Yes. Good. Well, in that case, perhaps I could have it?'

Chapter 13: The Market

I couldn't face going home straightaway; not after that exchange. So I decided to go shopping, always a disheartening experience but we were short of food. I needed meat or fish, anything with a bit of protein, which could be made into soup. I'd remembered to bring a string bag with me which I'd stuffed in my pocket. It was my "just-in-case" bag, *just in case* I came across something affordable. I caught a streetcar, entering, as by regulation, at the back. The tram was packed and the mass of passengers swayed this way and that with the motion of the vehicle as it made its way across town.

My mind wandered back to Viktor, sitting motionless in his chair. He was getting worse but every attempt to call out a doctor had failed. They were all far too busy dealing with people who mattered. As an ex-enemy of the people, no one wanted to know. I could just about persuade him to eat my offerings of thin soup, but that was about it. I knew he was dying; it was only a matter of time. I was being pulled from different directions and the strain was beginning to show.

We have our suspicions that there are unsuitable elements within the RAPA.' That's what Rykov had said. *I need you to find out information about your Dmitry Kalinin's colleagues and where they stand.*' It was like having a tiger for a pet. As long as you continued to feed it, it was satisfied, but as soon as the supply of food dried up, it would eat you up. There was no turning back, they had me where they wanted me; it was a lifetime commitment. I had to protect my brother from Rykov's clutches and if that meant informing on men like Mikhail, then so be it. As Dmitry's patron, he was the most obvious target. But there was always the fear that in denouncing Mikhail, he would be pressed into naming names. As a recipient of the Lenin Award, would Dmitry still be vulnerable? What choice did I have?

But for now, my thoughts turned to more pressing matters. I alighted from the streetcar near Gorky Park. Once freed from the claustrophobic atmosphere of the tram, I made my way through the bustling streets to the nearby proletariat shopping centre. The sun had come out but a brisk wind whistled through my coat. I stepped off the pavement and was almost run over by a horse-drawn taxi, the driver yelling at me to get out of the way.

Everywhere I looked, there were queues: queues for shoes and clothes, for crockery, medicines, and, worst of all, the queues for food which sprawled into the adjoining street. But the mood that prevailed was one of calm resignation; no one pushed, no one lost their temper – as long as everyone obeyed by the rules. And everyone dressed the same – women in headscarves, men in peaked caps, everyone in dark coats – the classless uniformity of the proletariat. I ambled precariously along the line and towards a shop with a large window. A large sign stuck over the stained glass proclaimed that no food was available without ration cards. Someone shouted at me to get back, assuming I was trying to push in. The people at the front bunched up as if denying me any space, glaring at me. I turned back and walked to the end of the queue where I found a young girl of about thirteen with windswept hair, wearing a red dress, its pattern long since obscured by dark stains.

'Been here long?' I asked.

'Half an hour,' she replied without looking at me, sucking a strand of hair. 'They reckon those up front have been here since the middle of the night.'

'Anything special?'

'Yeah, they got new potatoes in. And turnips. Won't be any by the time we get there.'

I smiled and walked away. I'd been tempted to ask the girl why bother carrying on queuing if she had so little expectation of getting anything, but I knew the answer. Vague optimism and desperation borne of hunger combine to make a powerful incentive.

I carried on walking, leaving behind the multifarious queues of people and decided to try my luck at one of the many small markets. I sometimes heard talk of the market nearby, next to the Church of St John the Warrior. I paced down the monotonous side streets, too small for trams but still busy with expressionless Muscovites. I knew the produce in the markets was more expensive than the State-run shops but while Rykov compensated me for my dirty work, I might be able to afford something without having to queue for hours with little hope of reward.

Eventually, I came across the market in a small square surrounded by tall, dilapidated accommodation blocks. There were only a few dingy stalls, and in front of each one, a crowd of people bustled, swaying and fighting for space. No orderly queues here. The stalls belonged to forlorn-looking peasants, half loaded with mouldering vegetables and disintegrating fruit. Further along, were the dreary outcasts, sitting cross-legged on the ground with a newspaper spread in front of them, on which were displayed bits of crockery, a scrap of lace, a drinking glass, a single boot.

I returned to the main thrust of the market and sauntered on the periphery of the crowd finding myself sucked in and involuntarily moved along by its rhythm. I heard the shouts of haggling, the expressions of disgust at so little being offered for so much. Some came away clasping bits of dried fish, a clump of vegetables, a half loaf of bread, a small hunk of meat. I could smell it all too, the aroma of stale food mingling with the dirt of the oscillating crowd. Further still, an open space where the sellers were not peasants but city workers who offered single items for sale: a few eggs here, a couple of slabs of dried fish there. Speculators, I thought: they had bought their goods from the co-operatives using their ration cards and were now trying to sell them at four times the price on the open market. They were playing a dangerous game.

Wandering back to the main thrust of the market, I came across a stall selling mangled slices of raw and cooked meat. My stomach churned at the rank smell of what was on offer. The two stallholders, their faces red, shouted and argued with the passing hoard. I knew I could afford their prices but wondered whether I could face even touching it. The overpowering smell became too much and I pushed my way back out of the crowd. I found myself following a bearded man dressed in a long black coat and split shoes. As we fought our way free from the bustle, I saw that he'd come away with a portion of cooked sausage, half unwrapped from its covering of newspaper. He shot a look at me, evidently pleased with his purchase. To my surprise, he sunk his teeth into the meat and ripped a chunk off. He raised the remainder of the sausage in the form of toast and grinned while his cheeks bulged and moved beneath his beard. But just as I was about to leave, I saw his expression change. Leaning over, he coughed violently and fragments of chewed meat spewed from his mouth. He staggered a few feet, still coughing and then started retching, his hand clutching his stomach. He retched again and, almost bent double, pawed at thin air. And yet, to my amazement, he summoned the strength to continue chewing. As I turned to leave, I noticed he had tears in his eyes, trying to force more of the sausage into his mouth, as hunger and repulsion fought for dominance.

*

I was exhausted but I had to keep going. I'd left the market with no more than a handful of heavily bruised potatoes and a few vegetables – still it was better than nothing. I'd been on my feet so long that a large split had appeared along the lining of the sole running all the way around the toe from one side to the other. But there was no hope of replacing them – shoes, as much as anything else, were in short supply. Someone once told me that the mass slaughter of cattle during collectivisation had caused an acute shortage of leather. I passed an optimistic balloon seller and a shoeshine stall. Half an hour later, feeling sick with dread, I was back home.

'I managed to get some vegetables,' I said breezily to Petrov as I stamped my feet.

'You've got your coat then?' Petrov was sitting at the table, a pile of papers in front of him.

'Yes, I'd paid a visit to Dmitry's, and, silly me; I left without it and had to go back. He said you'd been. Would you like some tea? How's Viktor?'

Petrov threw me a hideous look, and took a couple of strides towards me. Instinctively, I stepped back. 'Don't walk away from me, you whore,' he yelled. 'Do you like being there; do you like being his latest possession, his plaything? Huh? I told you, you weren't to see him again.'

'And I told you, I'm his model.' I stood rooted to the spot in the middle of the living room.

'And so I see; taking your clothes off. Who'd have thought that my wife was such a slut?'

'Better an artist's slut than a bureaucrat's lackey.'

My outburst shocked him – I'd never answered back before. 'You'd do well, woman, to think before you speak to me like that again.' He paced around and behind me. I summoned the strength to keep still, fearing he might strike me at any moment. 'So this is what I get, then is it?' he growled. 'I work all day to a standstill, but it's not enough for you, eh? You want cheap luxury, bourgeois decadence? Have you forgotten?' I was expecting this question, for it always came back to this. 'Have you forgotten that you owe it all to me? I saved you, Maria, I saved you. If it wasn't for me, you'd still be scavenging on the streets, sleeping in that hellhole. I know more about you than you think. That accountant – he told me things about you. How you appeared from nowhere, half-starving with your ragamuffin country clothes in tatters. You were on the run, he reckoned. What were you running from, eh? What were you, Maria – a kulak? Is that it, did I marry a kulak? You know I know people. One word from me and you'd be finished.'

'So I am your lackey then, your slave? A marriage based on blackmail. This is not a marriage, this is servitude. You're too proud to let me work, you won't let me have my own friends–'

'Oh, so all this is my fault? I do my best for you, Maria; these are difficult times. I'm the slave here. While I'm out working my balls off, you're…' His eyes began watering. 'You're taking your clothes off and parading naked in front of other men – and supposedly in the name of art. God knows, I mean it – if I catch you seeing that man one more time, I'll kick you out, back to whatever little hole you appeared from. I'll rip you apart as I did your brother.'

Did I hear him correctly? My brother? 'What did you say?'

'Nothing.'

'It was you,' I said in a whisper. 'You… you denounced Viktor.' The obviousness struck me like a slap on the face, taking my breath away. From a whisper to a scream. 'You denounced my brother, your own brother-in-law. How could you, how–'

'I had to, I had to do it,' he screamed back.

'You denounced my brother?' My vision blurred with tears.

'There were rumours. At work. I thought I was next – you and me. I did it for us.'

'Us? You did it for us?'

'We would've been next. It was us or Viktor. What could I do?'

'You beast. You killed my brother.'

'Killed? He's not dead.'

'He might as well be, you… you bastard.'

'You should be thanking me; it could've been you.'

'I wish it had been; anything to save me from spending another day with you.'

Chapter 14: The Faith

'Rosa, Rosa, have you heard yet?' said Ella and Claudia in almost perfect unison.

Rosa's eyes gaped open as she plonked her tray on the canteen table and quickly sat down. 'What? What's happened?'

'About Comrade Kalinikov. Haven't you heard?' said Ella, urging Rosa to lean forward. The expression on their faces was a mixture of fear and excitement.

'No, tell me.'

Ella glanced around and leant across the table, 'Comrade Kalinikov's dead.'

'Dead?'

Claudia added the detail. 'Yes, dead. He hanged himself.'

'No! Suicide?'

'Yes, they found him yesterday,' exclaimed Ella. 'In his apartment, hanging by the cord of his dressing gown. His wife and son were staying with friends out of town. They just came home and found him.' She clasped her hand around her neck as if to emphasise the point.

'But why?'

Ella rolled her eyes. 'Oh come on, Rosa, why do you think?'

'Because they purged him?'

'Yes, of course. No Party card, no job; no job, no apartment.'

'No apartment, no job,' added Claudia, slurping her soup.

'And all because he had his child baptised,' said Rosa.

'Exactly,' said Ella.

Claudia looked up. 'Who's going to take his classes now, do you think?'

'Shut up, Claudia,' snapped Ella.

Rosa shook her head. 'What would Comrade Stalin think?'

'I agree, he'd be appalled.'

'If only there was a way of letting him know.'

The three friends fell silent, each eating their dinners, lost deep in their own thoughts. Rosa had liked Comrade Kalinikov, even if his lectures could sometimes be tediously dull. But he had an aura of intelligence and respectability about him. People may not have loved him, but they certainly respected him – his knowledge of political and economic theory, dialectics and social materialism was beyond comparison. But recently, he'd become increasingly nervous as if he knew time and external forces were against him. Rosa had been shocked when the Purge Commission had expelled him, but not as shocked as she was now. That was the last time they'd seen him – squirming in front of Comrade Pletnev while confessing to the baptism of his eighteen-month-old son. *A superstitious renegade* is how Pletnev described him, *covering the innocent under a cloak of superstition.* Rosa remembered the woman behind her who'd stood up and declared she'd been at the christening and how proud Comrade Kalinikov had been. Would she have been so keen to denounce him, had she known her words were as effective as a death sentence? Rosa's face flushed as she also remembered the way she herself had clapped and stamped her feet with all the rest of the baying wolves, while Kalinikov sat there with tears streaming down his face. *Chuck him out! Chuck him out!* What a spectacle.

Ella broke the silence. 'It was the most terrifying moment of my life,' she said, as if to herself.

'What?' asked Claudia.

'Being up there, in front of the Commission. I honestly thought I was going to die. They don't take their eyes off you for a moment, and sitting there, surrounded by all those people, all of them willing you to fail.'

'We didn't want you to fail, Ella,' said Rosa.

'I know. Thank you.'

'"*So, what, Comrade Pavlovna, is your view of collectivisation?*",' said Claudia, mimicking the Commission Chairman.

'*Claudia*, shush, can't you see...'

'I'm sorry...'

'It's OK, I'm all right. It just shook me up a bit; it was so horrible.'

Claudia placed her hand on Ella's arm. 'But you survived, my girl, that's the main thing.'

Wiping a handkerchief over her eyes, Ella rose from her chair. 'I need to go; you two coming?'

'Rosa hasn't finished her soup,' said Claudia.

'Don't worry,' said Rosa. 'You two go. I'll see you later.'

Ella left quickly with Claudia following in her wake. Rosa sighed and settled down to finish her lunch. She thought about Ella's ordeal. Like Claudia said, Ella had survived. Her secret remained a secret. For once, the all-seeing eyes of the System had failed. But someone, somewhere had leaked Kalinikov's secret. Was baptism such a crime? The Party had decreed it was. Indeed the rejection of religion had always been one of the basic tenets of the revolution. As with the rest of her generation, Rosa had grown up as a devout atheist, religion played no part in her life; she couldn't understand it. Stalin was her only God. Surely, Kalinikov knew what a dangerous game he was playing. And perhaps there were other things too, things that the Commission hadn't made public, but knew about – certain irregularities in Kalinikov's life that singled him out as a dubious element. But *she* still believed, the alternative was inconceivable; she had to hold onto her faith in the system. Yes, sometimes it could be unpredictable but it had its reasons, its justifications, and she knew that. *You can't make an omelette without breaking eggs.* But did it mean it was right that Boris should also have been expelled? Like he said, his father had died when he was only five. But once again, the Commission must have had its reasons. Perhaps, they were right. Religion is in the blood and, like a hereditary disease, it cannot be shaken off easily. Once a Jew, always a Jew. *The apple never falls far from the tree.*

Rosa looked at her watch; she was planning on going to the library. Then, in the corner of her eye, she noticed the familiar sight of Boris standing at the counter, holding a cup of tea, a haversack flung over his shoulder. In an instant, their eyes met. What was he doing here, she wondered. She made to wave but Boris turned his back. Rosa watched as he went to sit at a table at the other end of the dining hall, his back still towards her. He sat down next to a group of three male students whom she knew to be friends of his. But as soon as he'd sat down, the friends rose as one and, without so much as a glance at him, went to sit at another table where they immediately resumed their animated conversation. Rosa looked across the hall at Boris's hunched back, a figure in solitude, his haversack at his feet. Above him, the banner: *"Food Co-Operation Opens The Way To A New Life"*. Perhaps, she thought, he hadn't seen her; his eyesight wasn't the best, even with those thick glasses he wore. But the distance between them hadn't been that big, surely he would have seen her. So why would he so pointedly ignore her? As soon as she formed the question, the answer came to her. She smiled, good old Boris, ever the faithful friend. By his expulsion, he was now considered a contaminated person, as just shown by his so-called friends. Perhaps, he was just being careful not to taint Rosa by his association? But then, she thought, he had no qualms about sitting with his male friends. Whichever way she tried to work it out, Rosa was puzzled.

The dining hall was thinning out; lunch was coming to an end and the students had other places to be, the kitchen staff were wiping tables and emptying ashtrays. The male threesome was leaving, still talking animatedly. There was no point, she decided, worrying about it when Boris was just there, a matter of a few feet away. She collected her bag and made her way across the hall. How small Boris seemed to be, his thin shoulders scrunched over, his head disappearing beneath the collar of his jacket.

'Boris?' He physically jumped at the sound of his name. 'I'm sorry, I didn't...' Her words floundered on seeing the expression on his face, a mixture of fear and loathing. 'I didn't mean to make you–'

'Leave me alone.'

'I'm sorry?'

'I said leave me alone.'

'I... I don't understand.' Nervously, she pulled out a chair and slowly sat down. Boris immediately leant back in his seat and pointedly turned his head away from her and pretended to fix his concentration on the other side of the hall. Rosa hadn't expected this, and it was upsetting her. She noticed his hands placed on the edge of the table, the left index finger tapping against the wooden surface. Why was he being like this? She had done something to upset him, but whichever way she stretched her mind, she could not think what. 'Boris, please…' she said quietly, 'what's wrong?' She felt condemned by his silence. 'What have I done?'

This time, it was she who jumped. The way he stood bolt upright, the chair scraping noisily against the floor, the glance of fury in his eyes as he looked down at her. 'You pretend not to know…?' By the time Rosa spluttered an incoherent word, Boris had grabbed his haversack and was striding across the dining hall heading directly for the exit.

In a flash, Rosa's jumble of confusing thoughts manifested themselves in anger. Rising to her feet, she surprised herself by the volume and the intensity of her outburst. 'No!' she yelled across the hall, 'I don't know, I don't bloody know.' Like a radio being switched off, the gentle background babble of conversation and kitchen staff at work stopped instantly. Boris too stopped. He'd reached the large double-swing doors. For a moment, Rosa thought (hoped) he'd turn around. But he didn't. After a pause, he pushed open the heavy doors and was gone. Rosa watched the doors swing back and forth and settle back into position, aware that all eyes were on her. She decided she wasn't going to allow him to walk away without explaining his behaviour. Gathering her bag, she hastily made for the exit. Boris was already at the far end of the corridor. She ran to catch up with him. By the time she saw him again, he was outside, trotting down the main steps which led down from the college entrance onto the gravelled drive, which, itself, led to the street.

'Boris!' It was raining heavily; people were scurrying up the steps, escaping the downpour. Rosa hurried after him, cursing him and wishing she'd brought her raincoat. 'Boris,' she cried out again. 'Please, stop.'

He carried on walking but slowed down with each step, like a large locomotive grinding to a halt. Finally, without turning around, he stopped next to the ornate fountain and allowed his haversack to fall from his shoulder and lie on the wet driveway. Rosa walked up from behind and circled around him to face him directly. And there they stood for a few time-stretching moments, facing each other silently in the rain, the gushing fountain next to them.

'I would have survived, you know,' he said.

'Yes, I know.'

'So why did you do it?'

She wished she could see into his eyes, but his glasses were too speckled with spots of rainwater. 'Why did I do what?'

'Does the guilt of betrayal lie so easily on your conscience? *You knew.* You were the only person I'd ever told because I thought, I believed, you were the only person I could tell.'

'Your father? But…'

'Yes, my father. Do you know what it's like to have had a father and never acknowledge his existence? We all ask each other what our parents did, don't we? It's one of the first questions we ask people. *What did your father do for the Revolution?* And they've always done something, haven't they? Yes, he fought the Whites and single-handedly killed a whole division of them, or he listened to Lenin preach. I remember him vividly, my father. Yes, he died when I was five and I love him to this day. And why? Because the man who took his place, beat the Jewish shit out of me daily for ten years. I was brought up speaking Yiddish and then I was suddenly forbidden to speak it. Even an utterance of it earned me a lashing – it was literally beaten out of me. And yet I tell people he's my real father and that I love him. Do you know how great this feels? To be able to tell the truth; to tell you how much I hated him, and still do. And that's how I felt when I told you about my real father. I may have only mentioned it in passing, *my father was a rabbi*, but oh, what liberation. Just a passing comment, that's all it was, but it felt as if I was standing on the rooftops, shouting it out for all Moscow to hear. Yes, my father was a rabbi and I'm proud of the fact, I'm proud I'm a Jew. Inside, inside, my heart was beating. *My father was a rabbi.* It was the first time I'd ever said it. And why you? Because I thought I loved you. Yes, OK, I know, you didn't love me back, I knew that, but I couldn't help my own feelings. I told *you* because I loved you because I trusted you. Trust is a non-existent thing, but I thought you were different. But you're not, you're even worse…'

'I never told a soul.'

'You liar!' Boris stepped away, then turned back and spat the words at her. 'It was twenty years ago; we lived in a small village hundreds of miles away. Even the all-seeing eyes of the NKVD would not make the connection. And yet, five minutes after telling you, they knew! You told them, or you told *someone* who told them.'

Someone. Yes, thought Rosa, *someone*. The realisation hit her, she staggered as surely as if struck by a physical punch. 'It's not how you think…'

'No? Stripped of my Party card, my ration card, my place at college. I'm only here now to pick up my things. Hauled in by the NKVD for a cosy chat, shunned by my friends, a week's notice to quit the apartment. But of course, don't let any of this shake your faith, Rosa; I wouldn't want to disillusion you.'

He scooped up his haversack and the rainwater dripped from its contact with the ground.

'Boris, please–'

But Boris was already walking away. He stopped and turned. 'Perhaps next time you see me, when I'm out there on the streets with the rest of the beggars, you'll dig deep in your pocket and help me out a bit.'

'No…' But Boris had reached the end of the short driveway, turned the corner and was gone.

The drive and the entrance to the college were deserted, the rain having forced everyone inside. With her hair glued to her face, Rosa fought for breath as rain and realisation drowned her in a spasm of self-pity and hatred.

Chapter 15: The Death

My every waking thought now was how to escape Petrov. It was so obvious to me now that he'd denounced Viktor to the NKVD. It wouldn't have taken much, just a whispered word; an acknowledgement from a Rykov-type bureaucrat and the damage was done. I had to leave. I envisaged various scenarios but the conclusion was always the same. Whatever way I looked at it, I was doomed. And yet I knew I had to do something. I was still young, I'd fallen in love; I had the rest of my life in front of me. But while I remained married to Petrov, I was still a prisoner under the camouflage. Now, each day was another day wasted, another day less of freedom, of love.

My problem, our problem – for it occupied Dmitry's mind as much as mine – became more intangible and more unassailable every day. Sometimes, during my more charitable moments, I couldn't believe Petrov would carry out his threat. But he would. I knew him too well. What he couldn't have he destroyed – the people who used to live in our apartment, the boss whose job he wanted, the assistants who threatened him with their very intelligence. Trotskyites – all of them, and where were they now? No man, no problem. Pride, jealousy and fear make for an unpredictable and dangerous combination. And these were people against whom he had nothing more than whispered allegations. But he took what little he had and used it to devastating effect. Against me, his own wife, he had a positive arsenal of ammunition, a long list of crimes against the State.

I'd been out all morning, shopping; this time with Anna and this time with more success – we'd queued for hours and came away with half a dozen sausages each. As we queued, I told Anna everything. Speaking in hushed tones, I told her of my love for her brother and Petrov's reaction. I told her that Petrov had denounced Viktor. I told her that I had a past to be frightened of. I didn't tell her what – it was enough that she knew.

'You could blackmail him,' she said quietly, so as not to be overheard.

'With what, Anna? There's nothing I could hold against Petrov, no chink in his armour, no Achilles Heel – apart from me. He travels light. He has no possessions, no friends, little family, no secrets, no skeletons. I'm his only item of baggage. My past is his only fault line.'

'Perhaps there's something at his work?'

'No, his work and I are separate entities. He rarely speaks about it – and even then only in terms of statistics and production levels. I doubt if he's ever mentioned me at work.'

'Just another bureaucrat without a personal life.'

'Yes. Work is a closed book, totally inaccessible.'

'So what is there?'

'That's the problem, as hard as I try to think, he remains invincible, beyond my reach. He has no weaknesses.'

'Does he drink? To excess? That'd be frowned upon.'

'No. Perhaps the occasional drink, but that's all.'

'Any weaknesses of the flesh?'

I laughed. 'No, Stalin and the Party are his only loves.'

'And that's how it's meant to be.'

'Wherever I start from, I return to the same place.' Of course, there was only one thing I *could* do. It wasn't something I could share even with Anna, but I always returned to it – and the thought of it made me shudder.

*

I invited Anna back for a coffee. Returning to my apartment, we picked our way through the poorly lit hallway, up the three flights of stairs, and down the semi-dark corridor. Our progress was hampered by boxes of litter, of piles of belongings, heaps of clothes, mattresses (occupied and unoccupied) and a continuous line of people – leaning against the walls, smoking, chatting, sleeping, children screaming and playing chasing games up and down the stairs, a mother breastfeeding on the landing, an old woman darning socks. Everywhere, there was such noise, people shouting, yelling, babies crying. Eventually, we got in.

Petrov was out at work and Viktor was still in bed. I checked up on him, as always. Immediately I knew something was wrong. 'Viktor,' I said. 'Are you all right?'

The room was dark; I opened the curtains and let the dim light through. Viktor lay in his bed, his head propped up on his pillows. His eyes were open but I knew – he was dead.

'Oh, my dear Lord,' I whispered. 'Viktor, oh Viktor. Couldn't you have waited until I returned?' I closed his eyelids, the sensation causing me to tremble.

I sat down on the edge of the bed.

After a while, Anna, who'd be sitting in the main room, came to see what had happened to me. 'Is everything all right?' she asked, standing at the door of the bedroom. 'Is Viktor all right?'

I shook my head, unable to talk. I watched her as she approached the bed. She grimaced at the sight of him and tried to disguise it. 'Oh, Maria. I am sorry.'

'I should have been here for him.'

'You couldn't be here all the time,' she said, rubbing my shoulder. 'It's over now; he needn't suffer any more. At least he died at home.'

'Yes. They can't touch him now.'

We sat in silence for a while, me on the bed, Anna on a chair next to me.

'What do I do, Anna? Who should I call first? A doctor? The undertaker?'

'Let's worry about that later. You're in shock, Maria. I'll make you a cup of tea.'

As Anna busied herself in the kitchen, I could hear a baby sobbing in the adjoining apartment. It started off as a bored sort of cry, but then worked itself up into an angry bawl, hardly drawing breath. Poor thing, couldn't someone see to it? Eventually, the baby stopped crying and a degree of silence returned, just the sound of people traipsing up and down the corridor, the sound of muffled talking.

'I put in an extra sugar,' said Anna, bringing in two mugs. 'You probably need it.'

'Thank you.'

'Tell me, Maria. Tell me everything that happened.'

'With Viktor?'

'Yes, with Viktor.'

I thought back to that terrible time, every last detail imprinted on my memory. 'Oh, Anna. Where do I start?'

'You know, don't you, Maria, that you can trust me? I mean, really trust me.'

'Yes, I know.' I stroked her arm with gratitude. 'OK, I'll tell you everything. I suppose it started when Nadya, Viktor's wife, came in to see me, with Rosa, screaming that they had arrested him. She was hysterical.'

'Understandable.'

'She told me how these men in their long black shiny mackintoshes barged in in the middle of the night, looking like messengers from the Devil himself, and started tearing the place apart.'

'Looking for incriminating evidence.'

'Yes. They ripped up the mattress and the sofa, flung all the drawers on the floor, smashed all the crockery. Of course, Viktor had done nothing wrong, and I told her to cling onto that.

'The next day, I went with her to the Lubyanka prison where we thought they might be holding him. We queued for hours with hundreds of other women, just like us, all desperate to know about their husbands, their sons, their brothers. They all had parcels — we hadn't. When we got to the head of the queue, the blank-faced official said he had no record of him. Then, we went over to the Butyrka prison and finally the Lefortovo and repeated the whole process — and all for nothing. Next day, we went through it all again, but this time, Nadya came prepared with a parcel: a few clothes, bites to eat, a book or two.

'Our lives had come to a standstill. I lived with this constant gnawing in the pit of my stomach; we both did. Every time we spoke to an official, it was with tears in our eyes. We both so desperately wanted to know where he was. He adored Stalin, we'd say; he was a communist to his last hair. We were wasting our time of course. They just stare at you with utter contempt and order you out of the way. Every night, I'd come back here and just cry my eyes out. Petrov couldn't understand; he said there would have been a reason for Viktor's arrest. Little did I suspect that he was the reason for it. All the neighbours were too frightened to talk to us any more. And the few friends we had, made no contact. I could imagine them all scrubbing my name out of their address books, concerned to wipe away any association with me. And Nadya. For them, we had ceased to exist. Viktor was another of the "disappeared".

'I wasn't going to give up. My brother and I had survived so much together; I had to find him. I had to remain strong because Nadya had fallen apart. She lost all her strength. So I carried on by myself, visiting all three prisons every day. Eventually, I found out that Viktor was being held in the Lubyanka, which was, of course, the first place we'd tried. I spent weeks going to the prison with my parcels and handing them over. I also tried getting into the offices of the NKVD, just in the hope of being able to help him in some way. Nadya even began blaming Viktor for his own downfall – he'd always been too *nice*. She was angry because he hadn't been vigilant enough; he should have denounced more people and saved his own skin. And then she began talking as if perhaps he *was* guilty, after all.

'One day while I was queuing at the NKVD headquarters, I was told to meet a certain officer at some specified time and place. Alone. This was very exciting; I'd been thrown a lifeline of hope. I naturally kept my appointment and was met by a man whom I've come to know well, too well. His name is

Rykov. He said he had a proposal for me, a sort of deal. He said I was the sort of woman they were always on the lookout for. By that, they meant I was presentable, intelligent, cultured. In short, he wanted me to be a spy, an occupational denouncer, and in return, they'd give me back Viktor. Of course, I refused, how could I? How could I ruin the lives of others, to subject scores of women to the same fate I was experiencing? So I said no. But he told me to think it over; there was no deadline to his offer.

'A short while later, Viktor was sentenced to ten years in a labour camp out in the Urals. It was all too much for Nadya. Poor Nadya. She died a broken woman. We took Rosa in. Petrov wasn't keen but even Petrov with his ice-cold heart knew we couldn't leave her in one of those orphanages. And so, I tried to rebuild my life, but it wasn't easy. For once, Petrov proved useful. I was the sister of an enemy of the people – it's bad enough but at least I wasn't the *wife* of an enemy of the people. Petrov used his contacts, denounced a few colleagues and was able to keep his job.

'I wrote every week to the authorities, requesting permission to visit Viktor. He was meant to have visiting rights, albeit, only once every couple of years. Finally, thanks to Rykov, my request was granted – I could go to the Urals.

'It took three days by train, three days in a third-class apartment, sitting on a hard bench, with little to drink or eat. I'd made the mistake of falling asleep before eating. When I awoke, the food I'd so carefully prepared and brought with me had been stolen. A horse and cart took me the ten miles from the station to the camp gates. Oh, Anna, a more forbidding place, you cannot imagine. The bleak watchtowers, the high walls, the rolls of barbed wire, the barren landscape. The camp was made up of long, uniform barracks with tiny windows. As

I waited to be admitted into the complex, a group of about one hundred prisoners were leaving for their day's work. Oh, what a pitiful sight. There wasn't a glimmer of life among them. These weren't men, but the remnants of men, with their thin, wasted bodies, their ragged clothes useless against the biting wind, barely able to lift their feet; their filthy faces and long unkempt beards.

'I presented my papers to the guard in the office and was searched by a female guard. Presently, I was shown to a small waiting room with a dried mud floor and, stretched from one window to another, a banner which read *Labour for Socialism*. I remember thinking the irony of the slogan bordered on the cruel. The door opened and in came an old man with a long shaggy beard, covered in lice, with haunted eyes and large dark blotches on his yellow skin. He was followed in by a guard holding a pistol. The guard pushed the old man towards me and said, "you have ten minutes". It was then I realised – this old man was my brother. Viktor. He'd aged a hundred years in three. He just looked at me and at first, I thought he hadn't recognised me. Then, he fell on his knees and started howling. I took him in my arms and, Anna…'

'Go on, tell me.'

'I feel ashamed to say it but it was all I could do not to retch, he stank so terribly. He pleaded with me, begged me, to do all that I could to get him out of that hellhole. His every waking moment was an utter torment.

'Oh, what a life, I cannot describe. They work all day in the most terrible conditions – breaking rocks, chopping trees, laying tracks, all of it the work of strong, hardened men. But these poor beings, the amount they have to eat is pitiful, lacking any form of substance. I told him, I told Viktor, I could get him out, he just needed to be patient, but I had the means.

And then our ten minutes were up. I'd travelled three days and nights for ten inadequate minutes. But what did it matter – ten minutes or ten hours, I'd seen what I needed to see, witnessed for myself what depths a man can endure.

'I came back to Moscow, my mind made up. I'd do whatever the bastards wanted me to do, anything, for I couldn't bear the thought of my Viktor suffering so horribly. I immediately went to see Rykov and said I'd be his spy, that I'd offer whatever evidence I could to incriminate others, to put them through that same hell Viktor was living, simply in order to have him back. It was someone else's turn. What had been an impossible decision suddenly became very easy. Rykov sat there and grinned at me. He knew all along that I'd come round in the end. It was Rykov who arranged it for me to visit Viktor. He knew what he was doing.

'And so I became an official spy for the NKVD. I've never told anyone this, how could I? For the last two years, I've kept my fortnightly appointment with Rykov; always Rykov. They even pay me. I started off keen; happy to denounce people I knew through Viktor's old work, passing on overheard snippets of conversation, of whispered doubts, and even my suspicions, however ill-founded. After the fourth session, Rykov declared he was happy with my work – I'd kept my side of the bargain, and so it was time for him to keep his. Within two weeks, Viktor was home. He was delivered here in a Black Maria. Unfortunately, in the three months since I'd seen him in the camp, he'd developed pneumonia. A doctor came to see him regularly for a while. There was no bed for him at the hospital, and, as an enemy, ex-enemy of the people, the doctor was not permitted to prescribe anything beyond the most basic of medicines, so naturally his condition worsened. The virus spread to his lungs and from then on, I knew it was only a matter of time. But still, I carried on, acting as Rykov's personal spy, too frightened to stop.'

Anna let out a deep sigh. 'Your story – about coming from Leningrad – I never really believed it. You see, when we first met, you were still new to Moscow, and you seemed so unversed in the ways of the city. At first, I thought it was because you weren't used to Moscow, but the more I thought about it, I realised that one big city is not so different from another. It wasn't Moscow that was new to you; it was city life generally. Any city. You'd come from the countryside.'

'I can't go back that far, Anna, I simply can't. But yes, Viktor and I came to Moscow and Petrov found me working as a maid for an accountant. He gave us a new identity. Also, Nadya and Rosa when they came. Don't ask any more.'

'And are you going to tell your Rykov about Viktor?'

'Of course. I have no reason to work for them now. Viktor's death ends our contract.'

We both looked at Viktor. There was no serene expression on his face, as I believed the dead often have. He'd died as he lived – in torment.

'I don't think Rykov will let you off that easily,' said Anna. 'And perhaps, Maria, you might need him.'

'Rykov?'

'Yes, Rykov. You are in danger; you know that, don't you? While you still insist on seeing Dmitry, Petrov's anger could be the end of you. But there's still time.'

'To do what?'

'To go back to your husband. Tell Petrov it's all over between you and Dmitry. Pledge him your future. He'll forgive you and in six months, it'll all be forgotten.'

'I can't; it's too late.'

'What do you mean, too late? What choice do you have?'

'I have no choice, Anna. I can't carry on with Petrov; it's like your brother said, I'm dying slowly from the inside. But Dmitry, Dmitry has given me a reason to live, a future. He's restored my sense of womanhood. Have you never known love, Anna?'

She didn't answer for a while; she just looked at me, her eyes blinking. After a while, I think she'd stopped seeing me and saw, instead, her own reflection. A small, wry smile flashed briefly across her lips. 'No,' she said, 'I have never been in love. And yet, I know what you mean. I also know you are in an impossible situation. Dmitry may be your future, but he will also be your downfall. If you don't go back to Petrov, he will denounce you, as he did your brother, of that I am sure.'

'Yes, I know. I know.'

'You must stop him.'

'How?'

'I have an idea.'

'Go on…'

Chapter 16: The Dacha

'Petrov, we need to sort this out, one way or the other. Come away with me, just for a couple of days.'

Petrov was scanning the front page of *Pravda*. Without lifting his eyes, he barked back at the suggestion. 'Are you mad? I can't; I've got too much work.'

'But I'm not asking you to take time off, just come away with me on one of your days off.'

'No. Anyway, where would we go?'

'Anna has a dacha, she said we could use it anytime we wanted.'

He rested the newspaper on his lap. 'Anna? A dacha?'

'Yes, Anna. Is it so strange?' We were sitting in our apartment on the settee. I had decided to lure Petrov away to the dacha where, I thought, we could talk out our differences. In his heart of hearts, he knew our marriage had nowhere to go, that it was finished. But I needed to convince him of the fact while persuading him he needn't let his pride ruin my life. Couples divorce, it wasn't new, sometimes it couldn't be helped. OK, the dacha didn't really belong to Anna, it belonged to Dmitry, but if he knew that, then there'd be no way I could persuade him to come away with me.

'What can we talk about there we can't talk about here?'

'Because, Petrov, can't you see? Our marriage is falling apart and–'

'And whose fault is *that*, exactly?' he said, stamping his leg on the floor.

'Yes, I know. But we need to talk, I mean really talk. I just think if we went away from all this… this claustrophobia, and had some country air, we'd be more open with each other. We'd put aside our pain and sort ourselves out. Just you and me. Think of it, Petrov, we could go for long walks and enjoy the delights of spring.' For the first time, his face softened, I was getting through to him. I pressed home my advantage: 'Who knows, we might even enjoy it. Anna says it's a lovely spot. We could cook some proper meals for a change, light the fire and have the whole place to ourselves.'

He picked up the newspaper and began reading again but I could tell he was thinking about it. He was tempted, that much was obvious, but would he concede? 'How far is it?'

'Not far, only an hour by train, we could go tomorrow night, Wednesday.'

He didn't speak for a whole two minutes. Instead, he read his *Pravda* but I could see his mind working. It made sense to him, but he hated it when I came up with an idea. Eventually, without lifting his eyes, he spoke. 'One night only. I need to get back to work.'

'Yes, that's fine. One night only. That's all we'll need.' I leaned back against the settee and closed my eyes. I was pleased, it was what I wanted. I had a plan, albeit one that left much to chance, and it involved large quantities of vodka. It didn't take much to get Petrov drunk but it had to be vodka.

Under the influence of wine, he became argumentative and aggressive, as Dmitry, himself, had witnessed. But vodka made him maudlin and dull. I soon tired of his sentimental discourses and either left the room or, if we were at home, forced him into bed. Never before had it occurred to me that within this sentimentalism might lie a story, a revelation. I needed him relaxed, feeling nostalgic, his belly full and sexually fulfilled. Then, I'd allow the vodka to do its work. But whatever Petrov told me, I knew that, come push to shove, his word was worthier than mine. I needed a witness, someone who could, if necessary, add credence to my testimony. That someone was Anna.

*

Dmitry's dacha was situated down a leafy lane outside a small village, about an hour and a quarter north-west of Moscow. The whole lane was occupied by dachas. The weather was foul, with fierce rain and a howling gale. We managed to cadge a lift from an old boy with a long grey beard, wearing a floppy peaked cap, felt boots and a pipe clamped between his brown teeth. We rode the two kilometres from the station in silence on the back seat of his two-wheeled cart pulled by a pony as decrepit as the man. The lane was picturesque in the extreme, a long straight road, about half a mile long, with lovely birch trees overhanging the lane giving it a tunnel-like appearance. On either side, a series of driveways led up to the hideaways of the privileged. The peasant bade us farewell with a dismissive wave as we skipped off the cart outside number nine, Dmitry's dacha, and lugged our overnight bags up the short gravelled drive. The dacha was a small, one-storey wooden affair with a tin roof and painted turquoise green, its windows and doors decorated with elaborate fretwork. A large hedge concealed it from its neighbours, and behind the dacha, one could see the edge of the woods, the large pine trees and the silver birches swaying in the wind.

'I'm impressed,' said Petrov, as I unlocked the front door.

'She's had it years apparently. Came through a contact at work.'

'I never knew she was doing so well.'

It was dark inside and the musty, stale air hit us as we walked in. I shivered. Petrov pulled back the curtains and flung open the blinds. The main room was small but didn't have that same claustrophobic feeling of Moscow apartments. A large table dominated one side of the sitting room, an old brazier stood next to the wall, its funnel zigzagging at angles into a hole in the ceiling and through the tin roof; two armchairs sat at opposite ends of the room, each a deep shade of crimson, either side of a woven rug.

'This place bears the hallmark of Dmitry,' said Petrov, idly looking at the series of small framed landscape paintings and pencil drawings, flanked by portraits of Marx, Lenin and Stalin. He was right, of course, I recognised the style, the concentration of detail, the vivid colours, the exaggerated contrast between the light and shade. On a small, cloth-covered table in the corner, was evidence of an artist at work – the paintbrushes, the coloured-splattered boxes of paint, the pencils and bottles of turpentine.

'Yes, it does seem so.'

'Funny, isn't it?' said Petrov, in a tone that implied there was nothing funny in what he was about to say. 'Once upon a time, not long ago, I'd never heard of the man but now he seems to invade every part of my life. Even a simple night away and he's all around me.'

'Well, it does belong to Anna, so obviously, he comes here too. Nothing funny about that. They are brother and sister, after all.'

'Hmm.'

I carried the bags through to the tiny bedroom where there was just enough room to walk around the double bed. A wardrobe occupied one wall. I opened the doors and found a couple of male shirts hanging inside. Everywhere, like Petrov said, Dmitry's presence lingered. I hid the shirts beneath the bed.

I busied myself in the kitchen, an area to the side of the sitting room, while Petrov slumped in the armchair, lit his pipe and opened the *Pravda*. This was a good sign – Petrov only ever lit his pipe when he was feeling totally relaxed. There were a few tins of stew which we could make use of and, of course, a couple of bottles of vodka. Within this scene of simple domestic harmony, my heart was pounding. But, while I was scouting around in the cupboards looking for pans, crockery and cutlery, I was having doubts and could feel the certainty draining out of me.

'Do you have to make so much noise?'

'Sorry.'

'What about the fire?'

'Yes, Petrov.' I hadn't realised until that moment, the place was so cold. Next to the brazier, was a basket of logs and kindling wood, and, next to it, an axe and a poker, and, to the left of the brazier, a small stack of dry newspaper. I placed four logs onto the hearth, crumpled up some newspaper on top of them, and finished off with some pieces of kindling. But the logs were too big and wouldn't allow the doors to shut. Despite hunting around in the basket, I couldn't find any logs of suitable length. I held a thick log, took the axe and split it down the centre. The axe embedded itself a third of the way down and splinters of wood landed on the mat. Another few strokes, and it was cut. After ten minutes, the fire was alight and looked strong enough to remain so.

Petrov had been watching me. 'You do that like a proper country girl,' he said with, I think, a hint of admiration in his voice.

'Some things you never forget.'

'So I see. Any chance of a cup of tea now? Or shall I make it?'

'No, you stay there and relax a bit.'

'Are you all right?'

'Yes, Petrov, I'm fine. And you?'

'Couldn't be better.'

As I hunted around the kitchen cupboards for a kettle, I told myself to be strong. I'd come this far, I couldn't back out now. I couldn't find a kettle and resigned myself to boiling a pan of water on the stove. The water had just started to warm up when there was a knock on the door. My heart lurched. It couldn't be Anna; it was too early, far too early.

Petrov looked up from his paper and removed his pipe. 'Who in the hell could that be?'

'I… I don't know.'

'Well, don't just stand there, see who it is.'

'Can't you?'

'Maria, please.'

'OK.' If it was Anna, she was three hours too soon. I needed time on my own with him, to take him to bed, to cook a warm meal. Anna's unexpected appearance was all part of the plan but not this early. I opened the door and staggered back. This wasn't part of the plan at all. 'Dmitry?'

'Maria? I saw the lights on. But what are you–'

'Didn't Anna say…?'

'What the hell is he doing here?' Petrov was on his feet, hovering behind me, clutching his newspaper.

'I could ask the same,' Dmitry retorted, removing his hat and coat and shaking off the rain. 'Aren't you going to let me in?'

'No,' snapped Petrov, as Dmitry edged past me. 'What's he doing here?' said Petrov to me. 'Did you know about this?'

'No. No, really, I didn't, Anna didn't tell me.'

'Nor me,' said Dmitry. 'I told her I was coming tonight. I often come here alone. She must've got mixed up. I was hoping to do some work.'

'Well,' said Petrov, 'you can turn right around and leave, thank you very much,' said Petrov, flinging the newspaper on the table.

Dmitry strode to the middle of the room and dropped his haversack next to the settee. 'I can't go back now; there won't be another train until morning. Don't worry, old man, I'm sure we can all muddle on together. You two have the bedroom, I'll just kip here; I'll be fine. Any chance of a cup of tea?'

'Yes,' I said, glad to step back into the kitchen area. 'I've just…' I could see the steam rising from the stove. Taking a tea towel, I picked up the pan by its handle.

'This is no coincidence,' growled Petrov, facing Dmitry, his back to the fire. 'You two have planned this, haven't you?'

'No, Petrov,' I said. 'Believe me, I had no idea.' It was true. Was Anna still going to come, I wondered?

'You're getting paranoid, my dear man,' said Dmitry. 'Why should we do that, eh?' Dmitry's composure didn't feel natural. The way he kept saying *old man* was false, it wasn't an expression he used, he seemed to be mimicking Mikhail.

'Don't patronise me.' Petrov spun around to face me, his eyes ablaze with fury. 'What are you up to, woman?' I edged away from him, my back to the fire, feeling its warmth against the back of my legs, still holding onto the pan of simmering water. I was frightened; I'd seen Petrov angry but not like this. He seemed to be trembling with fury, so beside himself, he didn't know where to direct his anger next. 'If the pair of you think I'm going to let you get away with it, think again.' He was speaking quickly, his voice a deep growl. 'The pornographer and the kulak – what a combination, the NKVD would have a field day.'

'Perhaps but they're never going to know, are they?' said Dmitry.

'No?'

'No, because you're not going to tell them. You're going to do the decent thing and let your wife go. My God, man, admit it, it's over.'

'No, never.' I watched as the two men circled around each other, like two male tigers, measuring their ground, waiting to pounce. The room wasn't warm yet, but I could see the beads of sweat forming on Petrov's shiny scalp, his eyes glaring behind his glasses.

'She's still young; she has a life to live, yet you keep her locked up like a caged animal.'

'She's my wife and that's good enough for me. I saved her but if need be, I'll destroy her. Both of you. If she even tries to leave me, she'll rot in Hell, and you too. I've seen what they can do to men like you, they'd crush your balls.'

'Listen to you, you pathetic little man.'

'Oh hark, the pretentious artist, the bourgeois lackey.'

'My conscience is clear. How's yours, Party man?'

I'd backed almost into the fire, still holding the pan, when Petrov made his lunge. A fist hurled towards Dmitry's face. Dmitry pitched his head to one side but Petrov's fist caught him in the chin. If it hurt, Dmitry made no sign of it. Instead, he squared himself and threw a punch back. I heard myself screaming at them to stop. Dmitry's fist caught Petrov fully on the nose. He fell back against the arm of the settee and ricocheted onto the floor, landing at my feet. I took a few steps back, not wanting to be within his reach. He shook his head and rubbed his nose, dabbing his blood, then hauled himself up. As he did so, he grabbed the fire poker.

'Please, Petrov, no,' I screamed.

'Come on, Petrov,' said Dmitry. 'This is stupid—'

'Oh, it's Petrov now, is it?'

Dmitry also stepped back, his eyes fixed on the metal stick. 'Put it down, man. This won't solve anything.'

'You think not, you bastard? I think it solves quite a lot, actually.' Petrov waved the poker back and forth in front of Dmitry's face, relishing his moment of power.

'Put it down, I said,' said Dmitry.

He didn't see it coming, nor did I, but he screeched in pain as the poker smashed against his arm. I screamed. Dmitry staggered back, cursing, clutching his arm where the poker had made contact. Petrov didn't hesitate and wielding it like a sword, struck him again, hitting Dmitry against his side. I heard the crack on his ribcage. My hand went to my mouth. Dmitry fell to his knees, gasping for air. Petrov stepped over him, grunting. He lifted the poker above his head, gripping it in both hands, his face screwed up. He was going to hit him on the head; he was going to smash his skull in, I could see it in his eyes; he wanted to kill him.

I was still holding onto the pan of water. I threw its contents onto the fire. Anything for a diversion; to stop Petrov from using that poker. The sudden sizzling sound made Petrov falter. He turned to see what the noise was and in that moment Dmitry leapt to his feet. As Petrov turned to face him again, Dmitry struck, punching him in the face. Petrov fell, landing heavily on his back. We watched him, waiting for him to get up, the silence broken only by Dmitry's breathing and the crackle and spitting of the fire.

'I think I've knocked him out,' said Dmitry.

Petrov lay there untidily but perfectly still, his legs at the oddest of angles. It was then that I noticed it – the blood seeping out from beneath his head, staining the bricked surround of the fireplace.

Dmitry stood staring at him, his mouth gaping, his face white, the colour drained away.

*

I don't know how long we stood there, looking at each other, without seeing the person in front of us. I could hear the rain lashing against the window, the deep howl of the wind. I am a little girl again – playing with Anastasia, my wooden doll, in the fields behind our home, waiting for my father to come home from the farm. I am a young married mother, living in another hut, only yards away from where I was brought up, waiting for my husband to come home from the market. It is my first night in Moscow, finding shelter in the backdoor of a closed restaurant, rummaging amongst the rubbish, my stomach aching with hunger. I am leaning against the counter in a small office on the fourth floor of a district police station, waiting with Petrov as the chain-smoking clerk fills in our marriage certificate. I am Dmitry's model, standing unashamed as Dmitry commits my naked image to the canvas.

*

How long it took to realise, I don't know, but I became aware of the thumping knock on the door. I could hear a voice outside in the rain, shouting, muffled.

'Dmitry, what do we do?'

'Huh?'

'The door. There's someone at the door.' How hollow my voice sounded as if belonging to someone else.

'What?'

'Dmitry, please…' But I could see from his eyes, he wasn't with me. He stood there, statue-like, comatose, holding his ribcage. The body at his feet, lying on its back, a dishevelled heap.

I had to answer the door, to stop the thumping.

I walked the few paces to the door as a woman walks to the gallows. I ran my fingers through my hair. Immediately, upon opening the door, I squeezed through and stepped outside, forcing back the darkened figure in a Mac. A short man, a head as round as a button, stared at me from beneath his rain-sodden hat with anxiety written all over his piggy features. He looked like a man who had come face-to-face with a medieval witch.

'Is-is everything all, all right?' he stuttered, arching his neck sideways to try and catch a glimpse through the closing door. 'I thought I heard shouting.'

'We're fine. Just a small argument. We're fine now.' I tried to smile, the crooked smile of a witch.

'It sounded like two men's voices.'

'My voice goes deep when I'm angry.'

'Oh.'

'Yes.' Self-consciously, I coughed.

'But everything's OK now?'

'Yes. Absolutely. Thank you for your concern. I apologise if we worried you.' I glanced up at the rain. 'We're getting wet.'

'No, no, it's… it's fine, I…'

'Yes, well.'

'Yes. I'll be…'

But he wasn't leaving; seemed to have no intention of leaving despite the rain. So with my hand behind me, I opened the door. 'My husband – he gets jealous,' I said as I squeezed backwards through the gap. 'Very jealous,' I said, closing the door.

I listened and after a few moments, I heard his steps fading into the wet night.

I turned, hoping that perhaps Petrov was not dead, that somehow I had imagined it all. But no, it was real enough. Dmitry was slumped in one of the armchairs, staring at the figure on the floor.

Part Two

Chapter 17
Moscow, 28-29 February 1992

Caroline and I were back at the Hotel Ukraine, lounging in the soft leather armchairs, each sipping a welcome glass of red wine. We sat in silence, our thoughts reeling from the tale Maria had told us. An elderly Russian gentleman wandered past us, dressed smartly in a thick suit and using a walking cane. He was old enough, I reckoned, to have lived through the latter Stalinist years. Had he too lived in a state of constant anxiety, had he known someone who was arrested, had he been an informal spy like Maria or Petrov? Perhaps, he'd been a victim and had spent years in a Siberian Gulag, living from day to day, eking out an existence. Everyone around us must have known what it was like to live within the all-seeing eyes of the KGB or the NKVD, as it was called in Maria's day. I was beginning to understand the true meaning of the word 'freedom'. One doesn't always appreciate what one has until one learns of the alternative.

From Maria's apartment, Caroline and I found the nearest Metro and caught a train to Moscow's biggest street,

Tverskaya Ulitsa, where we wandered up and down absorbing the atmosphere of rush-hour Moscow. We popped into Yeliseev's Food Hall where Rosa had been so dumbstruck. In those days, as Maria had told us, the street was called Gorky Street and the food hall was called Gastronom No.1, accessible only to the Party and police elite. Now, it resembled an upmarket supermarket but in the most beautiful environment, with its huge chandeliers and carved pillars. We bought a couple of four-ounce jars of caviar as souvenirs and idled our time amongst the lavish surroundings. It seemed strange to be walking in the steps of Rosa some sixty years later. As we stepped back outside into the cold, I had an image of dozens of unprivileged Muscovites, their noses pressed up against the glass of the shop front, eyeing the goods that were so inaccessible to them. And the cold! I found the cold rather bracing but then I knew I could easily escape it. The hotel was extremely warm, and our bedrooms were so hot, I woke up drenched in sweat. But how difficult it must have been without the proper means to heat one's apartment.

'She still hasn't told us this terrible secret of hers,' said Caroline, taking a large gulp of her wine.

'I think she has, her lover killed Petrov.'

'No, it was something else, something that happened before she came to Moscow.'

'Yes, you're right. But what could be worse than your lover killing your husband like that?'

'But it was an accident; he didn't mean to kill him. Perhaps she'll tell us tomorrow.'

'Yes, if she trusts us enough.'

'Oh, I think she trusts you all right.'

'You think so?'

'Definitely. She likes you, it's obvious.'

'I hope you're right.'

Caroline yawned and glanced at her watch. 'Well look, *Reech-hard*, it's late, I'm going to bed. Coming?'

'Not yet, give me ten minutes or so.'

'OK.' She leaned down and kissed me on the cheek. 'Don't be too late, eh?'

I smiled and watched her leave. I was so pleased Caroline was with me; I couldn't have come by myself, I lacked the courage. Caroline and I had only been together for about three months but already I was feeling very comfortable with her. I wished, just for once, that it would last. I'd been unlucky with my girlfriends. I don't know what it was – I entered into relationships very easily, but my difficulty was keeping them going. It was as if I was good novelty value but once that novelty had worn off, they found nothing left to interest them.

I decided to get myself a cup of coffee before going up to our room. The bar staff spoke broken English, so for once, I didn't need Caroline's help. I asked the barman for a cappuccino.

'Company?' said a female voice next to me.

I turned to see a woman, or rather a young girl, plastered with make-up and dressed provocatively in an extremely short skirt and an eye-popping low-cut top. 'I'm sorry?'

'You want company?'

'No, no, I'm all right, thanks.'

'Buy me an espresso,' she purred, then, turning to the barman, said something in Russian.

'Espresso for the lady?' asked the barman.

'No, no. *Nyet*. No,' I said as firmly as possible.

'No company?' she said, pouting her lips in a fake expression of hurt.

'No, thank you.'

I took my cappuccino and pointedly sat down with my back against the bar. I sipped my drink and tried to think of Maria and Dmitry, Anna, Rosa and Boris. All these names filling my mind. But somehow, I couldn't concentrate. Knowing that the young prostitute was sitting not far away, her eyes burning in my back, made me feel uncomfortable. I couldn't help but glance over my shoulder. It was a mistake. She was smoking a cigarette, her legs consciously crossed, exposing the top of her suspenders. Unfortunately, for a split second, our eyes met.

I watched a respectably dressed middle-aged couple come into the lobby from the cold. They laughed as they removed their coats and stamped the snow from their boots. I guessed, like me, they were foreigners, enjoying the novelty of snow.

'Company?'

I jumped and was annoyed that I hadn't noticed her stealth-like approach. 'No,' I said, furiously shaking my head. She sat down, nonetheless, which made me feel nervous, dreading to think how much it would cost me for the pleasure of this girl's company. Her make-up made her look older but I reckoned that under the disguise, she could have been no more than about sixteen. Her eyes were dulled and for a moment, I found myself pitying her for what must be the most tedious of work. Irked, however, that my evening contemplation had been interrupted by an indecently-dressed teenager, I gulped down the rest of my coffee and rose to my feet.

'Goodnight,' I said brusquely. And with that, I took the lift and returned to Caroline and the claustrophobic heat of my room.

*

Having sussed out how Moscow's Metro system worked, we decided against the expense of another taxi ride. The Metro stations were large and dark, with long, unending escalators, and Art Deco lamps at regular intervals. The signs were all written in the Cyrillic alphabet and Caroline and I had to read the shape of the letters to find our way. On the train, a young attractive girl with bright red hair smiled at me. I smiled back but Caroline noticed and glowered at me. I didn't dare look at the redhead again. I wondered whether my would-be escort from the night before had had any luck.

The buildings between the Metro station and Maria's flat were imposingly large and uniformly bleak. We trudged through the snow, still not believing we were in Moscow. Until just three years ago, the Soviet Union was on the other side of the Iron Curtain, and although I knew of people who'd visited, the idea seemed almost ludicrous. I had Russian in my blood but nothing would have enticed me to visit. As a youngster, the USSR was the feared enemy. I remember we all lived in genuine fear of a nuclear war. I actually used to have nightmares of the falling bomb, the huge mushroom cloud rising above London as the USSR and the West collided into World War Three. I had visions of Brezhnev's fat finger on the button, bringing to an end everything we'd ever known. My class once wrote a letter to him, asking him to remember the children of the world, to allow us our future. We really believed that Russian people were different from us – automated alien humans living an existence we wouldn't recognise. The only time we saw them was when we watched the Olympics on television. There they were, these muscle-bound men and men-like women, throwing the shot-put unbelievable distances, sprinting like devils, matched only by their Eastern European cousins, the Romanians, the mighty

East Germans. I remember almost weeping with pride when Sebastian Coe and Steve Ovett won their medals in Moscow '80, beating the Soviets on their home ground. This was more than sport, this was politics, this was ideology.

But now I was here, I felt as if I'd been before; it seemed like the most natural place to be. I embraced the drabness, the snow, and the cold as much as I adored the beauty, the architecture and the pure culture of Russia. The language, still so alien to me, sounded so noble within its harshness. The people had lived a history that was unique and they were still living it now. And none more so than my very own grandmother.

*

The door was opened again by Irina, drying her hands on her checked apron. Caroline said hello but Irina merely grunted and shuffled back into the kitchen.

'Richard, Karen, hello, my friends, come in, come in,' said my grandmother from inside. She was sitting in her red leather armchair, the yucca plant standing to attention behind her. The green cardigan had been replaced by a pale blue one but the kingfisher brooch was still there. Her face broke into a broad grin as we entered.

'Hello… Maria,' I said, aware of my hesitation.

I offered my hand but she laughed and said, 'Now that you know me as your grandmother, don't I get a kiss?'

I laughed also, to hide my embarrassment, and leant down and kissed her on the cheek, noticing the delicate hint of perfume. I wanted to call her *grandmother*, to acknowledge our relationship. I had never known a grandmother, never had a chance to call anyone by that term and I so wanted to use it. But it was like using an older person's first name without asking – it seemed inappropriate. Would she ask me or would the opportunity pass me by while I stood on ceremony?

Maria asked us what we had done the previous night. Caroline told her about the food stall on Tverskaya Ulitsa, the hotel and various landmarks we passed along the way. While Caroline spoke, I noticed that the curious wooden bear was now sitting on the coffee table, no longer on the sideboard. I wondered why she'd moved it. I stared at the large painting of the collective farm and realised this was Dmitry's work, the one he got into so much trouble for. I looked at my grandmother's younger image and wondered how anyone could interpret the hint of cleavage and the outline of breast as pornographic.

'When do you go to Saint Petersburg?' asked Maria, interrupting my thoughts.

'Tomorrow evening.'

'Oh, so soon. You have much to see in Moscow but I keep you here. I am a selfish old woman.'

'No, no, not at all. It's been fascinating hearing about everything.'

'It was a hard time.'

'Yes, I suppose it was.'

'So, tell me,' said Maria abruptly, 'you two – you will marry, yes?'

'Well, we, er…'

'We haven't known each other long,' said Caroline, her cheeks flushed.

Maria spoke to Caroline in Russian. Caroline nodded her head, smiled and said something back. Their conversation continued for a short while longer and finished with Maria laughing and slapping her knee. I looked at them both, wondering.

'Well?' I asked.

'I'm not allowed to say,' said Caroline with a smirk.

Naturally, this just intrigued me more but I decided against pursuing it, feeling rather pleased that Maria should like Caroline enough to talk to her confidentially.

'Irina!' yelled Maria. As if on cue, Irina appeared carrying a tray of tea. She laid it, or rather plunked it, on the table and exited without a word. 'She is shy but she means well. I think.'

Without being asked, Caroline started placing the cups on their saucers and stirred the tea.

'I tried your English marmalade – how nice it is, but I think your Bronzed Syrup is perhaps too sweet for my teeth.'

I smiled. 'The painting,' I said, pointing to the canvas, 'is it Dmitry's?'

'*The Workers' Rest*, yes.'

'So, the young pretty girl at the right – that is you?'

Maria laughed. 'You have your father's charm, yes, that is me.'

'That's Richard for you,' said Caroline, passing a cup of tea to Maria. 'Always the charmer.'

'You know, I am pleased you are here. I worry you may not want to come back.'

'Why? Why wouldn't we return?'

'After what I tell you yesterday. It's not natural to kill one's husband.'

'But it wasn't you that hit him,' said Caroline. 'And it was an accident,'

I stifled a laugh, not sure whether my grandmother was purposely being droll or whether it was a solemn statement whose seriousness had got lost in translation. But then I saw a hint of a smile and realised that, even in English, she knew the value of irony.

'That's why I don't want to marry,' I said.

Caroline and Maria laughed and exchanged, what I thought, was a knowing look as Caroline passed Maria her cup of tea.

Maria took a sip, then called out Irina's name again. Her maid appeared and the two of them exchanged a few words. Moments later, Irina had collected her coat and was gone. I noticed Maria's hand was shaking. A splash of tea spilt over and swam in the saucer. She looked at me, then at Caroline and then back at me. 'What I tell you now, I have never said before. It is very hard.'

'I understand—'

'No, you cannot begin to understand.' Her tone had changed, her eyes had lost their softness. Instead, she seemed almost frightened. I felt too nervous to say anything. I glanced at Caroline and she raised her eyebrows at me. Maria sighed. 'I was always hungry in Moscow, we all were, but I never complained because hunger means nothing when you... you...'

'Go on...' I almost said it, almost called her *grandmother*.

'When you are really hungry, so hungry you think you are about to die, *then* you know what hunger is. When we think of famine, we think of Africa, no? But we had famine too. Oh, they denied it, said it was all propaganda, the work of anti-Soviet agitators, but it was true. I know, I lived it. We all know of the Nazi camps, we know how the Jews suffered but no one now knows how we suffered too. They came to take our grain for the cities. Industry was everything. We peasants – yes, I was a peasant – we didn't matter. They take everything and left us with nothing. Millions died, *millions*. If we didn't die because we were hungry, they killed us off for being a kulak.'

'A kulak?'

'Yes, a kulak. It means a peasant who is richer than the rest, who exploits labour. It was absurd of course, you'd think kulaks lived in palaces, not mud huts. But Stalin wanted us liquidated. Yes, that is the word he used – liquidated. We worked hard, buy a cow. That makes us a kulak.' She paused and took a sip of tea. 'I have lived with this secret for sixty years. *Never* have I said a word. I have longed to tell someone but it is not a story one tells after dinner. But before I die, I have to say it. After you have listened, you may hate me and for that I am sorry…'

I could feel my heart beating – she'd waited more than half a century for this and, after all this time, Caroline and I were the audience she'd waited all her life for. She was terrified, unable to look us in the eye. I waited while she composed herself and wondered what could have happened to render an old woman so frightened and so full of guilt after all this time.

'I was young, twenty-five. My name was Matrena. It is the name I was born with. I changed it to Maria when I came to Moscow. I could no longer live with the name of my birth. I had a husband, an older man. His surname was Makarov and that is the name I always remember him by – Makarov. When we were hungry, we dreamt of food, and then we would wake up miserable because, of course, we had no food. That day, the last day, it was a cold May morning…'

Chapter 18: The Hunger

Matrena woke up on a cold May morning in her own home for the last time. She opened her eyes but, not wanting to face the day ahead, closed them again. It was the same every day, that fleeting moment of optimism abruptly suffocated by the grim realisation that she was still hungry. She scratched herself. Perpetual hunger had gnawed away at her soul, eroded her personality and diminished her thoughts to a one-track desire from which there was no escape. Hunger strips the mind of logical thought, chases away one's imagination. The mind is concentrated and constricted, like a man in a straitjacket, and any freedom of thought is crushed by the unbearable weight of hunger. One has so little energy yet sleep is hard to come by. When finally, it does prevail, sleep provides the only respite, the only satisfaction – for Matrena's dreams are filled with food. Huge banquets and unending feasts filled every corner of her nocturnal wanderings. She dreamt she was fat and awoke to find herself emaciated. With the hunger tearing at her insides, she placed her hands on her stomach, the stomach which, just moments before in her dream, had been bloated with food, was instead bloated with starvation.

Eventually, her husband, Makarov, came to drag her out of her pit. He sat silently beside her on the edge of the bed and stroked her arm. She looked for the dark attractiveness that used to characterise his face but saw only the lines of fatigue and hunger etched into his translucent, dry skin. Gone were the blazing green eyes, the blackness of his hair, the permanent smile. His breath was dry and stale, his gums white, his teeth a dark yellow. He was wearing the same clothes he'd worn for weeks (or was it months?). She no longer noticed the stench – she was too immersed in it herself. What catastrophe had brought them to this? Somehow, it could have been more bearable to blame a severely bad harvest, or adverse weather, or the workings of an external enemy; but no, it was man-made, and it came from within. Only in Russia could the people suffer so much at the hands of the Dictatorship of the Proletariat.

They both knew, at some point during the day, they could expect the usual visit. She always hoped it would come sooner rather than later, just to get it over and done with. It was like waiting for the Grim Reaper day after day. No, worse – at least the Reaper only bothered you the once.

The family congregated in the main room. It was dark and dank with smooth mud walls and a low whitewashed beamed ceiling. A thin blanket draped over the solitary window in an attempt to stem the whistling draught that played with the candle sitting on the table. A parade of bugs, croton bugs, marched up and down the improvised curtain. Makarov sat on a wooden bench at the end of the long, bowed table, a look of pity mixed with disgust as he stared at his two daughters, Natasha and Nicola, lying huddled together on a mattress next to the huge clay stove. What a pathetic sight they made, what with their swollen bellies, and skeletal arms and legs poking out from their filthy remnants of cloth, totally unaware of the flies congregating around the eyes, their thinning brittle hair crawling with vermin. Matrena knew they were too exhausted by hunger to wake up. She stood at the stove and lifted the lid of the steaming pot and poked in a fork. Breakfast, such as it was, was the same as yesterday, the day before and the day before that. In fact, she could scarcely remember a time when they had anything different, any variation on a slither of potato. She crouched down and, taking Natasha's hand, tried to smile. She could feel the bones of the little girl's fingers under the skin. Natasha and Nicola – her four-year-old twins with their faces of old, old women.

There was a knock on the door. They'd come early today, thought Matrena. At least they still had the decency to knock. Matrena looked at Makarov. There was no nervousness in his expression, simply dulled trepidation. He squeezed Matrena's hand but there was no point in trying to reassure her; they were all at their mercy. They'd been lucky so far, each extra day in their dank home a bonus. But Matrena felt it in her bones – today their luck was about to run out. Then came the second knock, no more impatient than the first. 'Enter,' growled Makarov.

The Chairman of the District Soviet entered. Matrena knew his name now, Comrade Yonov. A tall, stiff-looking man, nothing to look at, she thought, no soul, no heart, which made Yonov's grip on power all the more precious. Yonov was followed by his usual assistant, Ivanova, a woman with a slow eye and heavy eyebrows and the look of a condemned woman surviving by virtue of her uniform. 'Good morning, Comrade Makarov,' said Yonov with a chirpy tone laced with false sincerity. 'So, what's going on here, preparing for a feast then? Smells good.'

'You're welcome to join us,' replied Makarov.

Yonov lifted the lid of the pot and, waving away the steam, peered in. 'A potato – how imaginative.'

'And what would you suggest, Comrade?'

Replacing the lid, Yonov turned to Makarov. 'You don't fool me. Pretend to eat like paupers and as soon as our backs are turned, you feast like kings. Enough of this charade – you know why I'm here.'

'To take away my non-existent grain?'

'Don't give me that bull, I know you're hiding it, I've got my informers – people tell me things, y'know.'

'They can tell you as much as they like, I still don't have any.'

Yonov looked at the two girls on the mattress, their limbs intertwined, their eyes closed. 'Do you know what the punishment is for non-compliance of your quota?' he said to Makarov.

Matrena had heard this conversation too many times. She rose from her chair, making herself the centre of attention. 'Why do you keep on so? Every day, we go hungry and every day you ask the same stupid questions, make the same impossible demands.' She walked over and stood directly in front of Yonov, towered by his height. 'What do you want us to say that we haven't told you a dozen times before?'

She could tell that Yonov wasn't used to such arrogance from a woman. Her comments angered him and seemed to prick his professional pride. 'Hold your insolent tongue, you—'

Instinctively, Makarov stepped quickly forward and placed himself between Yonov and his wife. 'Don't you dare.'

Yonov slapped Makarov hard across the face. Matrena gasped and put her hand to her mouth. Makarov stood his ground breathing heavily through his nose, staring at Yonov, his eyes burning with fury. Ivanova edged to her boss's side, but Yonov had no need for her help. He reached inside his jacket and pulled out a revolver. 'Do you know what this is?'

Makarov watched it as he answered. 'A Mauser.'

'A Mauser – that's right. You have to hand it to the Germans – they know how to make guns.' Matrena could sense Yonov's satisfaction at having the situation under his complete control.

Yonov turned to address Ivanova. 'Take an inventory. Up in the loft too,' he said. Ivanova nodded and took a notepad and a pencil out from her breast pocket.

Matrena watched her suspiciously. 'What – what are you doing?' Ivanova pointedly ignored her as she licked the end of her pencil and started jotting lists in a well-used notepad. Matrena repeated the question, this time to Yonov.

'Shut up,' snapped Yonov, his hand still gripping the revolver.

Matrena knew the answer – they only listed everything once they'd decided to turf you out.

Makarov had realised it too. 'You're taking us away, aren't you?' he growled. Yonov kept his silence. Makarov persisted. 'Why, we haven't done anything wrong? On whose authority?'

'On the authority of this,' Yonov snarled as he waved his revolver in front of Makarov's face. Makarov stepped back. Matrena leapt towards Yonov, grabbing his wrist. 'Get out, get out, you bastard,' she screamed.

Ivanova came to her boss's aid and, between them they loosened her grip and flung her off. Matrena fell across the room, landing in a heap at the foot of the table. 'Try that again, you bitch, and I'll kill you,' yelled Yonov, still brandishing his revolver. Natasha and Nicola woke up, their eyes blinking into focus. First one started to cry and then the other.

Matrena's eyes were also welling up. 'Leave us alone,' she said.

Ignoring her, Yonov glared at Makarov. Barely able to disguise his glee, he pronounced their fate: 'With the authority invested in me by the District Committee for the Collection and Redistribution of Grain, I am arresting you and your family for: a., non-compliance with repeated requests to fulfil your quota of grain; and b...' He paused, trying to remember what the 'b' was.

Ivanova interjected. 'Kulak agent?'

'Yes, yes, thank you, Ivanova, I'm perfectly aware of that. And b., for being under suspicion of being a kulak agent. You are thereby–'

'We're not kulaks,' said Matrena.

'I didn't say you were, if you listen I said "under suspicion"–'

'And he said kulak agent not an actual kulak,' added Ivanova.

Matrena was aware of the underlying farce beneath the tragedy unfolding in front of her. 'Well, if we're talking semantics here, what exactly defines us as being either a kulak or a kulak agent?' The calmness in her own voice surprised her.

'A kulak: one who possesses property or wealth that favours him to the detriment of the rest of the village and contrary to the spirit of collectivisation.'

Ivanova looked up from beneath her eyebrows. 'And you should see how much they've got here boss – pots: three; pans:

four (one slightly dented); jugs: three; wooden bowls: five; wooden spoons–'

'Shut up, Ivanova.'

'Sorry, boss.'

Matrena could almost have laughed if it hadn't been for Nicola's simpering but she was quite prepared to continue the farce. 'And a kulak agent?'

A flash of realisation passed over Yonov's face. 'You bitch; you think you can take the piss? I've had enough of this; we're leaving right now.'

'Where are you taking us?' asked Makarov.

'Just you. I'm not touching those kids; your wife can stay here and bury them. They'll be dead by the end of the day.'

'I'm not going anywhere,' said Makarov, despite the muzzle of the Mauser pressed against his stomach.

Yonov stepped back a pace and lifted the revolver, pointing it first at Makarov's forehead and then slowly swinging it around to face Matrena. Matrena, realising the gun was aimed at her, felt her heart quicken. She stepped back towards the stove, glancing nervously at her husband but Makarov kept his focus on Yonov. Matrena, shaking with fear, crouched down near her daughters and grabbed a delicate little hand.

With his eyes fixed on Matrena, Yonov addressed Makarov, saying quietly, 'Listen here, you bastard, I'll count to five and if you're not through that door by the end of it, I swear I'll shoot. You got that?' He didn't wait for an answer. 'One…'

Matrena knew that her husband had no option and the sense of loss was already beginning to eat at her. She had lived all her life in this village. As a girl, she'd helped her father in the vast fields owned by the local family of nobles. She'd lived in this very house, with Viktor, her brother, and her parents and grandparents. She remembered the long evenings; all of them crammed into this dingy space, her mother reading Tolstoy and Pushkin to her, trying to explain the complex narratives. Then, of course, came the war. Viktor joined up in 1916, becoming a soldier of the tsarist army, leaving behind his pregnant wife. He fought the Germans in conditions he'd never been able to put into words. But the war wasn't going to plan; there were rumours of soldiers deserting en masse. Eventually, Viktor deserted too, refusing to fight for the imperialists, placing his loyalty instead with the workers.

'Two...' Towards the end of the war, Viktor was back in the village, reunited with his wife and joining Matrena in the fields, and now a proud father to a daughter. Meanwhile, the murmuring of discontent grew audibly each day. The word "revolution" was on everyone's lips. They stopped working the fields – it was no longer safe to be seen working under the 'bourgeois yoke'. And when it came, it broke forth like a dam, a torrent of revolutionary violence that shook the very foundation of Mother Russia. One could taste the excitement; they became drunk on the anticipation of a new beginning. The old order was on its head, now *they*, the workers and peasants, had the power: the Dictatorship of the Proletariat. She remembered the night the old estate workers looted the nobles' house. She and Viktor came away with a wheelbarrow full of treasure: a heavy carpet, a silver cup, a cigarette case and other bits and pieces of imperialist loot. But it was a strange musical instrument that really excited her brother. He found out later it was a bassoon. And then, they set the old house to flames. She remembered her sense of unease. But Viktor didn't share her concerns or disquiet – as far as he was concerned the nobles had it coming to them. The fire reached the moon, extinguishing forever bourgeois exploitation. The old life was gone and from the ashes they would build a new utopian reality. That night they couldn't sleep for excitement. For weeks and months on end, people took to the streets, and platforms were hastily erected, as, overnight, ordinary people became impassioned orators delivering adrenaline-stirring speeches and conjuring up fist-shaking slogans. New words became part of the everyday vocabulary; Bolsheviks, soviets, anarchists, Social Revolutionaries. And everywhere that name, again and again, Lenin, Lenin, Lenin.

'Three…' Then after the euphoria came the hangover; the bloody fallout, Reds against the Whites, the Civil War and its arbitrary death and executions. Matrena's village remained staunchly Red. She remembered too well the death of those regarded as White sympathisers. She watched as they were forced down the road that led out of the village, lined up against the wall of a decrepit barn and shot, their desperate pleas met with derision and ridicule. She cheered along with the other villagers as the shots echoed through the early evening air. She shuddered with shame at the memory. One could still, to this day, see the bullet holes peppered against the wall of the barn.

'Four…' But Matrena, Viktor and Makarov had all become adept at embracing and condoning violent change as a means of camouflage. The village had rid themselves of the bourgeois oppressors and for that, they were thankful. But the new masters, whom they had all readily embraced, became more ferocious, more stifling than the tsarist regime had ever been. And now, thirteen years on, in the figure of Yonov, it was pointing a gun straight at her head. She looked at Natasha and Nicola, huddling each other for warmth, too young and too weak to know or care what was unfolding around them.

She saw the blank, death-like expressions on their faces. Yonov was right – they'd be dead by nightfall.

'Five…'

She knew they'd been defeated, defeated by the power of a Mauser. Makarov knew it too. 'OK,' he said, stepping towards the door. For a moment, she thought she heard Yonov breathe a sigh of relief. Makarov reached the door and turned to face Yonov with a shrug of the shoulders.

She tried to speak but the choking in her throat prevented the words from taking shape.

Ivanova, having forgotten to check the loft, joined her boss at his side. 'Let's go,' said Yonov, pulling open the door.

Matrena watched as Makarov followed Yonov outside into the street, Ivanova behind them. He turned around at the door. 'It'll turn out all right,' he said in a hoarse whisper. 'You'll see.' She knew of course things wouldn't turn out all right – how could they? She knew she'd never see him again. For the first time in her life, she wanted to tell him how much she loved him. But she didn't know how to.

*

Matrena looked at her daughters and knew with a force that crushed her that they wouldn't survive.

She didn't cry but her whole body felt numb, her mind fuzzy with incomprehension, and her heartbeat seemed to have slowed down to a crawl. She rose from the floor and sat on the wooden bench, her eyes fixed on the closed door. The whole sequence of events had happened so quickly, she wondered whether it had happened at all. How long she sat there staring at the door, her mind empty of any thoughts, she did not know. Half an hour? Two hours? It didn't matter. The girls had fallen asleep again, still huddling to each other for warmth under the fast-diminishing heat of the stove.

They'd taken away her husband. Something told her she ought to run after them, plead with Viktor and Nadya nearby to help her. But she couldn't; her body was too weak and anyway, what could they do? Perhaps they'd taken Viktor as well. She had to think. Despite the many searches, Yonov and his men always managed to miss the sack of grain hidden in a concealed hole under the stove. That and a few potatoes was all they'd had these last couple of months. It was a starvation diet and now the sack was almost empty. What could she hope for then? With her husband labelled a kulak, she'd be beyond sympathy.

It was almost nightfall and still she'd barely moved. She realised she had to leave while she still maintained a degree of strength. She would call on Viktor and Nadya – assuming they were still there. But what about the girls? Still lying on their mattress next to the stove, their breathing was slow and laboured. It wouldn't be long now, she thought. Just as she finally thought she was about to succumb to tears, she mustered the strength to move. She mustn't cry, she thought, if she did, she'd never stop. She stepped outside, shivering against the cold. She looked up the street and scanned her eyes across the trees and the thatched houses lining the muddy track. Houses just like hers – small square blocks made of logs, compacted with mud and whitewashed, each with just a couple of small windows and a chimney. And how odd the trees looked without their barks, stripped of their dignity like old women stripped of their clothes. In their hunger, the villagers had resorted to eating every available piece of bark they could reach. She remembered also how once the village reverberated to the sound of dogs – there were dozens of them. But not a single dog remained – they'd all been eaten, as had all the livestock. There wasn't even any manure to eat any more. She'd done it all – fed herself and her family on a diet of dog, manure and bark. The sight of the village sprawled out in front of her and the deprivations its occupants had suffered made her shudder. She knew this view as well as she knew her own face; this had been her village all her life. But she never wanted to see it again. She shuffled round to the back of the house, which used to be piled high with logs. Wedged beneath the house was an axe and, next to it, one remaining log. She picked up the axe and mustering all her strength, she split the log into two.

Back inside, she threw the two halves of the log in the stove. She picked up the large pillow that she and Makarov shared. She knelt down beside the girls. She brushed away the flies from their faces and eased them as close to one another as she could. Natasha opened her near-lifeless eyes and stared momentarily at her mother before closing them again. Matrena smelt their little heads; the hair infested with lice and caked with dirt. The dry musty smell was unpleasant but she didn't mind – she was, after all, their mother. She kissed Natasha's forehead and then Nicola's. Still kneeling, Matrena closed her eyes, bowed, and clasped her hands in prayer and begged His forgiveness for what she was about to do. She hadn't prayed for a long time, but if there was ever a time she needed to pray, this was it.

She took the pillow. She crossed herself, not once, but twice. Once for each child. Without stopping to think, she pressed the pillow against their faces and pushed down, holding it there as her eyes clouded with tears. The girls suffered no pain, no distress. They never knew.

Chapter 19: The Store
Moscow, 1935

I had never been to a Torgsin store. Theoretically, they were open to the general public, but because they dealt only with foreign currency or gold, silver or other valuables, they weren't places frequented by many. I'd walked three miles to find the nearest store, my package wrapped in newspaper and in my string bag, tucked securely under the armpit of my quilted coat. There was no waiting queue outside this store, merely a small gathering of people looking wistfully at the abundance of the window display. I saw for myself the luscious blocks of cheese arranged in a pyramid, the carefully placed array of fruit and loaves. An old bearded man with a newspaper under his arm came up next to me, also to admire the display. He was wearing mittens and wrapped in a black but shabby overcoat and was leaning his head on his arm against the window. A shop assistant, a young woman, appeared on the other side of the window, tiptoeing carefully among the display, her arms laden with bananas and apples. The woman stopped in her tracks at the sight of the old man, bent down to deposit her bounty of fruit and then, using her hands, shooed the old man away. The man obligingly stepped back and, for the briefest of seconds, I caught his eye. His face was gaunt, his skin pale beneath the coarseness of his grey beard which was streaked with black, like oil stains on dirty snow.

With my package still tucked under my coat, I dismissed the old man from my thoughts and felt the slight thrill of privilege as I pushed open the door and entered the store. The high-ceilinged hall, hung with chandeliers, smelt of a mixture of delicate perfume and fresh bread. Here, was a counter selling leather boots and shoes – practical or elegant, all shiny; there, a display of the thickest of fur coats; elsewhere, a display of meat, the flesh gleaming with freshness, the thick sausages, the generous cuts of bacon; and over there, butter and cheese, all deliciously yellow. In the background, I recognised the scratchy music, a symphonic piece by Rimsky-Korsakov, whose nineteenth-century romanticism was back in fashion. I breathed in, the music soothing my nerves, and felt dizzy in such an atmosphere of opulence.

I joined the queue at the pay desk. It may have been a Torgsin store, but the rules were the same. First, you queued to exchange your cash (or, in this case, your foreign currency or goods) for ration cards. Then, you queued to purchase your goods, and then back to the pay desk to hand back the spent cards. There were about twenty people ahead of me. It was quite the shortest queue I'd seen. A gentleman in front of me turned around and raised his eyebrows in acknowledgement. He was clean-shaven and even smelt of scent but I noticed that his neat outward appearance couldn't hide the dark stain on his long overcoat, the patch on his trouser knee. He leant towards me and whispered, 'I've got my gold wedding ring. How much do you reckon that'll get me?' He opened his fist and I saw, resting in his blotchy, red palm, the band of gold. 'It's chunky enough, don't you think? My wife doesn't want me to sell it, but I tell her, you can't eat gold.' He closed his hand on the ring and I noticed the blackness under his fingernails.

I smiled politely. No, I thought, you can't eat gold; you can't live off memories when your stomach is empty. The man shuffled forward in the queue and I followed him. The music had changed to Tchaikovsky's First Piano Concerto. I closed my eyes – Viktor had loved this piece of music, being the first record he'd bought. He'd played it constantly. And then, after his arrest, I had sold the gramophone player to pay for the daily packages I delivered to the Lubyanka prison, but I still had the record.

Eventually, the man in front of me was being served. Behind the counter, with its shiny till and abacus, stood a heavily made-up middle-aged woman, her face ludicrous in its layer of powder, her unnaturally auburn hair tied tightly in a bun, her fingernails painted bright crimson. She took the man's ring and couldn't help a grimace as their fingers touched. She glanced at it with an expression of disinterest and passed it to a male colleague behind her, a young man dressed in a tight, dark blue suit with waistcoat and watch-chain, his hair greased back with a severe central parting. He peered at the ring through an eyepiece for a few moments then, without removing the eyepiece, shook his head. 'One,' he said, passing the ring back to his female assistant.

'One bond,' she said abruptly, handing the ring back to its owner.

'What do you mean one bond?' asked the man leaning forward, leering at her.

'One bond – that's all it's worth.'

'But what will that buy me? A sausage, one single sausage? Maybe two?'

'Your choice. Take it or leave it.'

'It must be worth more than that – it's gold, isn't it?'

The young man with the eyepiece interrupted. 'Poor quality, I'm afraid.'

The older man stared at his ring. 'But it's my wedding ring,' he said quietly.

The woman leaned up. 'Next,' she said.

The man looked at me, his face creasing with lines of rage and indignation. 'You bastards.'

'Next!'

'You stuck-up bastards.' In the corner of my eye, I could see a squat man in a brown uniform fast approaching. The older man had seen him too. 'Bastards,' he said one more time as he turned to leave, but his voice had lost its venom, instead sounding pathetically hollow.

I watched him leave, being trailed from a discreet distance by the brown uniform. '*Next!*' repeated the counter assistant with obvious impatience, bringing my attention sharply back into focus.

'I've got something that may interest you,' I said, producing the newspaper-wrapped article from my bag. The mere size of it interested both the counter assistant and her eyepiece colleague behind her. They watched as I unravelled the last layers of newspaper, putting each one back into my bag. Denuded of its umpteenth layer of wrapping, the final package seemed rather small. But nevertheless, the golden bust of Tchaikovsky looked impressive on the countertop, the chandelier lights reflecting off its shiny curves.

The young man came out from behind his desk, his eyes focused on the bust. 'Well, what have we got here then?' he said. He was impressed, I could tell, and I felt a small prickle of pride that my brother's moment of glory was still able to dazzle. The man picked up the bust, commenting on its surprising heaviness, and inspected it, turning it this way and that. It was about six inches high, with a green felt base and the inscription *Tchaikovsky Prize for Youth Musician*. 'I think you'd better come with me.' With that, he scooped up the bust and beckoned me to follow him. 'This way,' he said.

I followed him through the store and the crowd of staff and customers, past the stalls and counters, the convergence of smells, and through a *staff only* door and up to the second floor. He knocked on a door, waited to be summoned, and walked in. Behind a large desk, was an elderly man with a pince-nez, his grey hair parted and greased down; an older version of the floor manager. He eyed me suspiciously, obviously surprised to be visited by a member of the public. The younger man placed the bust on the desk and whispered an explanation. The older man inspected the bust in a similar fashion, removing his pince-nez and peering at it through a magnifying glass and occasionally nodding his head.

'Hmm, interesting.' Looking up at me, he asked, 'Where did you get it from?'

'My brother won it.'

'Impressive. Go on.'

'Best new musician. He played the bassoon.'

'Doesn't he want it any more?'

'My brother died – a week ago.'

'And so now you want to sell it?'

'I have little choice,' I said, disappointed that the director had offered nothing by way of condolence.

'Hmm. Well, it's solid all right, it's a good piece of craftsmanship; excellent even.' He sat back in his chair, his elbows on the armrests and arched his fingers. He remained silent for a few moments, his eyes still fixed on the bust standing on the blotting-pad in front of him. Eventually, he sighed and spoke, gazing at me from above his pince-nez. 'I can offer you Torgsin bonds to half its true value.'

'Half?'

'Yes.'

'Is that all?'

'What else are you going to do with it? No one's going to want to buy a piece of sentimentalism like this, even such a good piece of sentimentalism,' he said, waving his hand towards the bust. 'And Tchaikovsky? Mawkish codswallop. Trust me, your average Joe Public doesn't have the means and most of my fellow Torgsin directors wouldn't touch it. You won't get better than half. You could try and prove me wrong but I warn you, you'd be wasting your time. Now, had it been Shostakovich, I'd offer you almost its full value. And Prokofiev, well, the sky's the limit… But Tchaikovsky? No one's got time for Tchaikovsky any more.'

'Half?'

'Half. Now, if you don't mind, I've got much to get through. If you don't want it, then leave.'

*

Half an hour later, I was sitting in a small café in a narrow street, half a mile from the Torgsin store, the bust of Tchaikovsky tucked away in my bag between my feet on the floor. I hadn't been to a café in over three years, I could barely afford to. But today, I was determined to counter the humiliation I'd felt at the hands of the Torgsin director. I still had a little money coming in from the NKVD; otherwise, I may have accepted the director's humiliating offer. But not yet.

I bought a small coffee and sat at a table next to the window and watched the uniform black figures pass outside. I cupped my hands around the mug and breathed in the delicious aroma.

It was a few months before his arrest when Nadya and I watched Viktor play Mozart's Concerto for the Bassoon in B Flat and receive a standing ovation. It was his moment of creative glory, the highlight of his brief musical career. Many times, after his arrest and Nadya's death, I resisted selling his bassoon, but eventually, circumstances forced me into parting with it. But never the bust. I'd always been determined not to sell it, however desperate the situation; it was too integral to his life. After his return from the prison camp, I placed it in Viktor's brittle fingers and watched as he caressed the golden contours and ran his finger along the inscription. A reminder of a life long since gone.

I missed him. As much as I'd become accustomed to living without him, there had always been hope. Hope is such a giver of strength, however desperate things seem. With hope, there's possibility and the motivation to continue the struggle. In many ways, life was more difficult following Viktor's return. The fight was finished but far from won because the price had been so high – the fortnightly visits to Rykov's office, my double life as an informer, as a State spy. The nights I lay wide awake wondering whether this was the night my unfortunate victims would receive the knock on the door, the silhouette of the uniformed men in the doorway, the Black Maria parked on the kerbside outside their home. How well I knew that moment, that moment when one's normal life is brought to an abrupt end, when the nightmare of mere existence starts. It's so sudden, like the switching off of a light, the swift plunge from light to dark. The intensity of it is terrifying, watching these forbidding men searching through one's life, ordering you around with intense threats. Yonov and Ivanova. I'll never forget them. It was like having a hand reach inside your chest and tear out the heart.

And the Viktor of those last few months was not the Viktor I'd grown up with. There was nothing in his spectre-like appearance that resembled his former self, the gifted young bassoonist, the fervent revolutionary, the steadfast servant of the State. And this is how they re-paid him. I could have accepted the physical change if I could have seen something in his eyes, some light, some glimmer of his former self. But even that was gone; they'd taken that away too. His eyes were lifeless and dull. That was what pained me the most. Without a hidden spark, I knew he had no fight left in him.

Viktor. Along with his wife, the only person who knew me as Matrena and knew me as Maria. Matrena had already died from within, but what about Maria? Every day, I think of them, of my little girls. I imagine them growing up, of the games they'd play, of how they'd look. No one knew of this inner torment I carried within me for so many years. But by never revealing the truth of my darkest moment, I felt as though I was denying them a right to an existence. By never speaking of them, it was as if they never lived. I was the only living person who knew that they'd ever been alive at all and I was failing to acknowledge the fact. But I had no choice. I had been a kulak – despised and condemned from the moment Stalin had ordered the liquidization of the kulaks as a class. My poor husband Makarov had had the misfortune to own a couple of cows and a few chickens and even an old mule. His Bolshevik leanings counted for nothing – he was a kulak and that was that. They couldn't make him join the collective but they stole the grain from under our noses while our children starved. And then they took him. I never knew what became of him; I doubt if I ever shall. Perhaps, he is still alive, eking out an existence in the frozen East somewhere. Perhaps the memory of our girls lives on in him too. But somehow, I doubt it. I fear he perished along with all the thousands and hundreds of thousands of peasants tarred with the kulak brush.

And so, Natasha and Nicola, starved to death by politics, exist only in my memory and in my dreams – they might as well have never been born for the mark they left on this world.

For two days, Viktor and I scrambled around in the forest surrounding our village, surviving on insects and bits of bark scraped off the trees, sucking the snow off the leaves, until we came across the railway track. We followed it, for what seemed like hundreds of miles, to the next village where we waited, hiding behind the station, scavenging for edible roots in the mud. This village lay directly west of our own and we knew the westbound trains would ultimately be heading for Moscow. My brother and I stowed away on the next train and two days later, found ourselves in the communist capital of the world.

I sipped my coffee slowly, concentrating on the delight of swallowing the hot sweet liquid, enjoying, for the second time that day, a sense of decadence.

Chapter 20: The Job

Vladimir had a job to do. Rykov had told him to question Maria on what she knew about the discovery of a body in some woods directly outside the dacha belonging to her friend's brother. Rykov was tightening the net around the Russian fucking-Association of Proletariat Artists, as he called them. He wanted to see them dead and buried but Dmitry's position was, for the time being, secure. They couldn't arrest him now that he was about to receive his Order of Lenin; it'd make the Politburo look foolish. Another year, and it'd be all right; enough time would have lapsed, enough time for a former recipient to have strayed from the rightful path. But then the phone call from the Criminal Investigations Unit had juiced things up. A crime is a crime, at least one of a non-political type. The Politburo wouldn't interfere in the investigation of a suspicious death. An old man, apparently, had been walking his dog in the woods early one evening, when the dog went wild over a particular spot. The old boy could see the ground had been recently disturbed and returned home to fetch a shovel. A couple of feet down, and there it was – the freshly buried corpse.

Vladimir was glad to be given the excuse to interview Maria, for the hope he might see Rosa. He hadn't seen her since their trip to the closed store and it was bothering him. It was partly his fault, he supposed, work was heating up by the day – the number of arrests they were having to make because of the purges was putting the department under huge pressure. He was working every day – ten, twelve, fourteen hours at a time. He was exhausted, both physically and mentally, and in desperate need of a break. The thought of a few days off at his mother's dacha was like an unreachable oasis in this drab city with its drab, frightened people. The fact that it was his department that was the main source of terror passed him by.

Vladimir had never been to Rosa's apartment but desperate causes called for desperate measures. Whenever he'd been to the college, he couldn't find her. He was usually palmed off by one of her friends, the overweight one or the overly made-up one. Each of them guilty in her own way of vanity. The former for being so damn plump during such austere times, the other for paying herself far too much attention – both were equally obscene. He wouldn't have minded so much if they could tell him where Rosa was, but every time they said she wasn't in or they didn't know where she was. Frankly, he didn't believe them.

And so, Vladimir found himself outside the block of flats in a dismal backstreet on the outskirts of the Arbut district. He got the address easily enough; it was plastered all over Maria's files. He found the main door to the apartment block open and wandered in, blinking as he got accustomed to the dim light. He climbed the three flights of stairs, appalled by the amount of debris and clutter impeding his way. Do people have to live like this, he wondered, where was their pride? As he turned into the corridor, he almost tripped over a couple lying entwined in each other's arms on a tatty old mattress. He turned his face away, unable to hide his utter contempt for them. Everywhere, there were people, wasting their time away. He couldn't believe that Rosa lived in an apartment with all this human filth on her doorstep. At the sight of him, they stopped their chatter and stared at him, leaning back further into the walls. He enjoyed the effect he had on these people, striking them dumb by his mere presence. Maybe they knew – he wasn't a uniformed officer, but perhaps the long black Mac, the way he walked, the authoritative look he'd cultivated, spoke more to them than the outward appearance of the uniform. He was a man to be reckoned with, a man of the . NKVD. He knocked on Rosa's door and as he waited, he became aware that the corridor folk were edging around him. He turned to face them, and en masse, they backed away, shrinking away from the glare of his contemptuous look. He turned back to face the door and allowed himself a little snigger – it was like the pantomime. The door opened a fraction and he saw Maria, wiping her hands on her apron, peering at him. 'Vladimir?' she said, understandably surprised to see him.

'Maria Radekovna, can I come in?'

*

I hesitated for a moment when I saw Vladimir standing at the door. My eyes flickered from him to the others behind. With a quick nod of my head, I opened the door and allowed him through. I was about to close the door when I noticed that the corridor mob had inched forward to within touching distance of me. I knew what they were thinking – if I was taken away, my flat would be up for grabs. But they were confused, I could tell, the police never worked alone, what was he doing there? But I was in no mood to enjoy the moment, the appearance of Vladimir at my flat was torturing me. I closed the door and found him standing in the middle of the main room, his nose twitching with displeasure, taking in the sordid details of his surroundings. I felt as if I should offer him a seat but felt too embarrassed by the state of Viktor's armchair to do so.

'I'm sorry to bother you but I wonder if you could tell me where your niece is?'

Oh, so that was it, I thought, it was a romantic call, not a call of business. I sighed with relief. 'I haven't seen her today.'

'Pity. Any idea what time she'll be back?'

'No, she might not be back.'

'You don't know whether your niece will be back tonight? Does that not worry you?'

'No, you don't understand. She spends most of her time at college.'

'Ah, of course, I see.' Vladimir absorbed the information. 'Well, if she happens to drop in, tell her I was asking after her, and hope she's all right.'

'I will.'

He sat down on the edge of Viktor's armchair. 'So how's your friend, the artist? What was his name?'

'Dmitry.'

'Ah yes, Dmitry.' He knew very well. 'And tell me, how are you getting on with RAPA; found out anything of interest yet?'

'My appointment is not for another few days. I thought this was just a social call.'

Vladimir shrugged his shoulders. 'It is but I might as well get something out of it. So?'

'My report must be delivered to Comrade Rykov, and Comrade Rykov only. But I will tell you that I intend to hand in my notice.'

Vladimir snorted. '*Hand in your notice?* You're talking about the NKVD here, not some women's flower-arranging co-operative, you can't just hand in your notice when you feel like it. Remember the deal, your brother–' He stopped and glanced around the apartment. 'Where is your brother?'

'He's dead.'

'Oh.'

I knew what he was thinking – I now had all this space to myself, it wasn't right, what with whole families living in corridors. 'He died a few days ago.' I waited a moment, wondering whether he might offer his condolences. He did not. '*That* is why I'm handing my notice in. You brought him back as good as dead, and now he is.'

'No, no, hang on; don't make it sound as if it's somehow our fault. We don't have a say in how the camps are run.'

'Yes, but you made damn sure he got sent to one.'

'Yes, and what would you suggest? He was an enemy of the people, he *confessed*, he held up his hands and said, *OK, I did it, I was a capitalist spy, I admit it.*'

'So be it, but *I'm* not going to spy for you any more.'

'Rykov won't like it – he decides when you're finished, not the other way around. Especially now he's got you earmarked on the RAPA case. Not that it matters much, RAPA's already as good as dead in the ground – nationally, it's fast falling out of favour. Rykov's keen to get in on the act and expose your friend's subgroup, the Moscow East, isn't it? Where is he anyway? We need to speak to him.'

'Why?'

'You see, a body was discovered in a copse not far from a dacha registered in the name of your friend Dmitry. We haven't seen the body yet, but it's being sent over for an autopsy, but our country bumpkin colleagues tell us it is recent; it'd been unearthed within forty-eight hours of death. Now, I'm not a criminal policeman, I'm on the political team, as you know, but, in this instance, the two seem to be merging. We have a witness who gave a lift in a pony and cart to a couple from the train station to the gate of this dacha and a neighbour who spoke to the woman. Did your associate talk to you about spending some time there?'

'No.'

'So, it wasn't you in that pony and cart then?'

Although my heart leapt at the assured assumption, I carefully paused and waited a few measured moments before replying. 'No, certainly not. He doesn't know me well enough to invite me to his dacha.'

'So what were you doing last Wednesday and Thursday?'

'I was at home.' That wasn't difficult, I was always at home.

'Remind me, Maria Radekovna, what's your husband's name?'

'Antonov. Petrov Antonov.' Again, he knew full well but he still made a show of writing the name down in his notepad.

'The boss has asked me to request your presence at an identity parade as soon as we can get the neighbour over here.'

'Oh.' I turned and looked out of the window to the street below.

'Would that be all right with you?'

'Yes, of course. I have nothing to hide.'

Chapter 21: The Ordinary Man

The college was abuzz with activity; it was the evening of the Chekhov performance. Vladimir had seen the poster on the door of the main entrance; the same poster he'd seen dotted around in various shops in the district. He'd come to deal with another outstanding issue – Rosa.

He stood at the end of the main college corridor and surveyed the scene – students in nineteenth-century costume, others with clipboards, lecturers waving bits of paper, all walking hastily in different directions. The atmosphere was soaked in nervous excitement. Envying their enthusiasm for something so simple, he ambled down the corridor, looking out for Rosa or one of her friends. He turned left at the end of the corridor and down another that led to the main hall. It was here the performance was taking place in little over two hour's time. He looked through the round window of the heavy double-swing doors and saw the stage. He was impressed – the painted scenery at the back of the stage depicted a late nineteenth-century nobleman's drawing room, complete with swaying curtains on either side of a large French window, framed pictures of aristocrats and hunting scenes. In the middle of the stage was a large polished table, decked with full dinner service, with large candleholders and ornate serving dishes. To the side, a large sofa plumped up with cushions. He wondered where they'd managed to commandeer so much stuff. All of the lights in the main hall were switched on, and the place was awash with yet more excitable students.

A voice from behind him told him to mind his back. A thin, middle-aged woman carrying a tray of champagne flutes pushed her back against the door. Vladimir offered to hold the door open and went through first to hold it open for her. Before she had the chance to disappear, he quickly asked her if she knew where Rosa was. She did and nodded in the direction of the drama department where, she said, she'd be getting ready. Vladimir thanked her and made his way back to the main corridor. Most of the classrooms were off this corridor and sure enough, halfway down, he saw a door with the sign *Drama Department* written on it. The small window had been screened off from the inside with a dark cloth. Vladimir knocked. The door opened a fraction, and an older woman with suspicious eyes asked brusquely what he wanted. Yes, she said, Rosa was there, she was busy, but she'd see if she had a minute. Vladimir thanked her and waited in the corridor. A few moments later, Rosa appeared at the door, surprised at his unexpected appearance.

As she stepped out into the corridor, Vladimir eyed her costume. She was quite the bourgeois lady with her flowing light green dress and bustle; her hair tied and held up with a decorative clip, and, in her hand, a parasol. 'Rosa,' he said, 'you look… you look stunning.'

'Thank you.'

'Can I see you for a minute?'

She glanced up and down the corridor. 'OK, but I don't have long, we're having a final dress rehearsal in a few minutes. We'll go outside.'

Once outside, in front of the college's main entrance, Rosa stood next to the fountain, drawing a line in the gravel with her parasol. Vladimir wasn't sure where to start. 'So, how have you been? I haven't seen you for ages.'

'Busy. What with the play and college.'

He noticed that she hadn't yet looked him in the eye. 'Yes, of course. I, er, was sorry to hear about your father.'

'Are you?'

Now she looked at him but he was taken aback by her coldness, by the sharpness of her dismissive response. 'Well, yes, I saw your aunt, she told me.'

'You saw my aunt?'

'I came to see you, to see how you were.'

'I'm surprised she didn't throw you out. But I suppose she's too frightened of you.'

'I... Why should she do that?'

Rosa thrust the spiked end of the parasol into the gravel with such vehemence, it stuck. 'Vladimir, I thought for a while I liked you, I thought I could trust you. Vladimir the Librarian. Oh, what a laugh you must have had about that. What an idiot you must've taken me for. Everyone knew, everyone but me. I mean, I defended you, told them they were wrong. You said you were a librarian and I believed you.'

'Yes, I know, I'm sorry, but I had to lie to you to protect you.'

'It wasn't much of a lie then, was it? Access to the closed stores, theatre tickets, cinema, the restaurants. I only fell for it because, I suppose, I wanted to. But to anyone else...'

'Didn't you enjoy it?'

'Of course I enjoyed it, who wouldn't? But that's hardly the point, is it? You lied to me. You lied.'

'I had no choice, Rosa, believe me. My job, it's… it's not the kind of job one announces to the world.' He waited for a response, hoping, at least, for an acknowledgement of his predicament, but nothing was forthcoming. She'd picked up the parasol and was idly jabbing the gravel with it, making rows of neat holes. It was irritating him beyond reason but why, he couldn't work out. 'Who told you?' he snapped. 'I need to know, who told you?'

'No one told me, like I say, it was obvious to all but me.'

It was only obvious, he thought, because someone had told them, and it wasn't difficult to work out who that someone was.

'My father, did you have anything to do with that?'

'No, I swear, I had nothing to do with your father's case, it was before my time. Look, it's a job I have to do. I won't pretend that I don't enjoy it sometimes, seeing the conspirators brought to justice, the uprooting of class enemies, but sometimes…' He glanced around, wanting to make sure they were alone. Lowering his voice, he continued, 'I know sometimes we might be a bit overzealous, we make mistakes. I expect your father was a mistake.'

'Ha!'

'But I'm an ordinary man doing an extraordinary job. And now that I'm in it, I can't leave; I know too much of what things are like from the inside.'

'Does that mean you want to leave?'

Two students, both girls, came out from the college, and, giggling, trotted down the steps and passed the fountain. Vladimir waited until they were almost out onto the street before replying. 'No,' he said simply.

Rosa turned her parasol upside down and rubbed the gravel and dirt from the spike. 'I have to go now.'

'Rosa…'

'Boris is back,' she said, as she sauntered away from him, towards the steps.

'Back?'

She stopped on the bottom step and turned around. 'Yes, the college made an appeal to the Politburo on his behalf, saying they couldn't perform the play without him. They said that since he wasn't technically under arrest, he could do the play but he's not allowed to resume his studies.'

She made to climb the steps but Vladimir hastened after her and grabbed her wrist. She tried to free herself, but he tightened his grip. 'Boris. He told you, didn't he?'

'*What?*'

'It was Boris who told you I worked for them.'

'Don't be ridiculous. Let go.'

Vladimir released his grip and, with his arm suspended in mid-air, watched her climb the steps and push open the large college doors and disappear inside. His heart was thumping, his teeth clenched. He suddenly felt very alone. That bastard little Jew was ruining everything – he'd squirmed his way back into the college and he was poisoning Rosa against him. A vision flashed across his mind – the image of Rosa huddled within the arms of the Jew boy, a gloating, triumphant smirk across his face. Vladimir could feel the acrid phlegm burn the back of his mouth. He spat violently, trying to rid himself of the spit from his throat and of the mocking vision from his mind. This was it, he thought, he was going to have to deal with the Jew once and for all. And this time, the Jew wouldn't come back.

Chapter 22: The Damned

I kept asking myself – was I a murderess? No, it was an accident but somehow I still felt as if I had turned into a monster, a cold-blooded monster. The question kept bouncing in my brain as I caught the tram to my dreaded appointment with Rykov – our routine chat. Dmitry and I were free to start our lives together. Isn't that what we wanted? But far from rejoicing in our solitude, we avoided each other, wallowing in self-pity and reciprocal resentment. The days lacked structure, all sense of normality disappeared like water down a plughole. I hadn't seen Dmitry since Vladimir's visit. I tried to ring him, to tell him that we were in danger, that Rykov wanted me for an identity parade. But he hadn't answered. The neighbour at the dacha would recognise me – how could he not? But Rykov's job was political. If I proved useful to him, he might think my services were too important to allow me to fall into the hands of the criminal police. I was as dependent on Rykov as ever.

The cool spring air was doing me good but nothing could chase my demons away. I had the feeling they'd be with me for the rest of my days, forever tormenting me, teasing my subconscious with a feather. I passed a church near the northern end of the Arbut. Across the door was a banner proclaiming *Support the war against superstition!* The influence of the Godless Society was everywhere, counting the days until they could finish off, for once and for all, the believers in their own St. Bartholomew's Massacre. The church was now just a shell, the inside transformed into a large warehouse. The church bells, I knew, had long since been removed and melted down for scrap metal. But it was still a church, and I had to avert my eyes for fear God was watching me. I remember when they sent the army to tear down the church in the village. Many of the villagers, armed with pitchforks, tried to bar their way, desperate to save their tradition. I wanted to join them but Makarov held me back. He was right; the Red Army soldiers quickly crushed the picket and shot the ringleaders.

Religion is the opiate of the people. How long I'd resisted the Godless Society. Once, out of love, I killed two small girls and I needed God, I needed to believe in a God who would look kindly on my desperation and pardon my sins. But now, I had played my part in the killing of a man, my husband. I didn't dare think of God, for what would He make of me now? Would *He* see it as an accident? Would He forgive me this time? However hard I tried to justify it to Him, and to myself, I felt beyond His forgiveness. I walked with my hands thrust deep into my pockets, my eyes fixed on the pavement in front of me, unable to look up at the people walking past me. Petrov had stood between me and my freedom, but as I lived in a country where the Dictatorship of the Proletariat terrorised its own, how could I ever expect to be free? Even though Petrov was gone, I felt as suffocated as ever.

Poor Petrov – I never gave him the child he so wanted. At first, I also wanted children. I felt that another child would ease the pain but Natasha and Nicola are too entrenched within my psyche to be so easily supplanted. Not a night goes by when I don't dream of them and every morning I awake with their names on my lips. They smile at me in those last few moments of unconsciousness, their bright eyes and laughing voices, wishing me good morning as I open my eyes. It took years to get used to those few moments of panic when I realised I was awake and they had gone. I'd shut my eyes, desperate to see them again but my awakened self lacked the strength of my subliminal mind. During the daytime, I can only visualise them in those last few months and weeks and on that fatal day. Sometimes, I can't wait for the hours to pass, for the day to fade away, can't wait to slip back into my dreams where I know I'll find them, waiting for me, forever laughing and playing and calling me 'Mama'. Makarov is sometimes there too, but always in the distance, that half-smile playing on his lips as he watches on proudly.

After the first couple of years, I became frightened that a new baby would erase my dreams, would deny me my possession of Natasha and Nicola. But then I realised that I did want a child, I just didn't want one with Petrov.

How strange it felt to be thinking of Petrov as part of my past. I looked back on that evening and shuddered. It had only been a few days, but it already felt as if it was a lifetime ago, somebody else's lifetime.

*

'Well, come in, Maria Radekovna,' said Rykov as I entered his office. On his desk was a cup of something hot, still steaming. 'Take a seat.'

I sat down. I waited for him to comment on the weather. But instead, he launched straight into business. 'So, I understand young Vladimir has asked you to appear at an identity parade?'

'Yes.'

'Good. Now, I'm sure there'll be nothing to worry about. This man, the neighbour chap, will be with us the day after tomorrow. Two o'clock. That suit? Good. Our country colleagues tell us they've found traces of blood near the fireplace. Interesting. So, tell me again, what is your relationship with Kalinin? Your Dmitry?'

Of course, the neighbour would recognise me. Even in the dark, with the rain, he would recognise me, the medieval witch. The way he stared at me, open-mouthed, disbelieving. Two days time, two o'clock. So casually said, as if Rykov and I were arranging a coffee date. There was no escape; nowhere to run to.

'Maria Radekovna, did you hear what I said?'

'What? I'm sorry?'

'You were miles away.' He laughed. 'Usually, when people sit there, I have their undivided attention. So, let's try again. How well do you know this artist?' Then, rather unexpectedly, Rykov rose to his feet and walked to the side of the room where, leaning against a wall, was a board of some sort covered by a dark green cloth, which I hadn't noticed before. 'One thing that worries me still, if I may, is this reluctance of yours to admit the extent of your friendship with our friend, Comrade Kalinin.'

'But I've told you, I know his sister well, so by association—' My words stuck in my throat as, like a magician, Rykov whipped the cloth away and there, under the full glare of the room's lighting, was the painting, my Mona Lisa–like smile grinning at me as if greeting an old friend. Rykov stepped back to admire it. There I was, in my full naked glory, being examined by an officer of the NKVD.

'It's a good likeness,' said Rykov, with a mischievous glint in his eye, turning back and forth to compare the two of us. I felt as exposed as my portrait and felt the need to fold my arms across my breasts as if he could see through my clothing. 'So, tell me, Maria Radekovna, is your friend's brother quite so familiar with all his casual acquaintances?'

I couldn't look at him. I tried to focus on the painting but that was worse. 'I – I just… he needed a model, that's all, his usual model was sick–'

'His usual model? But there are no other paintings like this at his apartment.'

'No,' I said humbly. 'It was the first.'

Rykov stepped up to the painting to examine it from close-up. 'Quite a brazen example of titillation. Very nice titillation, if I may say, but it's hardly a work of socialist realism, is it?' I didn't answer, not thinking I needed to. 'I said, *is it?*'

I jumped; the vehemence in his voice frightening me. 'No,' I said, conscious of the quiver within my monosyllabic answer.

'So, how do you feel when you see this? Do you feel *proud?* Whoring yourself to the first man who tells you to strip your clothes off?'

'He's an artist.'

'Oh yes, I don't question his talent, but that doesn't excuse your part in this. Don't artists usually pick up the cheapest bit of skirt they can find? You're an intelligent woman, Maria Radekovna, I know that, but you deem it right to degrade yourself like this? Where is your shame, your sense of dignity? Hmm?'

He was right, of course, but at the time it seemed so right, so damn romantic. But now, under his scrutiny and in this office, it seemed exactly as he was describing it: sordid, cheap and degrading. His expression summed it up for me, his disgusted look. I remembered the way Dmitry had seen me that night – audaciously confident and beautiful. But the beauty was fading with every second. I remembered the confidence I felt that night, as if the whole world was about to change, as if we were on the threshold of the bright new tomorrow we were always being promised. But how pitiful it all looked now, pitiful and downright silly.

He returned to his chair. 'So, what have you got for me this week? Anything to report?'

'Yes. I've been to a meeting of RAPA.'

'You have? Good. And anything come from it?'

I sighed. How I hated this moment. 'Is this necessary any more?'

He glared at me and I felt myself shrink into the chair. 'I'll pretend, just – this – once, that I didn't hear that. Have you or have you not anything to report?'

'Yes.'

He took a sip of his drink. 'Good.' He waited while I stirred myself for another denunciation. 'Well, go on,' he said. 'Don't keep me in suspense.'

Chapter 23: The Play

The corridors were deserted. So too were the classrooms, the offices and the canteen. Not a soul was in sight. In the distance, Vladimir could hear the sound of the actors on stage; their exaggerated voices reverberating through the narrow corridors. The only other sound was that of three pairs of shoes on the parquet floor. The two uniformed men marched side by side a few feet behind him, both of them identical caricatures of themselves – burly, squat-faced, squared-shouldered thugs in corresponding long black mackintoshes. Vladimir was nervous; he always was before an arrest, especially one where he was in sole charge, and, even more especially, after his last solo experience. He felt the inside pocket of his jacket for the umpteenth time, checking once again for the reassuring presence of the revolver.

Arresting someone was always difficult but when it went to plan, it was an exhilarating experience, especially when you believed the arrest was justified. The look of horror on their faces, the intense fear in their eyes, the incredulous denials; one could almost draw a diagram illustrating the various stages of response. And because one was always so on edge, one was liable to do anything to complete the arrest. It was a formidable escalation of fear upon fear with violence only ever a hair's-breadth away. Apart from the pressure one felt from one's superiors, there was always the risk it wouldn't go according to plan. And the pressure from above was real enough because woe betide the arresting officer who fucked up. Once was just about forgivable, twice was not. And Vladimir had used up his only chance. Hence, it wasn't just an act, one couldn't help but turn into the hard bastard people thought you were, simply from the adrenaline-induced fear of incurring the wrath of someone like Rykov. That the prisoners would plea, beg, break into hysterics, and lose all semblance of dignity was expected, but there was always the chance they might actually fight back, try to run away, throw themselves under a tram; those were the sort of things one worried about.

The women were always the worst. And the pregnant women especially so. That's what happened last time. Rykov had charged him with the responsibility of arresting a woman suspected of being (and subsequently sentenced as) a saboteur. The problem, as he found out when he arrived at her apartment at four in the morning, was that she was heavily pregnant. Rykov hadn't thought to warn him. Perhaps, he didn't know, or hadn't thought it important. She was a screamer, not the terrified kind, but the aggressive type. She refused to budge and, eventually, his thugs were forced into physically carrying her out, struggling to contain her huge belly. The bitch scratched one of the officers right across the eye, drawing blood. The officer's mate punched her in the mouth and then, the stupid bastard who'd been scratched thumped her in the stomach. Half an hour later, she miscarried in the back of the van; made an awful mess. Rykov was furious.

She had been Vladimir's responsibility. He couldn't afford any more mistakes. The bosses liked their suspects brought in cleanly – it was their job to apply the pressure.

Vladimir turned the corner into another corridor that led to the double doors of the main hall. He heard Rosa's voice bellowing out from within, her words wrought with embellished emotion. He slowed up as he approached the doors, the footsteps behind him following suit. What chance did he have with her now, he wondered. Their encounter just a few hours earlier hadn't gone well. Why was she so damn angry with him? He'd always taken her for a true believer, a young communist of the first order. Surely then, she should have embraced his proletariat duty as a worthy occupation. Was that not a cause for pride? Was a soldier not held in the highest esteem, and what was he, if not a soldier? But Rosa had shown no acknowledgement of this, no recognition of the sacred cause he was serving. Even his concession that her father's imprisonment had been a mistake had fallen on deaf ears. A concession that, if truth be known, was both unnecessary and based in falsehood, for Rosa's father was as guilty as they came. He was disappointed and even disturbed by her reaction, but it hadn't dented his feelings for her because he knew the root cause for it. Somebody had poisoned her mind and for her own sake, it had to stop. As the daughter of an enemy of the people, Rosa's own situation was far from secure. If she allowed herself to be taken in by counter-revolutionary thoughts, she could find herself in an unenviable position. It was like a rotting tooth – it took harsh measures to deal with it. And this particular rotten tooth was about to be removed.

Vladimir pushed open the left-side door, sneaked into the darkness of the main hall and stood to one side. The two uniforms followed and took their places on either side of him. They'd entered almost unnoticed, only a few people in the back row turned their heads momentarily, and a lecturer approached them. He was, presumed Vladimir, about to ask them for their tickets but then stopped at the sight of the uniformed thugs. Vladimir nodded at him, and the lecturer backed away. Vladimir couldn't help but consider it ironic that the two people currently on stage were Rosa and Boris. Was there a wave of electricity between them? No, he thought, just the clumsy transaction of dialogue between two amateur actors. A tingle of satisfaction went through him at the thought that poor unsuspecting Boris had no idea what the evening had in store for him.

"'How they keep on talking, talking all day long.'"

Vladimir was disappointed in Rosa's performance. He was no expert on acting, but he could see that her presentation was stilted, the way she stood awkward. Boris was even worse, his words sounded so insincere, so boringly flat. Even he, thought Vladimir, could inject more life into the character of Andrey Sergeyevitch. The set, at least, was impressive. He'd seen it earlier when he came looking for Rosa, but now under the stage lighting and floodlights, it was still more sumptuous. The lighting had transformed the painted wallpaper from the simple yellow of before to a vibrant mustard colour. The French windows looked out on a scene of a bright green lawn and weeping willows. The set designer had put the actors to shame.

"Our garden is like a garden passage; they walk and ride through. Nurse, give those people something.'"

The characters of Olga and Masha had come onto the stage, and Vladimir recognised the waif-like figure of Rosa's friend, Ella, and her overweight friend, Claudia. At last, here was some acting! Ella's mere presence had transformed the production. She spoke her lines with conviction and finesse.

"Let us sit together, even if we don't say anything…"

Ella's ability was having a positive effect on the others. Both Rosa and Boris seemed more at ease delivering their lines to Ella's character. Although he hadn't seen it for years, Vladimir knew the play well enough to know that they were fast approaching the end.

"Our soldiers are going. Well, good luck to them."

He felt for the revolver in his jacket and breathed deeply. He thought back to the pregnant woman in the van driving through the deserted night-time streets of Moscow. Her screams of agony as the baby miscarried, trying to muffle her screams with his gloved hand, the officer pulling on her hair to try to keep her still, while the other drove, occasionally turning around to thump her. It was barbaric but at the time he could have quite happily shot her there and then and pushed her out of the van and into the river. Never again, he thought, this time he wouldn't allow for any mistakes. At least this time, it wasn't a woman.

"If only we knew, if only we knew…"

Rosa, Claudia and Ella froze their expressions and their movement as the heavy green curtains drew together. The audience clapped. He joined in, clapping softly as the curtain drew back, and the three principal characters, the three sisters, bowed. Vladimir noticed, with an inward smile, that his two assistants had taken his cue and were also politely clapping. The curtains closed and reopened, and all the actors had come onto the stage, bowing to their audience, lapping up their applause, enjoying the artistic high, the creative buzz. The curtains drew close again, and the hall lights flickered on. The applause stopped as suddenly as it had started, and Vladimir blinked as his eyes accustomed to the harsh glare of the ordinary lights. The assistant to his left looked at him expectantly. Vladimir shook his head. No, not yet, he thought, let him enjoy it, let him enjoy his moment of glory, his last few minutes of freedom.

The audience had begun rising to their feet, collecting their belongings, making their way to the exits. Vladimir watched them as they passed, many of them casting him a furtive glance, quickly looking away before catching his eye. It was time, thought Vladimir. He nodded to his assistants and led the way.

They walked up onto the stage and followed the stage exit to the left as taken by the actors. It led to a high-ceilinged room, its doors propped open by buckets of sand. Vladimir could hear the gaggle of excited voices coming from within, congratulating themselves, the relief it was all over. *Now, here's to The Cherry Orchard,* Vladimir heard one say in a voice that cut above the others. As he approached, he saw the gathering of students milling around inside the room, heard the clink of glasses, felt the warmth of satisfied artistic pride. It seemed such a shame, he thought, to be breaking it up.

He knocked gently on the opened door as he stepped inside. Only the few nearest the door saw them at first, then some others, and then, like a ripple effect, a few more. People stopped talking in mid-sentence, their mouths hanging open, glasses poised near lips. A lighted match wavered and then burnt itself out. All eyes turned to them, their unexpected and unwelcome visitors. He eyed them each in return, his gaze flickering from one face to another. This, he thought, was power.

From the midst of the gathering, emerged Rosa, still dressed as the nineteenth-century lady of leisure, an apparition of the bourgeois past. Behind her, he saw Ella and, not far away, Claudia and next to her, Boris, dressed in a tuxedo and bow tie. Rosa was holding a glass of red wine, her eyebrows knotted in confusion at Vladimir's appearance. 'Vladimir? What… what brings you here?'

'I'm here to carry out an unpleasant assignment.'

'I don't understand. Here? Now?'

A large woman with pleated hair and flushed cheeks approached him. 'What's the meaning of this intrusion?' she asked.

'Who are you?'

'Ramzin, I'm the head of drama here. So I ask you again, what's the meaning of this?'

Vladimir flashed his identity card at her. 'Business.'

If he expected her to be cowed by the letters, NKVD, he was to be disappointed. 'That's all very well,' she said, 'but this is most inopportune. Can't it wait?'

'I fear not, I have my orders.' He walked past her, his eyes fixed on Boris, whose face wore the expression of depressed resignation. The few people between them parted like biblical waves. He felt like a central character in a play; the actors were now his audience. Someone coughed. He could feel the presence of his assistants at his shoulder, his worthy supporting cast. He cleared his throat. 'Comrade Gershberg?' he said, mustering up as much authority as possible, 'I would ask you to come with us, please.'

Boris took a deliberate sip of wine, swallowed and then said, 'May I ask why?'

'Yes, quite,' said Ramzin. 'Why?'

'I am not at liberty to divulge the peculiarities of the case at this particular juncture. If you would follow me, please.'

It was Ella who stepped forward, so splendid, remembered Vladimir, as Olga. 'You can't just take him,' she said. Vladimir cocked his head to one side. She turned to Rosa. 'Rosa do something, tell your... your *librarian* that Boris is innocent.'

'Innocent of what?' asked Vladimir. A murmur of discontent rippled around the room.

'Innocent of whatever he's guilty of, of course.'

The murmur was getting progressively louder. Vladimir didn't like it, he wanted to go. He turned to his men and gave them the nod. Passing around him, they marched up to Boris and stood on either side of him, their mackintoshes pressing into the boy's back. He tried to take one last sip of his wine, but one of the thugs grabbed hold of his wrist and lowered Boris's arm. Boris placed the glass back on the table.

Rosa came up to Vladimir and looked him directly in the eye, so close their noses almost touched. 'What's this about? Tell me,' she hissed.

'I'm not allowed to say, but I've got to take him – those are my orders.'

He nodded a second time at his boys and, this time, they each slid an arm under Boris's armpits.

'OK, OK, get your hands off me. I'm coming. Can I take my coat?'

Vladimir nodded and allowed Boris to retrieve his coat from the back of a nearby chair. Boris slipped the coat over his dinner jacket and declared, 'I'm ready.' He sounded like a man about to catch a train, thought Vladimir. With that, Boris marched freely out of the room, without looking left or right, and so briskly that the two guards had to readjust their step in order to keep up with him. Vladimir followed them. By the time they'd reached the stage, the murmur had reached full volume, a crescendo of shocked voices and gasping conversations. But amongst it all, there was still the occasional sound of a clinking glass.

*

The drive from the college back to the Lubyanka was a short one, only fifteen minutes at that time of night. The four men sat in total silence as the Black Maria glided through the streets. Vladimir sat to the left of Boris, staring out of the window but keeping Boris firmly within his peripheral vision and firmly within his concentration. The job of arrest wasn't done yet, but at this rate, it was going down as one of the easiest, trouble-free arrests in the annals of the NKVD. He'd never heard of anyone asking for their coat and then saying they were ready. The Jew was scared, Vladimir could tell that much but, it had to be said, his inner resolve was admirable.

Chapter 24: The Accusation

Dmitry's apartment was a mess – clothes all over the floors, drawers pulled out and turned upside down. He looked almost as dishevelled – unshaven, his hair unruly and in need of a wash. He wore his arm in a sling and told me his ribcage had been heavily bandaged.

'They've been.'

'Yes – as you can see,' he said dryly. 'Fairly obvious, really.'

'But you weren't here?'

'No. They took my painting.'

'Yes, I know. Dmitry, we *have* to leave.'

'Where?'

'I don't know but we can't stay here; they're onto us, they could be here any time. They found Petrov's body and are shipping it over. They discovered traces of his blood and they found the man who knocked, the neighbour. I have to do an identity parade. Once this man has recognised me, we're done for.'

His expression now remained impassive as he sat on the sofa, his elbows against the armrest, his fingers touching. Next to him, on the side table, was a cup of tea gone cold.

'Dmitry?'

'What can I say, Maria? As you say, we're done for. If they didn't have someone trailing us before, they certainly will now. They'll have us covered, they'll know of every move we make from now on. And anyway, where would you suggest we go?'

I hated the way he framed the question; it sounded so damn formal. But unfortunately, it was how he'd spoken ever since our return from the dacha. Things were not going well.

'Anywhere.'

'But where exactly, Maria? We could hardly return to the dacha; we don't have enough money to start afresh somewhere new, and we could hardly turn up on the doorstep of some old relative of mine, even though I have dozens of them dotted around. How would I explain you? I couldn't just turn up with a new *girlfriend* unannounced.'

'Why did you say *girlfriend* in that tone of voice?'

He looked startled by the accusation. 'I'm sorry, I didn't mean to.'

No, perhaps he hadn't meant to, but he had. The death of Petrov had shocked him more than I initially appreciated. He seemed different now, it was almost as if he was resentful of me – that I'd come into his life and effectively destroyed it. I couldn't blame him. This was meant to be the start of our lives with each other. But it wasn't how I'd imagined it to be. There was no joy in our new-found freedom.

He hadn't mentioned that dreadful evening but I know, like me, it was never far from his mind. After we'd cleaned ourselves up, we set to cleaning away the evidence around the body. Silently, we wiped away the blood and scrubbed the whole main room clean – twice. But still, as it proved, it was not enough. Dmitry winced continually as he worked, his arm and, especially, his ribcage hurting. Petrov, we left to last. The whole dacha looked as it should have except for the immediate area covered by the body. Dmitry needed to steel himself before even approaching it. He tried to pick Petrov up by the ankles but the trousers slipped back and Dmitry accidentally made contact with the skin. The unexpected texture of the skin went through him like an electric shock. He reeled back, his face aghast. Finally, we decided to roll the corpse up within a carpet. Psychologically, it made the job easier but Dmitry was still surprised by the heaviness of the corpse. I was not. I remembered very well the effort it took to carry first Nicola and then Natasha out into the woods behind the village, and they were a fraction of Petrov's weight. Between us, we carried Petrov out into the cold night, across the garden and into the forest behind the dacha. How far we carried him, I don't know but it seemed an immeasurable distance. Dmitry then returned to the dacha to fetch a spade. He was gone an age. I paced up and down swinging my arms around myself, desperately trying to keep warm.

It took Dmitry such a long time to dig a hole – the ground was so hard and, despite his injuries, he refused my help. But he didn't want to be left alone with the corpse so I had no choice but to endure the biting cold. All the time I felt on edge, half expecting to be discovered at any moment. But it was the middle of the night; no one was ever going to pass at this time in the pitch-black forest with the wind ripping at their faces. It hadn't been the first time I'd found myself in such a situation.

And how long did Petrov remain undisturbed? One day? Two? And now, he was being brought back to Moscow. It was like expecting a visit from a ghost. Dmitry and I were no closer now than we were while Petrov was still alive; if anything, we were further apart than ever. We seemed to be falling out of love as quickly as we'd fallen into it.

'I don't know, Maria, I don't know what to do – except to wait for the inevitable.'

Dmitry slumped back into the chair and closed his eyes, a tuft of black hair falling across his forehead.

The knock on the door made us jump. We stared at each other. Had they come already? 'Don't answer it,' I whispered.

'We have to answer it.'

Of course, he was right. They'd only break the door down; we were caught. I stood up and went to the door, my hand shaking madly. With my fingers gripped on the handle, I felt as if my life was about to take another turn for the worse. I opened the door, and there, standing in front of me with his hat in his hands, was Mikhail, his small round glasses shining under the hall light. I had to stop myself from throwing my arms around his neck, such was my relief.

Dmitry's relief was also evident as he stood to greet his old friend and patron. 'Mikhail, you old dog, what a relief it's only you,' he said with a laugh.

Mikhail smiled weakly. 'I know the feeling,' he said.

'Well, it's lovely to see you, come in, come in, take a seat.'

Mikhail sat down on the settee and glanced around at his surroundings. 'Have you been burgled?' he asked.

'If only.'

'Hmm, I see.' What little hair he had was greased back and positively shone. He turned down my offer of tea. 'That's a peculiar object.'

'That's my bear,' I said. 'Inside there's a bottle of eau-du-cologne.'

'How unusual.'

'So,' said Dmitry, 'what brings you here?'

Mikhail sat forward, his hands gripping his knees. 'An ill wind, I'm afraid to say, old man. They've arrested Mamontov.'

'*What?*

Rykov hadn't hung around.

Mikhail continued. 'They took him in yesterday.'

'It doesn't necessarily mean anything.'

'Are you kidding? You've always been too optimistic for your own good, Dmitry, how could it mean anything but the worst? They've got their claws out for us. RAPA's as good as finished; it was only a matter of time. I always thought Mamontov was the mole but it looks like I was wrong. Someone else has been informing on us. Someone within our ranks. And for what? For following the Party line to the tee? We virtually gave up art as a pursuit of the talented and allowed ourselves to be straitjacketed into drawing-by-number industrialists, eulogising the hammer and sickle, and this is what we get. I don't understand it. Perhaps, we were too dogmatic. We made too many enemies along the way, too critical of those who didn't follow our path. I mean, that's what I preached all along, we had to maintain a degree of tolerance, but oh no, idiots like Mamontov insisted there was no room for manoeuvre and look where it's got us. We became so damn rigid, we couldn't go back. And all we managed to achieve is to alienate those who could have supported us. So when Stalin wonders whether we've become too big for our boots, they're in there like a shot. So, that's the end of us. God knows what they'll force out of Mamontov. Those bastards will have him in there now, pissing in his mouth, forcing him to implicate us all. He'll tell them about me, he won't have any choice.'

'The Bukharin petition?'

'Yes, my moment of madness. How proud I was of myself, standing up for a principle. But they executed him anyway and they'll never allow me to forget that I signed that blasted piece of paper.'

'I thought you'd publicly recanted,' I said.

'Yes but a fat lot of good that'll do me now. You'll be OK, old man, especially now that they've announced your award in *Pravda*.'

'Have they?'

'You've not seen? Good Lord, you must be the last to know. Did you not get a letter?'

'No, I haven't... not yet.'

'Well, let me be the first to congratulate you, old man.'

'Thank you. Thank you very much.'

'Congratulations, Dmitry,' I added.

He smiled weakly. 'Anyway, I'm not so sure it'll protect me that much.'

'No, of course not, nothing in life's a certainty but there's a chance you might survive a little longer than the rest of us. They won't want to arrest you straight after honouring you with an award that's got Lenin's name on it, but be careful, they'll have you within their sights, waiting – your time might come yet.'

'I know.'

'You may have enough time to ingratiate yourself into the next fad. If you can, use your award well, it might open doors for you, go wherever it takes you.' I noticed a line of perspiration on his forehead.

'What are you going to do?' asked Dmitry.

'I don't know.' Mikhail pulled a handkerchief from his pocket and wiped his scalp. 'Just wait, I suppose. What else can I do?'

'Mamontov might hold out.'

'Fat chance, the spineless git. No, forgive me, I didn't mean that.' He blew his nose. 'No one deserves to suffer at their hands. No one. In their hands, you're guilty before innocent; what chance does anyone have?'

Dmitry opened his mouth as if to say something but then thought better of it and kept his silence. What could we say to console him? There was no point in trying to persuade him he might be spared because we all knew he was right; the poor man was living on borrowed time.

'I don't mind so much about myself, it's my wife and my boy. How's it going to affect them? It's just the thought of not seeing them again — that's what terrifies me. I love them so much…' The thought of his family was too much for Mikhail; he burst into tears, huge muffled sobs filled the air as he buried his face into his handkerchief. Up to this point, I'd been standing behind Dmitry's armchair. Dmitry and I looked at each other, each reading the awkwardness in our thoughts. I hardly knew the man, but the sight of this proud man sobbing in front of me was too much to behold. A moment later, I found myself sitting next to him on the settee with my arm around his shoulders. His body jerked at my touch.

Looking sideways at him, I wanted to say something but the words wouldn't come. He blew his nose again with quite some force and wiped his eyes with the back of his hands.

'Let me get you a tissue,' said Dmitry.

As soon as Dmitry was out of earshot, Mikhail whispered to me. 'It was you, wasn't it?'

I felt my heartbeat quicken. 'I'm sorry?'

'It was you; I know it was.'

'What do you mean?'

'It was you who informed on us. You have to tell Dmitry now, to warn him.'

'I can't tell him now.'

'So you're not denying it. If you don't tell him this instant, I will.'

Already, Dmitry was back. 'Here we are, Misha.'

'Thank you, old man. Forgive me for my undignified outburst, I – I couldn't...'

'Shush now,' said Dmitry. 'Don't apologise, we understand.'

'Yes,' he said through his handkerchief. 'That's the problem, isn't it? We all understand too well. It shouldn't have to be like this but it is. That's exactly how it is, this is the way we live, this is where communism has taken us, and I abhor it for what it's done to us.' He paused for a few moments and took a deep breath. 'They're taking all of us, one by one. It's my turn next; it's no use pretending otherwise. And then, it could be you next, you can never tell. When is your award ceremony old man, is it tomorrow? I've lost track of time.'

'Yes, tomorrow – Labour Day.'

'So it is. I'll try and come along if I can.'

Dmitry smiled. 'Yes, do. I'd like that.'

They talked more but I felt unable to listen. I wanted to be sick. How did Mikhail know? What could I do?

'We're like a row of dominoes,' said Dmitry, quietly to himself.

'A row of what?'

'Dominoes. Remember, Mikhail, me saying that to you? One falls, we all fall. I never actually thought it would happen though – not to us.'

'So, what do you think, then, eh, Maria?'

'I'm sorry?'

'Who do you think our mole is? Who's the wolf in sheep's clothing?'

'I… I really don't know. You sure you wouldn't like that cup of tea?'

Just as I thought my heart might cave in, there was another knock on the door.

'That's Anna, my sister,' said Dmitry.

'How do you know?' asked Mikhail.

'It's her knock.'

I'd never been so relieved to see her. She'd come, she said, to offer her brother her congratulations – she'd seen the announcement in *Pravda*. As Anna, Dmitry and Mikhail chatted, I wandered around the room, trying to look nonchalant. In the corner, behind an armchair, I found what I was looking for. Quickly, I bent down and pulled the telephone wire from its socket.

'You all right, Maria?'

'What? Yes, I thought I saw a button on the floor but it wasn't.'

'This could make you famous,' said Anna. 'Everyone will know your name now. Just think,' she said to Mikhail, 'my brother – the famous artist.'

'And we in RAPA are very proud of him. Listen, old man, I ought to go. I just wanted to come and say my farewells – just in case. I've got to… to make the most of it. It could be our last night together as a family.'

'I'll come with you,' I said.

'Leaving so soon?' said Dmitry.

'Shopping. You know.'

'I'll wait for you to get your coat,' said Mikhail, waiting by the door.

'Go out the back way,' said Dmitry, looking out the window.

'Nice to see you again, Anna,' I said. 'Sorry to have to rush.'

As Mikhail turned to leave, he said to Dmitry, 'Pray for me.' And with that, we were gone.

*

Mikhail walked fast and I had to trot to keep up with him. 'Please, Misha, if I tell him it would destroy us.'

'And if you don't tell him, they will destroy him. And don't call me Misha – we don't know each other that well. Anyway, I thought you had a husband?'

'Had. He walked out on me.'

'He did? How strange. Where would he go?' He stopped abruptly. 'So, why did you do it?'

'I had no choice. How did you know?'

'Obvious. You come to one meeting and then next minute they arrest Mamontov. A coincidence, I thought. But no, I knew it was you.'

'Like I say, I had no choice.'

'Well, I'm sorry for you, Maria Radekovna, but, frankly, I have more pressing concerns, including what will happen to my friend Dmitry.' He looked at his watch. 'It's five o'clock. I give you two hours to tell him. I might not have much time. I will phone him at exactly seven. Now, if you'll excuse me.'

'But Mikhail, please…'

He didn't stop. I watched him march off, his hands deep in his pockets. I tried to think, to pull together my jumbled thoughts. OK, so he rings Dmitry at seven. Will Dmitry have spotted the disconnected telephone wire? Probably not. So, Misha, Mikhail, gets a dead line. If he thinks it's his last night of freedom, would he be prepared to go out in the dark to tell his friend directly? Possibly. I had to assume he would. And how would Dmitry react if he knew? Even if I told him the reasons he would still feel betrayed, I was sure. Would he hate me so much to tell the police about Petrov? Unlikely, I thought, but I had to make sure it didn't get that far. I knew what I had to do – and the thought turned me cold.

I waited a few moments before following Mikhail. He never looked back; it didn't occur to him that I might follow him. I made a note of where I was going, mentally leaving behind a trail of breadcrumbs. We wound down through various backstreets until we came to a small square, Bolshaya Square, with a fountain at its centre. I saw him enter a block of apartments and, stepping into the entrance of a building opposite, I watched. Sure enough, after a minute or so, I saw a light come on – third floor. I wondered whether his family were in. I saw him come to the window. I stepped back into the shadows. When I looked again, he was gone.

Chapter 25: The Wait

As the Black Maria swung off the road and forced its way through the crowds, Boris knew his current existence had come to an end. How odd it was to be chauffeured in a rich man's car while wearing his tuxedo and bowtie. Anyone looking in would assume *he* was the man with the power. Despite the coldness of the night, Boris felt himself drenched in sweat. The car paused at the sentry box and then passed through the imposing iron gates. Boris peered ahead and saw the outline of the building silhouetted against the night sky, every window alight. His heart, already fast, beat even faster. *This*, he knew, was the Lubyanka, the most feared building in Moscow, the NKVD's main interrogation centre. The name, by itself, was enough to reduce men to quivering wrecks. Of those who entered the Lubyanka, very few came out the front way. You either came out in a box or were herded out the back into a waiting van and hence to start the long journey to some godforsaken place. Boris clenched his eyes shut and felt the sting of the sweat.

The long dark corridor smelt of disinfectant and carbolic soap. Vladimir went in front, then Boris, and the two assistants behind. Boris tried to keep up, but his legs felt weak with fear. He followed as Vladimir swung sharply left and opened a door into a small room. Inside, behind a table, stood two non-uniformed officers. Boris noticed how they thrust their chins up and stuck out their chests at the sight of Vladimir.

'Another one for you,' said Vladimir to them, before turning on his heels and leaving, taking his henchmen with him.

The room was bare, just grey walls and ceiling, not even a photograph of Stalin to relieve the monotony. Boris looked at his two new hosts, both wearing suits as grey as the walls. The taller, balder of the two, sat down at the table and picked up a pen. 'Name?' he asked without looking up. Boris answered. He then gave his address and age. The man clicked his fingers and Boris realised he was pointing to a door he hadn't noticed, behind the desk. The second man opened the door, and Boris made his way forward, fearful of what lay beyond.

This room was even smaller. To one side, was a camera perched on a tripod. The second man positioned himself behind the camera and pointed to the wall opposite. Boris stood with his back against the wall and faced the lens. The flash temporarily filled the room with its furious white light, while the vision fluttered on his retina for a good few seconds. 'Profile,' said the man. Boris swivelled to the left and the flash went off again. 'Out.' Boris returned to the first room.

The first warden was waiting for him in the middle of the room. The man behind him pushed Boris forward. 'Remove your belt and your shoelaces,' said the first man. Without hesitating, Boris obeyed.

Boris stood and waited while the first warden made a few notes, resisting the urge to pull his trousers up, which he could feel sagging annoyingly low on his hips. He glanced at the second man, who immediately averted his gaze. He wanted to talk, to ask them what was going to happen to him, but he knew to keep his silence. These men were hard, thought Boris – not just in the physical sense, but within their hearts. They had no more compassion for him than a worker in an abattoir has for the condemned cow. He was, and forever more would be, an object in a harsh, unrelenting system.

'Empty your pockets,' said the first man. Boris did as he was told but all he had was a packet of cigarettes, a box of matches and a few notes concerning the play.

'Watch.'

Boris took his watch off and handed it to the warden. The man made a few more notes before saying, 'Take your clothes off.'

'What?' Had he heard correctly, why would they want him to remove his clothes? But the man remained silent, his face devoid of any expression beyond boredom. Boris removed his dinner jacket and looked around for a chair or somewhere to place it. Finding no obvious means, he dropped the jacket on the floor. He untied his bow tie and then removed his dress shirt. He was about to drop the shirt when the warden clicked his fingers and held out his hand. Boris passed him his shirt. The warden took it and passed it to his colleague who proceeded to pull off all the buttons. Boris watched for a few moments. 'Clothes,' bellowed the first man. Boris jumped. Reluctantly, he removed his shoes and unbuttoned his trousers. Finally, he was standing in only his underpants, his hands clasped delicately in front of him.

'And those.'

He could feel his lips trembling through fright and cold. He swallowed and, summoning the strength, slowly pulled down the white, thin material and carefully stepped out of them. The warden clicked his fingers again. Boris passed him his underpants. He stood shivering in front of them, his hands now firmly cupped over his genitals and watched as the second warden hacked at the underpants with a knife. Eventually, the man extracted the elastic and threw the pants back at Boris's feet.

The first man stepped up to him. Boris noticed something in his hand. He stepped back, his body tensing up in expectation of pain. 'Keep still, you bugger.' His eyes flickering, Boris drew a sharp intake of air and prepared himself. 'Open your mouth.' Boris's muscles relaxed for a moment as he realised the implement in the warden's hand was merely a torch. The tension returned as he opened his mouth. 'Wider.' The fingers went in like two dry grubs. 'Look up.' The torch flicked on and Boris gagged as he felt the fingers poke under his tongue, against the roof of his mouth and at the back of his throat, darting roughly from one to the other. Then he felt a fat finger hook around one cheek and pull violently to the side. The warden tilted his head and used the torch to peer inside. The process was repeated for the other cheek.

It wasn't so much the pain as the unexpectedness of what happened next that made Boris cry out. The warden grabbed his bottom eyelid and yanked it down. Blinded by the flash of light an inch away from his eye, Boris tensed up as he awaited the second inspection. The pain was momentary but it was the fear of sudden pain that made his shivering more intense.

'Head back.' Boris complied but the warden still pushed his head further back with a swift jab beneath the jaw. The torchlight shone up into his eyes and Boris realised his nostrils were being inspected. Then, the warden twisted Boris's head first one way and then the other, as the light shone into his ears. What, wondered Boris, could he possibly hide in his ears, his nose, his eyelids? There were more obvious places if he so wished to try, and the thought of it drove a stab of fear through his heart.

'Hold your penis and pull back... oh, you're a Jew boy.' Boris shuddered. He opened his mouth but then closed it again. There was no point in asking for any concessions, these men had done this a hundred times or more. What was another frightened victim to them? His penis felt light and useless in the cold moistness of his hand. The warden bent down and, with his torch, inspected Boris's appendage. Boris grimaced. 'Lift your penis up.' This was part of the game, the ritual of humiliation, the degradation of the individual for the benefit of the State. 'OK, let go.' He wouldn't cry, not in front of these men. There'd be worse to come, an even greater humiliation to come; he knew that now.

'Right, turn around, bend over, legs apart and touch your feet with your hands.'

This, thought Boris, was it. The humiliation was complete.

*

The cell was small – about four feet by nine. The floor was wet, there was no ventilation and the place stank of stale air, urine and filth. There was a wooden bench attached to the wall and nothing else. A bright light bulb hung from the ceiling. Boris shivered; it was cold. Without the buttons, his shirt hung open. He sat on the bench and wrapped his arms around himself. But then, the peephole in the door opened and a voice boomed at him. 'On your feet, you Jewish shit. Catch you

sitting down again, I'll come in and break your balls – got it?'
Boris rose to his feet, the ground squelching beneath his lace-
less shoes. His trousers and underpants were on the verge of
falling down and he had no choice but to grip them in place.

He heard a noise – a scream – coming from not far away.
It was a horrific sound. It was followed by another, and then
another. There were screams all right – loud, piercing screams.
Boris's heartbeat quickened. He could even hear the sound of
the lash between each shriek of pain. The lashes continued
without pause, and each scream was more terrifying than the
last until he wondered whether a human was really capable of
such a noise. Boris paced up and down the nine feet of his cell,
his hands clenched over his ears, his trousers and pants
flapping around his thighs, trying to block out the sound of
terror. But each time he removed his hands, the screams were
still there. After a while, the beatings stopped, and Boris heard
the angry, bestial shouts of a man, followed by the tormented,
pleading voice of a woman. This time, the sound from the
beating was not a lash but a dull, sickening thud. The
anguished noise that followed was much the same. How can a
man inflict so much pain on another person, let alone a
woman? Was this what he could expect?

He sat down on the wooden bench and immediately
sprung up again, remembering the guard's threat. His head
throbbed, he felt so damn exhausted, he so desperately needed
to sleep. Was it possible that only a few hours before he was
standing on stage next to Rosa? Was it just a few hours? It was
hard to tell, he had no idea what time it was, whether it was
day or night. All he knew was that this was Day One of his
new life. Ironically, the make-believe world of the play had
been his last contact with reality. Already, it seemed to belong
to another lifetime. Now, he was in a new reality and it was

still only the first day. The first day of what? Ten years, fifteen, twenty-five? Thousands and thousands of days.

He realised the screaming had stopped. Now, there was a heavy silence. He strained his ears for a sound, a hint of a voice. There was nothing. Only the sound of his own breathing, coming in short bursts. Unable to keep his eyes open, Boris felt the heaviness of his eyelids.

Why was he here? The question had, up to this point, hardly bothered him. It was enough to know he was here. Logic and reasoning barely came into it. What had Vladimir said? *The peculiarities of your case.* Peculiarities of your case – what exactly were those, he wondered? His father the rabbi? Or rather, his attachment to Rosa, daughter of an enemy of the people.

He swayed as his head suddenly felt unbearably heavy. In his mind's eye, he was in a forest, a pine forest, it still smelt of piss but at least the view was heavenly with the rays of sun slanting between the trees. It was the forest outside his parents' village, near Vyatka (he could never get used to its new name, Kirov). He's running and then diving behind a fallen tree and hiding, crouched against the damp forest floor. He peeks over the top of the trunk. In the distance, he sees his parents walking side by side. But nearer by, calling out his name, is his younger sister, giggling to herself. He ducks down again and listens as the sound of her feet comes closer. Then he leaps out from behind the fallen tree with a loud whooping noise, his arms outstretched. His sister jumps with surprise and then collapses in laughter. Boris laughs too. He can't stop laughing, his whole world echoes with laughter. His parents laugh, the forest laughs, the sun laughs. Why, even God laughs.

His head fell abruptly against his chest and Boris woke up with a start. His knees ached, the coldness seemed to have permeated his joints and the dampness of the floor had seeped through to his feet and legs. He wished he could turn off the glaring light bulb. He started shivering, his whole body shaking with cold. He needed a pee. How long had he been asleep? It could have been two minutes or two hours. Were they going to make him stand forever? His tiredness was overriding everything, even the hunger. When was the last time he ate? Just before the performance? And when was that? Twelve hours, twenty-four? How long had he been in the cell? He'd become bewildered by timelessness. He paced to the end of the cell and leaned against the dampness of the solid wall. The coldness of the stone soon passed through his jacket and shirt and he moved away from it. If only he knew what time it was. He looked down at the bench, the hard wooden slab now looked as inviting as a four-poster bed covered in large, soft blankets.

Boris thought of Rosa. He visualised her eyes; wide and dark, her sleek hair, her beautiful smile that melted him every time he saw it. The times he fell asleep with her image imprinted on his drifting thoughts, only to wake up to find she was still there. He had so wanted her but he'd placed her on too high a pedestal, to the point she'd become unobtainable, like a precious vase one can't bear to touch for fear of breaking it. He felt his heart constrict at the thought of her using his secret like a weapon. She knew what he felt about her and yet she still yielded it. *Yes, she told me you're a yid.* Had she really hated him so much for loving her?

Just then, the peephole swung open and an eye appeared. 'I need a pee,' said Boris quickly.

'Piss in the corner then,' came the answer before the eye disappeared again. What choice did he have, he had to relieve himself. Instinctively, he went to unbutton his fly, only to realise the buttons weren't there any more. He grimaced as he urinated in the corner furthest away from the bench. Pigs lived better than this.

And then, the screaming started again.

*

Boris reckoned he must have been there at least a whole day on his feet, cold, without food, water or sleep when they finally came to fetch him. He could feel his spirit draining away. The heavy iron door creaked open and a guard appeared at the opening. 'Out,' he'd said.

Boris walked out of the cell, his knees shaking and his calf muscles throbbing. He felt an inexplicable gratitude towards the guard for having come to him, for having opened the door. 'What time is it?' he asked.

'Dunno.'

'Please, tell me, what time is it?'

'Shut the hell up. Walk.'

The guard followed behind, jangling his keys loudly, as Boris made his way down a long, carpeted corridor. Occasionally, he noticed an enclave built into the wall. On each side, he passed numerous doors, all uniform grey, each with a number. The moment of euphoria had already passed, instead came the sense of dread – where was he being taken to, what lay ahead? Apart from the guard's keys, there was no sound, the carpet absorbing their footsteps. The silence was unnerving. There must have been hundreds of people in this building but all he could hear was this false silence. But then, in the distance, there was the faint sound of more jangling keys. The guard placed his hand on Boris's shoulder. 'Back here,' he said urgently, 'quickly.'

Boris turned around and went to where the guard was pointing. Boris realised the guard meant him to stand in an enclave. Boris stepped inside and looked at the guard. 'Face the wall,' he was told. He turned around, his vision taken up entirely by the grey stone. The second set of jangling keys passed by. After a few minutes, the guard instructed him to proceed. As Boris made his way down the corridor, he realised the purpose of that little charade: the jangling keys were to alert others of their approach. Obviously, they were so determined to isolate the prisoners from one another, they weren't even permitted to set eyes on each other.

The guard took Boris up a long flight of stairs and Boris noticed the nets spread across the banisters. No chance of suicide there, he thought. Then down another long corridor. Eventually, Boris was told to stop. They'd come to a grey door marked with the number '421'. The guard knocked, waited for permission, and then opened the door.

Boris walked into the heavily carpeted room and was almost blinded by the shaft of light that shone through the window. As his eyes adjusted to the brightness of the day, he saw a table with a man sitting behind it, his hands clasped on the table in front of him, his head tilted slightly to one side. He wore a small pair of glasses pressed against his large blue eyes. Behind him, stood the familiar sight of Vladimir, a supercilious grin on his face. And, more worryingly, to Boris's left, stood a bear of a man, with huge, squared shoulders and the neck of a bulldog, his hands behind his back. Boris thought he heard the sound of knuckles being cracked. The slam of the door closing behind him made him jump. He glanced around;

the guard had gone. He could feel the sweat running down his back. He turned back and faced the man behind the desk.

'Good afternoon,' said the man with a curling smile. 'I do apologise for having kept you waiting for so long. Let me introduce myself. My name is Rykov.'

Chapter 26: The Arrest

'Hello. Could I be put through to Firefox, please.'

'Who shall I say is calling?'

I cupped my hand over the mouthpiece. 'Oxford Blue.'

'Wait.'

I was phoning from the communal phone on the ground floor. This, in all the months I'd been working for Rykov, was the first time I'd rang him. Above the telephone was a sticker proclaiming, *Socialism – united we stand!* At the end of the corridor, a couple of children were sitting cross-legged on the floor playing a game of cards.

'Oxford Blue. Have you news for me?'

'Yes. It's about our latest subject. He plans to go on holiday – tonight.' One of the children screeched with delight scooping up a pile of cards.

'Is he indeed? With family?'

'Yes. The plane leaves within a couple of hours.'

The line went dead. Rykov had heard all he needed to hear. He knew Mikhail's address and, thanks to me, he knew he was at home, at least for now. United we stand.

I returned upstairs to the flat and thought about making something to eat. But I had no appetite, just a deep empty feeling of nothingness. Instead, I busied myself dusting the apartment – snow-white clean, as Petrov would have demanded. I could hear the baby next door crying. I realised how alone I was in the world – no Petrov, no Viktor. Dmitry seemed to be slipping away from me. And I knew I'd be seeing less and less of Rosa – she had little reason to visit now. Poor Rosa, I was concerned for her. She was already suffering from the angst of disillusionment and it was a bitter pill to swallow. The arrest of her friend, Boris, had been a severe blow. Worse still was the thought that her supposed "boyfriend" had more than an influencing hand in Boris's downfall. Rosa had already sworn not to have anything more to do with him. Frankly, I wasn't sure whether I was relieved or not. Undoubtedly, Vladimir was not the sort of man I wanted my niece to be associated with, but equally, who could be better placed than to protect her interests – and mine?

Why they had arrested Mamontov – I had not mentioned him to Rykov. But over the years we had all come to realise that logic had no place in the world we lived in. I wondered what Mikhail was doing at that precise moment. Putting his children to bed? Making love to his wife? Rykov wouldn't go himself – he left the dirty work to Vladimir. Vladimir with his large ears. Poor, poor Mikhail. I'd ruined a good man's life, torn apart a loving family. However much I dusted or listened to the sound of the baby, or thought of my loneliness, I could not dislodge the image of Mikhail from my mind, with his hat in his hands and his apocalyptic words. But it was him or Dmitry – or me. I couldn't stand it any longer – I had to make sure I was safe. Throwing on my coat, I hastened back out.

Thirty minutes later, I was back in Bolshaya Square. The light on the third floor was still on. A family at home. I had to wait almost an hour, pacing up and down, by which time I felt chilled to the bone. No one, except for a black cat with its illuminated eyes, took any notice of me. Even the cat got bored of me and slunk off. I thought of my brother. Of course, I hadn't wanted him to die but now that he was gone, I couldn't help but feel hugely relieved. But this sense of relief troubled me. His survival had held my life in check for too long. I felt as if I couldn't do a thing while Viktor sat there all day long, let alone plan anything. But now, just as my future was opening up, it was closing again. The warden in charge of the block had been to see me – I had two days to move out. Two days. In some ways, it was a relief. Since Viktor's death, my neighbours had become even more unbearable. They were knocking on my door at night to keep me awake, spoiling my cooking in the shared kitchen, and stealing my utensils. They wanted me out as quickly as possible; each one of them believing it was their turn next to be allocated an apartment. Although moving in with Dmitry was a possibility, the idea had somehow lost its appeal. In some ways, the idea of simply disappearing appealed to me. I even thought about the village – the place where I'd left Matrena behind. It was dangerous and uncertain but it was a means of getting rid of Rykov.

Finally, a Black Maria appeared in the square, as quiet and as sleek as the cat. It parked near the entrance to Mikhail's block of flats and two men emerged and stood for a moment within the rays of a streetlight. One of them, in his long mackintosh, was Vladimir. The other was smoking. Vladimir fished a piece of paper from his pocket. Having read it, he looked up at the windows, then nodded at his colleague. The men walked up the few steps to the main door. The second man threw his cigarette behind him into the road. I watched it fizzle in the dark, as the door swung back and forth. I had no need to stay any longer. I knew what was coming next.

Chapter 27: The Parade

The day had come. I found myself standing in a line down a corridor with another dozen women, all vaguely similar to me in terms of their age, height and colouring. We stood in silence, as ordered, and waited. I felt no sense of fear, no panic. Instead, I was resigned to whatever fate had decreed. My husband was dead; I had played my part. Whatever the justifications, I had sinned, and there was no escaping that. And everyone knew it was far better to be a criminal prisoner than a political one and the sentences, even for murder, were more lenient. I thought of Mikhail and shuddered to think of the degradations he would be suffering now based on no more than my say-so. There was a strange consolation that whatever punishment I may have to suffer was no more than I deserved. But I had lost Dmitry in the process. He had changed – I had changed him. I felt hollow inside – everything I had done had been for nothing. Petrov deserved better.

'Right, stand straight, look straight ahead. Do not say a word.' A uniformed policeman walked along the line, inspecting us. Satisfied with his motley crew of women, he took his place at the far end of the line and nodded at a colleague standing next to the door. In came the man. I couldn't see him, and didn't want to, nor need to, my eyes focused on the brick wall opposite me.

The process was conducted in total silence. He paused at each woman. I was, I think, seventh in line. He stopped in front of me and our eyes met momentarily. It was him all right. He was probably thinking exactly the same about me. But if he recognised me, which surely he must, he showed no sign of it. Instead, he carried on to the next woman and so on down the line, eventually reaching the policeman at the end, who escorted him out of the corridor.

Moments later, the policeman was back. 'OK, thank you, ladies, you may return to reception where you can collect your fee. Thank you for your time. The accused will come with me.'

And with that, the line dispersed. I followed my policeman and was taken up two flights of stairs and deposited in an office. On being shown in the dark room, I was greeted by Rykov sitting behind a desk. But this wasn't his usual office, or indeed his usual place of work. 'Maria Radekovna,' said Rykov. 'Take a seat.' This office was small, not so opulent as his own office, low ceilinged and featureless bar the usual portrait of Stalin hung on the wall.

He shuffled some papers, wrote a note on one, then laid everything to one side and fixed his eyes on me. His curling smile seemed exaggerated, it seemed as if a cartoon mouth had been cut out and pasted onto his mouth. 'He recognised you immediately,' he said. It came as no surprise but my hands still gripped the side of the chair. 'So, let me tell you where we are. Your husband was reported missing by his assistant at work. So we asked her in to identify the body. This helpful lady had the forethought to bring a photograph of your husband and you from her boss's desk at work. You OK?'

'Yes. Fine.' I hadn't realised Petrov had a photograph of us both on his desk at work. The thought stabbed me in the heart. Rykov must have noticed it in my eyes.

He continued. 'Using the photo, our country-bumpkin colleagues tracked down an old chap who gave the couple a lift from the train station late afternoon, last Wednesday. He recognised both of you. And now our helpful neighbour has identified you from the parade. So, tell me, what exactly happened last Wednesday at the dacha?'

I told him. I told him everything. There was no need to hold anything back. 'Yes, we killed him,' I said by way of conclusion. 'But it was an accident and if Dmitry hadn't hit him, he would have killed Dmitry.'

Rykov stretched his arms, his fingers interlocked. 'So it was more important to you to have your artist friend alive than your husband?'

'I wasn't really weighing it up in that way. I threw the water on the fire, hoping the diversion would calm them both down.'

'How resourceful,' he said, scribbling another note. 'They will want to question you, of course, and who knows, they might say accidents happen and let you go. But I doubt it. I've requested to be permitted to speak to you first – to help in my own investigations.'

'Should I be grateful?'

Rykov shot me a furious look. 'I don't really care how you feel. But as soon as I let you go, you will be under their jurisdiction. I want you to know, your friend, Dmitry, is finished but, worse for him, his is a political charge. The RAPA colleague you told us about has been most obliging in his information. Comrade Mamontov confessed everything. We now know all the heinous goings on within that little organisation. The so-called Russian Association of Proletariat

Artists turns out to have been nothing more than a cover for counter-revolutionary espionage. We thought as much but we simply needed the proof. And now, thanks to your friend's accommodating colleague, we have it. We owe Comrade Mamontov a great debt of gratitude. And now that we have your friend's old patron under our protection, Mikhail what's-his-name, we're expecting confirmation of Mamontov's confession any time now. You remember that fuss at the locomotive factory, of course. Yes? Well, old Comrade Trifonov may have got himself in a schoolboy fluster over a bit of cleavage but his suspicions were well-founded. We have much to thank him for as well. Well, before his own arrest that is. So, we need to speak to our friend Dmitry Kalinin. But first, we want him to receive his award. His Order of Lenin will make the case more high profile. Makes us look good,' he said with a wink.

'So, in short,' he continued, 'your friend is under arrest and you're wanted for questioning. You can go home tonight. Enjoy your last evening of freedom. Do not think of doing anything rash. Should you even as much as yawn, I will get to know about it. Tomorrow, you will be at the ceremony with Dmitry. I'm sure your presence will make Comrade Kalinin much more accommodating. We will be accompanied by his sister, Anna, isn't it? And your niece.'

'Rosa? Why drag Rosa into this?'

'I want to ensure your cooperation.'

'You're taking Anna and my niece as hostages?'

'If you want to put it that way. Also, as her guardian, I should warn you… your niece has not been as forthcoming as we might expect from our loyal youth. We had reason to question a doctor recently. An abortionist.'

'No, not Rosa.'

'No, let me finish. Not Rosa but a friend of hers, by the name of Ella. I forget her full name now. She, the dirty little whore, had an abortion. This disgusting, low-life doctor performed the termination, denying Stalin a future citizen for our glorious motherland. When we questioned the young lady in question she confessed your niece knew all about it. So why, I ask, did Rosa not denounce her friend to the Purge Commission for the foul, anti-Soviet bitch that she is? We also interviewed a young acquaintance of hers, a Jewish boy, and he certainly confirmed that Rosa is in need of some attention.'

Chapter 28: The Park

Dmitry and I were being swept along with the immense Labour Day crowds as it snaked forward towards Gorky Park. Draped across the broad gates at the park entrance was a huge banner inscribed with Stalin's dictum *Life has become better, life has become more cheerful.*

Once inside the gates, I felt myself in a different land — such was the joyous atmosphere, the shrieks and laughter, the smiling faces, the happy families. Never had I felt so at odds with the people around me. There were thousands of people, all determined to enjoy their public holiday of the Revolution and, as if to mark the occasion, the sun had, at last, come out. Surely, I thought, as my life had collapsed around me, Gorky Park had never been as brimming and alive as this.

Dmitry put his arm around me. Without looking at me, he whispered, 'Don't turn around, but have you noticed our friend?'

'Friend? What friend?'

'We're being followed. A little chap in a corduroy jacket and a peak cap. You hadn't noticed?'

'No–'

'Don't turn around.'

'Rykov did say.'

'There'll be others too; you can be sure of that.' He sighed. 'Seems odd, doesn't it? They're allowing us our last day of freedom. Like a condemned man's last meal. We might as well enjoy it. How are you feeling?'

'Strangely calm.'

'Yes, me too. I'm sorry, Maria,' he said, taking my hand. 'I suppose we never stood a chance, did we?'

'No, I'm sorry. I've thought of it often – there you were, leading a comfortable life, playing within the rules. Then I came in and destroyed it for you. It is me that should be saying sorry.'

'I would have fallen sooner or later.'

'And now there's nothing we can do. It's almost a relief.'

Dmitry smiled. He knew what I meant.

We still had an hour to kill before we were due to present ourselves at the *Stage of Soviet Artistic Endeavours* where Dmitry was due to receive his award.

Near the park entrance, in neat orderly rows, was a series of cardboard battleships and tanks. Further along, Dmitry and I stopped and watched a demonstration of community dancing. A conductor was holding forth at the microphone, behind him his band, instruments at the ready. In the partitioned square in front of him, stood a dozen or so pairs of young grinning girls, dressed in knee-length red and white dresses, with large red bows in their hair. The conductor described the steps of the dance as the girls demonstrated the moves. Then, they repeated the show but this time, accompanied by music. The demonstration completed, the conductor invited the watching public to join in. A few couples stepped forward but most, like ourselves, were too abashed to participate. But then, the young girls sprang in different directions into the crowd and started dragging protesting couples into the square. We were among the press-ganged and soon found ourselves facing each other, embarrassed grins fixed on our faces, hands intertwined and at the ready. 'This is ludicrous,' said Dmitry. 'What are we doing?' There must have been about twenty couples. The music started and the conductor delivered his instructions as we skipped to the left, circled around the edge of the square and back in towards the centre but not without a few wrong turns and several collisions with other, equally inept couples. Dmitry had, I found to my amusement, a poor sense of rhythm. At the end of five, rather excruciating minutes, he was bent double with laughter and apologising for his 'two left feet'.

We'd made our escape before the next dance routine was introduced. 'How can we laugh at a time like this?' I asked.

'The laughter of the condemned.'

We strolled idly through the park, feeling detached from everything around us, our eyes caught by various attractions and unusual sights. We saw food stands selling sausages, bacon rolls, melting cheeses and frothy beer. The State could provide when it needed to. Ahead of us, we could see the Ferris wheel and, nearer by, came the screams and shouts from the bowling alley. We stood and watched a parade of *Pathetic Enemies*. A brass band passed first, playing a tongue-in-cheek dirge followed by the procession consisting of costumed characters lampooning the enemies of the revolution. First came the religious cavalcade: angels, gods, priests, and the figure of Jesus. Then followed the capitalists – children dressed in suits and eyeglasses, with cushions stuffed down their fronts, and fat cigars between their lips. One child, much to our amusement, had added the delicious touch of smearing tomato sauce around his lips – the blood-sucking capitalist. Lastly, there were the similarly obese Tsarist nobles, counts and barons and their self-important generals.

Elsewhere, we came across a junior chess masterclass with pairs of well-dressed children sitting at small tables, listening to advice and concentrating on their next move, their parents hovering nearby. But perhaps the most popular spectacle was the parachute jumping. Queues of people waited patiently to climb the steps to the top of a stone tower which, according to the notice, was 130 feet high. From there, people jumped off and parachuted to the grass below. I urged Dmitry to have a go but by now, time was against us – at least, that was his excuse!

The *Stage of Soviet Artistic Endeavours* was comparatively small compared to everything else we'd seen in the park. The temporary platform was fitted with an arched-shaped wooden roof, across which was the usual banner proclaiming another of Stalin's phrases: *The artist is the engineer of the soul.* There could have been no more than about fifteen rows of chairs. At least, virtually every seat was taken and more people milling close by, watching a string quartet playing Stravinsky. Dmitry led the way as we skimmed past the standing audience and made our way to the back entrance of the large wooden structure.

'This is where we part,' said Dmitry.

'Good luck.'

'Thank you.'

I leant up to kiss him. He wrapped his arms around me, pulled me in and kissed me hard on the mouth. It was only then, as the noise of the park receded into the background, I realised how loud everything had been. The intensity of thousands upon thousands of people talking excitedly, of couples laughing, of children screeching, of music playing. But now, as we kissed, the noise diminished into a distant rumble, a muffled murmur far, far away. Dmitry pulled back and we gazed at each other. At the very last, I seemed to have won him back. But it was already too late.

Without another word, he turned and walked briskly up to the burly man standing guard at the stage door with a *No Entry* sign. Having had his invitation carefully scrutinised, he was allowed in. As he stepped through the door, I raised my hand to wave goodbye, but he didn't look back.

*

I wandered along the rows of seats, finding one near the front, while also keeping an eye out for our mysterious companion. The string quartet was still on stage, performing a piece I think was Mozart. The viola player was female, otherwise, the others were male and they were all young. My neighbour, a grey-haired man with a slightly pockmarked face, told me, during pauses, that they were students from the *Workers' Academy of Music*. The next piece, he told me, was by Shostakovich.

But by now, I was no longer able to concentrate. I could feel my stomach churning. I was feeling nervous for Dmitry, for me, for Anna and Rosa. I wondered where they were.

What was happening to our world? Here I was, listening to Shostakovich, a thousand smiling faces around me, but behind each smile, there was a tale to be told. Stalin's purge had, like the most contagious of diseases, permeated into every sphere of life. There was barely a soul who had not been affected in some way, however indirectly, by the shadow that had been cast over the whole Soviet Union. And now, in my bid for freedom, I had thrown myself under that same shadow.

287

Life with Petrov had been so suffocating but, as I was now beginning to realise, it had been stable. Like a cheap trickster with a tablecloth, I had whipped that stability from the table with one fell swoop. But instead of finding everything still neatly in its place, the entire edifice had come crashing down around me. I missed him in a strange way. I had wanted to be rid of him but not in that way; he didn't deserve such a fate. I had swapped suffocation and stability for love and uncertainty. It no longer seemed the attractive proposition it once did.

*

The quartet finished with a piece by Rimsky-Korsakov. The audience applauded while the musicians took their bows and exited. A few people around me rose, deciding to find another attraction to amuse themselves with, and left. No one took their places so that the seats were no more than three-quarters full. I peered around and then I saw him. Sitting about five rows behind me, the man in the corduroy jacket and peaked cap. Our eyes met for the briefest of moments.

After a couple of minutes, a short, plump man wearing the most obvious of wigs appeared on the stage, clutching a large piece of paper. He was wearing a shirt and tie but had removed his jacket. The darkened rings of sweat stood out around the underarms of his white shirt. The heavy bags under his eyes conflicted with the smoothness of his skin, making him look older than he was. He coughed into the microphone at the front of the stage, dug around in his trouser pocket and pulled out a pair of glasses. I leaned over towards my neighbour and asked who this man was. My neighbour looked at me with surprise — obviously, I was meant to know. This man, I was informed with unnecessary emphasis, was none other than Nikolai Kopelev, Deputy Commissar for the Arts Ministry.

With glasses fixed, the Commissar held up the sheet of paper and began to read.

His speech was similar to the one Mikhail had made at the unveiling of Dmitry's *The Workers' Rest*. He talked about how important it was for the arts to work in tandem with politics and industry to achieve the ultimate utopia, which we, as a nation of workers, were already well on the road towards achieving. How the fight must always go on, the need for ever greater vigilance to guard ourselves against the ever-present enemy within and the persistent enemy lurking on the outside – the decaying capitalist countries, the emergent Fascist serpent. The speech went on in this vein for an indeterminable amount of time, so that even my sycophant neighbour had trouble stifling the occasional yawn.

There was a disturbance to my left, somewhere behind me. 'Why can't they just sit down,' muttered my neighbour to his wife sitting on his right. I half-heartedly turned around and was only dimly aware of a small group of people shuffling along a row of seats. But then I craned my neck further and my heart somersaulted. I must have let out an audible cry for my neighbour asked if I was all right. Our mysterious companion had gone. Instead, sitting in his place, were Anna and Rosa, flanked by Rykov and Vladimir.

Chapter 29: The Ceremony

Vladimir's heart was also thumping. Once, not so long ago, he'd hoped to win Rosa's hand. Instead, here he was, holding her hostage. What a situation for a young man to find himself in. Next to Rosa, was her aunt's friend and, to Anna's right, his boss. Circumstances had forced him into situations that had totally alienated him from her. And those circumstances were all down to the Jew and that moron up there on the stage. Look at him, the floppy-haired lout, with his fellow artists, all standing in a line, waiting to receive their meaningless medals.

And where did that leave him with Rosa? Nowhere. They might as well be a hundred miles apart as to sitting next to one another. He tried to watch her from the corner of his eye. God, she was beautiful, with her jet-black hair and her wide dark eyes. He twisted his head a little more. Rosa noticed and turned to face him. He held her gaze, wondering how to say sorry with his eyes but, feeling ashamed by her disgusted glare, turned away. Vladimir still wasn't sure whether Rykov intended to arrest Rosa and Anna, or whether he was simply using them to bait Dmitry. Rykov was fond of using hostages as a means to break prisoners. Vladimir had seen it for himself; the most resolute of men, who could withstand any number of beatings, simply had to see a loved one within the walls of the Lubyanka and they'd cave in within seconds. Boris, on the other hand, proved to be the least resolute of prisoners, not that Vladimir expected anything different from the lily-white Jew. Barely had the thug's fist cracked his jaw and he was confessing. But until he knew what he was confessing to, they had to hit him some more. The rubber bat against the soles of the feet helped remind him. He was, he eventually remembered, a leading member of a Jewish counter-revolutionary conspiracy who planned to assassinate Stalin and overthrow the Party. Amazing what they learn at college these days.

The day was getting hotter and Vladimir wanted to remove his jacket but knew he couldn't. He slipped his hand into the inside pocket and felt for his revolver. Sometimes he shuddered at the degree of power that had been entrusted to him.

On the stage, Nikolai Kopelev was handing out the Order of Lenins to the artists, shaking each one enthusiastically by the hand. Dmitry was last in the line. Rosa and Anna clapped as each recipient received their medal. Vladimir followed suit but when Rykov leant forward and glared at him across the two women, he immediately stopped. Dmitry took his turn, bowing before the Deputy Commissar, shaking his hand and receiving his award. Vladimir glanced at Anna and noticed the defiant energy with which she clapped. Dmitry shook the Commissar's hand again and made his way to the stage exit.

Kopelev thanked the audience for their attention and then also hastily exited. Around them, people collected their bags and belongings and rose to their feet. Vladimir and the two women looked at Rykov.

Leaning forward to speak to Vladimir, Rykov said, 'Right, take the girl and arrest him. Keep her close and any fucking about, show him the Mauser. Me and Anna will wait here.'

Vladimir nodded. 'You'd better take my hand,' he said to Rosa. 'I'm sorry, Rosa, I really am,' he said quietly once they were out of Rykov's earshot, pushing their way through the drifting crowds.

'I suppose you're going to tell me none of this is your fault.'

'What else can I say? Do you think I want to do this?' Realising perhaps he was speaking too loudly, Vladimir glanced around nervously and lowered his voice. 'I used to lie awake at night, my head full of you, swimming with your image. I'd fall asleep dreaming about walking hand in hand with you. But never, never in my wildest dreams, did I ever think it had to be like this.'

'You never said.'

They were behind the wooden stage, near the door with the *No Entry* notice. Vladimir caught sight of the burly guard and pulled Rosa back a few yards. 'Rosa, look at me,' he said, lowering his voice still further. 'I can arrest a person at the drop of a hat – man, woman, young or old, I've got nerves of steel. I can stride into the best restaurants, buy the sort of luxuries that most don't even know exist, but when it came to you, I was like a simpering child.'

'Am I under arrest?'

'I don't know.'

'Vladimir, tell me.'

But before he could answer, the stage door swung open and there, in front of him, a few yards away, stood Dmitry. A second later, Maria appeared, running up to Dmitry and flinging her arms around him.

'Maria,' said Rosa under her breath.

Vladimir stepped forward but Rosa, still holding onto his hand, yanked him back. Vladimir glanced at her, his eyes narrowing with determination, and, for the briefest of moments, he was a policeman again. But Rosa's frightened expression stopped him in his tracks.

'Help them,' she mouthed, gripping his hands still tighter.

Vladimir stared at her, his mind whirling with impossibilities. He looked down at their hands, their fingers, moistened by sweat, locked around each other. He suddenly felt very heavy as his insides lurched within him. He realised he'd never really had to make a decision, at least not a *moral* one; the word had never concerned him. Things were decided for him, circumstances had always dictated the course of his life. If not circumstances, then Rykov. All his life, he had bathed in cruelty. It's what made him so damn good at his job. Cruelty and loyalty. And now Rosa was forcing him to question his twin gods. His mind flashed to a memory. He was at school with his older brother who'd been given a bloody nose. It took all of Vladimir's powers of persuasion to force his brother to say who the tormentor was. Once he'd got the name, Vladimir walked up to him and demanded an apology. The older, bigger boy laughed at him. He didn't laugh for long. That day was a turning point in the young Vladimir's life; the day he realised the depth of his courage and strength, strength that often bordered on cruelty, and he soon embraced it in its many brutal forms.

'Stay here,' he said to her. 'Don't move until I come back for you.' He strode up to Dmitry and Maria, still with their arms around each other, wrapped in their own world. It was

Dmitry who saw him first, his arms dropping, his expression heavy with foreboding. Maria followed his gaze and, on seeing Vladimir, her face whitened.

'So, you're not going to let me enjoy my moment of glory?' said Dmitry.

'I have Rosa with me.'

Maria looked across and saw her, standing only a few yards behind.

'You will follow me,' said Vladimir. 'Quickly, around the corner.' There was something in his voice that made Dmitry and Maria obey without hesitation. Once out of earshot from the burly man at the stage door and away from Rosa and from the milling passers-by, Vladimir spoke, his face peering up to Dmitry's, only inches away. 'I can give you an hour, no more.'

Dmitry and Maria exchanged glances. 'What do you mean?'

'Go to ground, leave Moscow, get the fuck out of here, I don't care, but if you don't act now, you won't get another chance.'

'Why are you doing this?' asked Dmitry.

'It doesn't matter. You will need to hit me.'

'What?'

'Hard.' Vladimir straightened and braced himself.

'You're asking me to hit you, a NKVD man? This is the sort of opportunity that most people would gladly pay for.'

'Get on with it,' said Vladimir through clenched teeth.

Dmitry hit him.

Vladimir staggered back. He put his hand to his mouth and looked at the trickle of blood on his fingers. 'Again.'

Dmitry obliged.

This time, Vladimir almost fell but managed to stay on his feet. Blood seeped from his nose. He smiled. 'That'll do,' he said. 'Now go.'

Dmitry made to step forward, to offer his thanks, thought Vladimir, to shake his hand. But Vladimir turned abruptly and walked back around the corner.

*

Vladimir found Rosa where he'd left her; she hadn't moved an inch. She was obviously expecting to see her aunt and Dmitry behind him. Her eyes widened with incredulity as she realised Vladimir was by himself. 'They got away from me,' he said, holding a handkerchief against his bleeding lip.

Rosa opened her mouth but then closed it again. Vladimir seized her hand and led the way back towards the front of the stage to where Rykov would be waiting for them. Vladimir was walking quickly and Rosa pulled his hand to slow him down.

Coming up next to him, she whispered, 'Thank you.' He looked at her from the corner of his eyes and winked.

Chapter 30: The Apartment

We had to wait for so long for a streetcar; it seemed as if all of Moscow was on the move and, because of the festival, there were fewer streetcars than normal. Every minute we waited, we felt as if our futures were slipping away from us. We couldn't speak, could barely look at each other. Vladimir told us we had one hour to make good our escape. One hour. How easily we can distort time. But however we distort it, we can't control it, it does exactly the opposite of what one wants. Just when one wants to stop it, the seconds and minutes hurtle by like an overflowing stream. This is how it felt now as I looked down the street and willed the streetcar to come. I would happily wait hours at a time for every future streetcar, just let this one come now. The warmth of the sun settled on our backs. One brief sentence had been enough to decide where we had to go. I did not have my internal passport on me. If we were to make our escape out of Moscow, then I had to have it. But then where? Dmitry thought he had a solution, an old acquaintance who owed him a favour. We could impose ourselves for a day or two before slipping quietly out of the city. Our apartments would soon be unsafe to return to. The all-pervading eyes of the NKVD would prevent our return. The future suddenly seemed a frightening place. How unpleasant it is not to have any idea where one might be in a week's time? A month?

A year? How would we start again? I knew the feeling; I'd been through it once before. That all-consuming existence when one lives from one day to another, never knowing what misfortune hung around the corner, never being able to trust anyone, too frightened to catch people in the eye for fear of betraying oneself. And still, there was no streetcar and no means to get back to my apartment. I wanted to be sick; I felt so weak. Dmitry took my hand, his palm wet with sweat. We were as powerless as each other. The image of two little girls flashed across my mind.

When finally, our streetcar approached, I almost wept with relief. We had already lost twenty minutes; the journey would take another twenty minutes, possibly as much as thirty. We were first in the queue but a number of people had gathered at the stop behind us. Dmitry and I stretched ourselves out, determined to keep our place. The streetcar drew up and it was packed. We had to fight and push our way on. People cursed us, tried to block our way, tried to push us off. I wanted to scream, I wanted to scratch my nails across their ugly, contorted faces. Together, with the force of people behind us, our determination provided the impetus and we clambered aboard. We clung on, almost falling out the back, as the streetcar speeded its way back towards the city centre.

*

We ran up the stairs to my apartment. It was only as I was unlocking the apartment door, I realised how empty the block was. Everyone was out, enjoying the sun, enjoying the public holiday. Either that, or they were waiting for a streetcar. I looked at my watch. It had taken us almost an hour from leaving Vladimir to getting back. How precise was he being when he said an hour? Would they know to come here? I imagined the Black Maria speeding through the city, screeching to a halt in front of Dmitry's block. I could see them breaking in his door and then, on finding it empty, returning to the car.

'Where is it?' asked Dmitry.

'Here, in the sideboard.' I pulled open the drawer where Petrov and I kept all our official documents – work permits, ration books, his Party membership card, Trade Union card, various passes – and our internal passports.

'Well?'

'I – I can't see it.'

'What do you mean, you can't see it?'

My stomach lurched as I realised my passport wasn't there. Desperately, I rummaged through all the sheaves of paper, hastily discarding them and throwing them onto the floor. I felt my strength draining from me with every passing second. I turned to him, tears brimming, 'It's not here.' I felt as if I was pronouncing my own death sentence.

'For Christ's sake. Where else then? What about the other drawers?'

I pulled the next drawer open with such haste, it fell to the floor, spilling its contents. Dmitry fell to his knees, scattering pieces of paper in his desperate search for the familiar blue booklet. I checked the last drawer, filled with letters and Petrov's work-related reports, minutes, orders and memorandum. I was exhausted, my head throbbed and my eyes were clouding over with tears and panic. I wanted to curl up in a ball, close my eyes and pretend I wasn't living this nightmare.

'Try the bedroom,' urged Dmitry.

I straightened up, panting, debilitated. I feared I was about to faint. 'It won't be there,' I said breathlessly.

'Well, it's got to be somewhere,' shouted Dmitry. 'Think, Maria, for the love of God, think.'

'I'm trying, but, but… Petrov's hidden it.' I noticed I'd referred to him in the present tense.

I saw the colour drain from Dmitry's cheeks. 'In that case, we're done for.'

'No, wait. The mattress.' And yes, sure enough, there it was, beneath the mattress.

'Oh, thank the Lord,' said Dmitry.

It was at that point, we heard the pounding at the door.

*

Moments later, I found myself grappling with the window lock. My inner self seemed to have already vacated my body and to be looking down, watching myself, watching as Dmitry pulled me back from the window by my waist, my arms flailing, my reddened face contorted with fear and anger. His words came to me through a clouded haze, words that on the surface sounded like calm reassurance but in reality, could not hide his own terror. We were four floors up, he said urgently, if I jumped, I'd be jumping to my death. Did I care? I spat back through clenched teeth.

My inner self reconnected with my outer shell at the moment the door burst open and there, in front of us, stood four breathless people, which, in such a small room, constituted a small crowd. It took a few moments for my glazed eyes to adjust. Behind Rykov and Vladimir stood Rosa and a dishevelled-looking Anna.

Anna had aged and seemed to be ageing as I looked at her.

'Good afternoon, comrades,' said Rykov, removing his hat politely. 'How nice to make your acquaintance again, Maria Radekovna.' Vladimir had been true to his word and given us an hour, almost to the minute. I tried to catch his eye but he was purposely avoiding me, twisting his gaze this way and that, anywhere but look at either me or Dmitry. Somehow, I felt embarrassed; embarrassed that having been given the gift of the hour, we had failed him. But unlike him and his boss, we did not have the luxury of a car. Rosa lurked behind him, a sweep of her black hair falling over her eyes. How beautiful she looked, but so helpless.

With his hands in the pockets of his light knee-length coat, Rykov made a point of circling around Dmitry as Dmitry stood as a statue in the middle of the living room. 'So, this is the famous Dmitry Kalinin, recipient of the Order of Lenin for contribution to the advancement of socialist art and socialist realism, and pivotal member of the Russian Association of Proletariat Artists, and, no less, the man who has the

299

nerve to hit an officer of the NKVD. That takes some doing. I salute you, Comrade Kalinin. I apologise for having dragged your sister here, and Maria, for bringing Rosa. Although you and I, young lady,' he said, addressing Rosa, 'have our own issues to discuss.'

Rosa whitened, stepping back against the front door. Anna stood by her side and took her hand. The two women had never met before today but it's strange, I thought, how circumstances can bond.

Rykov continued, still orbiting his prey. 'And how sad it is that the association is no more. The Moscow East Division, certainly, is a thing of the past. Such an austere association, who'd have thought it would turn out to be just a front.' He noticed Dmitry's eyebrows rise. 'Yes, Comrade Kalinin, you heard me correctly: a front for anti-Soviet agitation and propaganda. Your colleague Comrade Mamontov spilt the beans, and then your old pal, Mikhail, is, as we speak, confirming it all. Couldn't wait to tell us all the sickening, traitorous details.'

'Bullshit,' snarled Dmitry. My heart stopped a moment at his effrontery.

'Well, you would say that, wouldn't you? But it's amazing how many times your name cropped up. Again and again, isn't that right, Comrade Vladimir?'

Vladimir didn't answer, assuming, as I had done, it was a rhetorical question. 'I said isn't that right, Comrade Vladimir?'

'Yes – yes, boss.' I realised at that moment that he was as nervous as the rest of us; only Rykov was enjoying himself, savouring the moment of capture.

Rykov then circled around me; like the Devil on my back. 'And you, Maria Radekovna. How empty your block is today. Think how disappointed your neighbours will be when they realise what excitement they've missed. I saw your husband only a few days ago, did you know that? No, of course not, why should you? He was lying on the cold slab, his body as white as snow, the poor sod.' Rykov then stopped and faced us. 'What a lot of questions I have for you both.'

'We have nothing to say,' said Dmitry.

What happened next, happened so quickly, I didn't realise until later how much I screamed. Rykov whipped his revolver from his coat pocket and smashed it, sideways on, against Dmitry's face. Dmitry fell back, toppling into me, using the sideboard to maintain his balance. Anna and Rosa collapsed into each other's arms for support; Vladimir stepped forward as if backing up his boss. 'You filthy dog, you treacherous bastard,' bawled Rykov, the revolver pointing at Dmitry's chest. 'You think you can stand up to me, but when I'm finished with you, you'll be begging for death to come release you.' Suddenly, he swung around to face Anna and Rosa, and fired. Anna and Rosa screamed as they dropped to the floor. Plaster from the wall fell about them, splattering their hair. Dmitry made to move but Vladimir had also produced his gun and had Dmitry within his sights.

'Next time,' said Rykov breathlessly, 'next time I'll aim for her heart. Five seconds. I give you five seconds to get your ass out that door.' Stepping back, he lifted the revolver and aimed it directly at Rosa. 'One…'

Rosa lay huddled on the floor, whimpering, Anna's arms wrapped around her, a tangle of legs spreading out from beneath them, their faces pressed against each other, their tears mingling. I glanced at Dmitry, his eyes fixed on Rykov, his mouth gaping open.

'Two…' My life had lurched to this moment. My name is Matrena. I cross myself, not once, but twice. Once for each child. The girls suffered no pain, no distress – an easy transition from this miserable life to the next, without a sound, not even a whimper. Poor, poor pathetic girls, they never felt a thing; they never knew.

'Three…' The wind whistles outside, the light fading, slowly drowning the inside in darkness. The world feels dead, our existence forgotten. I'd expected my heart to be pounding, instead, it had slowed down to such an extent, I wondered whether it was beating at all. I can't remember how they looked; my mind, in an effort to protect itself, has conveniently forgotten the details. But how heavy were those hessian sacks with their dismal contents as I dragged them outside and into the woods. Viktor had dug a hole for me. He was weak but it was May, the soil was soft. He never said a word or asked me anything. Alone, I lowered them into the grave, kneeled, and said a prayer. I prayed that God might realise that by denying them their existence, I had saved them from further torment. They had known nothing but misery in their short, pathetic lives. May He forgive me.

'Four...' I didn't cry for months. Survival and self-preservation never allowed me the luxury of tears. It was only when I'd become ensconced into my new identity, when I was alone for the first time within the warmth and safety of these four solid walls; when, for the first time, I could look into a mirror and not expect a shadow behind me; when I'd finally stopped running and hiding by turn – that was when I cried. And how I cried.

'Five...'

I am crying now and I don't think I shall ever stop.

'Put the gun down.' The words, so quietly spoken, felt as though they'd seeped through the floorboards.

'What the...' Rykov realised and looked incredulously at his assistant. Vladimir had swung his gun around from pointing at Dmitry and was pointing it now at his superior.

Rosa sat up a little, her face soaked, her eyes widening. 'Vladimir?' she said in a bewildered whisper.

Vladimir kept his eyes firmly on Rykov, his hand shaking slightly. 'I said put your gun down, boss.'

The look of incredulity on Rykov's face vanished in an instant as he burst out laughing, 'You stupid... stupid sod,' he said between bouts of laughter. 'What the...'

Dmitry, standing on the balls of his feet, glanced from one to the other, not sure how to react.

Rykov still had his gun pointing at Rosa. 'I'll kill her, then what would you do? Kill me? You wouldn't have the guts, you wouldn't...' He trailed off, realising that he'd tutored the boy in his own image, that perhaps his young shadow was indeed worthy of having the guts. His arm, still pointing his gun towards Rosa, slackened a fraction as he tried a different tact, 'And how do you think you'd get away with it? You can't kill me and sweep my existence under the carpet. Vladimir, we haven't come this far together for it to end like this. Vladimir? Vladimir…'

Rykov's arm stiffened. Vladimir saw it. A gun fired. I screamed as the shot rang out and echoed and bounced around the four walls.

Vladimir almost fainted at the realisation of what he'd done. Rykov lay in a heap, his hands clutching his stomach, unable to prevent the blood gushing through his fingers, his revolver inches away. How quickly the blood came, drenching his shirt, forming a pool on the floor. His legs shook violently, his eyes rolled to the back of his back.

Huddled in the corner, near the front door, Rosa and Anna were crying hysterically, clutching each other for support while Dmitry and Vladimir stood over Rykov watching Rykov's fingers clasp and unclasp. I'd backed myself against the window, my hands shielding my eyes from the scene before me.

Through my fingers, I saw Dmitry kick the gun away from Rykov's reach. 'He's not dead,' I heard him say to Vladimir.

Vladimir nodded. 'What do we do?'

'Well, we can't leave him here.'

'And we can't take him anywhere.'

The conclusion, horrendous although it was, was obvious. We all knew it. Rosa pulled herself away from Anna's arms and unsteadily rose to her feet. 'We have to take him to a hospital.'

Vladimir shook his head. 'No, he won't live that long.'

'Couldn't we just leave him?' asked Anna.

'Too risky,' said Vladimir. He glanced down at his hand and looked at his revolver as if surprised to find it there. He took a step towards the crumpled figure of Rykov and knelt down next to him.

'Vladimir?' said Rosa. 'What – what are you doing?'

He placed the end of the gun against Rykov's temple, the perspiration glistening on his brow. He took a deep breath, braced himself and pushed the muzzle hard against the skin.

Anna covered her face with her hands. Dmitry put his arm around Rosa's shoulder, and Rosa buried her head into his chest. Only I watched intently, barely daring to breathe.

I could see the shaking in Vladimir's hand. With each passing second, as Rykov's laboured breathing became more audible, Vladimir's shaking got worse. Then, he suddenly rose to his feet and swung around with frustration, his eyes filled with tears. The moment had gone; nothing would make it come back. But the problem still persisted.

I crossed myself – just the once. Vladimir was facing me as I approached. I held out my hand but it took him a few seconds to realise what I meant. He passed me the revolver. How heavy it felt, and so large in the smallness of my hand.

Dmitry stepped towards me. 'No, Maria.'

I stared into him. How far we'd come in such little time. I was no longer even convinced whether it'd been the right thing to do. But now it was done and it was too late to question it. His mind, I am sure, was drifting through the same territory. He stepped aside.

Following Vladimir's example, I placed the muzzle against Rykov's temple. I couldn't afford to hesitate. For a moment, I thought I saw Rykov open his eyes.

But only for a moment.

Epilogue

Four deaths. But history, as they say, is a foreign land, and so, who was I to sit in judgement?

Maria looked at her watch. 'Oh dear, it is dark, you must be hungry and tired, listening all day to my horrible story.'

'No, no, not at all,' said Caroline.

'Yes, but I must eat. Irina leaves me something, but it is not enough for us all.'

'Don't worry,' I said. 'We'll go now. But can you just tell us, what did you do with the… the body?'

'Dmitry and Vladimir hid it in the locked wardrobe in the bedroom and Anna and Rosa wiped away the evidence – that much I can remember. But the details escape me. Did I cry, did I curl up into a ball, did I pray? I don't know. All I see is the gun on the floorboards, the light from the window reflecting in its barrel.

'You know, it was many days before they found him. And when they did, hundreds of people were arrested. In the end, they find their scapegoat and he was found guilty and shot. But still, hundreds of others died too. But we five – Anna, Rosa, Vladimir, Dmitry and I, we all escaped. But as five people, we never saw each other together again. We all became new people with new histories. Vladimir and Rosa disappeared in one direction, Dmitry and I in another. Only Anna remained here in Moscow.

'Vladimir and Rosa, I heard many years later, were married but it was not to last. What happened to Vladimir, I do not know. Rosa married again in 1946 but that too wasn't to last. After the war, the suspicions and paranoia of the pre-war came back, and she was arrested and sentenced to ten years. Whether she ever survived the Gulag, I shall never know.'

'Poor Rosa.'

'Yes, born in the year of the Revolution. Only Anna found any peace. She re-assembled the pieces of her life and married Mikhail in 1940.'

'Mikhail? Dmitry's patron?'

'Yes. He was lucky. He served only five years in the gulag. When he came back, his wife and children had disappeared. Together, he and Anna lived the life of good proletariats – humble and cautious but content. Sometimes, she wrote to Dmitry and me. Her last letter came in 1953, the year of Stalin's death. She told me of Rosa's arrest and exile and it made me feel sad – it was like she was writing about a passing friend. She and Mikhail were still living happily together.'

'What happened to Dmitry and you?'

'Dmitry and I moved from town to town, trying to live – doing work where we could find it, for shelter and food. We got married. We had one child – a son. Dmitry's dream was to start painting again. But in 1941, on the eve of the war, he worked in a munitions factory. And with the war, he was enlisted into the army.' She paused for a few moments and her fingers played with the kingfisher brooch on her cardigan. 'Dmitry, your grandfather, Richard, was killed in the streets of Stalingrad in forty-three.'

Caroline and I exchanged glances.

My grandmother continued. 'Not long ago, I paint a copy of *The Workers' Rest*. The local gallery even exhibited it for me. Just think how proud Dmitry would have been! A collector saw it and returned the following day with the original. In a moment of sentimentalism, she present me with Dmitry's painting – as a gift. That is why you see it now, after all these years.' I followed her eyes and gazed at the painting. 'Look at her. I know her so well but behind her mask, she is no more than a stranger. But I am still here and the Soviet Union is dead. Two revolutions, two turns of a gigantic wheel...' she said something in Russian, her words trailing off.

Caroline leant forward and took her hand and spoke to her in her native tongue.

'You must hate me now,' said Maria, fishing in her cardigan pocket for her handkerchief. 'All those things, those dreadful things…'

'No,' whispered Caroline, 'of course not.'

'No?'

'Caroline's right – what else could you have done? We can't imagine what it was like but we understand, Grandma…'

'*Grandma?* She looked at me through a haze of tears and gulped. 'You called me… thank you, thank you, Richard.'

*

Twenty minutes later, Caroline and I were outside the apartment block, standing in the snow, breathing in the cold night air. Beyond the faint rumble of traffic, everything seemed so quiet. We were hungry and the numbing wind battered our faces but we couldn't move. It was as if we needed time to acclimatise to the present before throwing ourselves into the frenzy of the Moscow metro system. I looked up to the block looming above us in the dark and my eyes scanned the lights on the fourth floor. Somewhere, behind one of those windows, sat my grandmother. I imagined her sitting in her leather armchair, with a tray on her knee, eating the supper left by Irina, watching the television news. In a few hours time, we were due to be on the night train to St Petersburg. I didn't have any choice. I so very much wanted to go back up, to see her one last time, to hear my name pronounced as *Rich-hard*, to kiss her goodbye again. The thought of leaving her behind, of leaving this wonderful city, bit into me. She was part of me – the only family I had left. For so long, I'd lived without the comfort of family. I was strong, independent, totally self-reliant. But not any more. Forty-eight hours and everything was turned on its head. Having found her, I didn't want to leave, I didn't want to be alone any more. The thought of being back in London with her so far away, with only the sullen Irina for company, was unbearable. I imagined buying her Christmas presents and writing the name *Grandma* on the tag. I wanted to do her shopping for her, to pop in unannounced – just to see if she was okay.

'Come on, Richard, I'm cold.'

'Caroline, what were you and Grandma saying to each other in Russian?' I surprised myself with how easy it was to say *Grandma*.

She pulled the earflaps of her hat tighter against her face. 'When?'

'Earlier on this morning, when you both laughed. I asked you what you were saying and you said it was a secret.'

'Oh, that.' She smiled.

'Well?'

'Don't worry, I'll tell you later.' She started walking away from me.

'No. Tell me now.' I watched her as she stopped beneath the glow of a street lamp and turned around, her gloved hands clutching at her scarf beneath her chin, her shadow reaching towards me. The shaft of light, illuminating the falling snow, fell at an angle across her face.

'Richard, do you know what day it is?'

'February twenty-ninth, why?'

'Exactly, a leap year – Maria reminded me. But I told her I was going to already – tonight, on the train.'

As I stepped towards her, I thought I saw a figure at one of the many windows on the fourth floor. 'Going to do what already?'

She pulled me closer and kissed me, our cold faces touching, our numbed lips thawing under the warmth of our contact. 'Richard,' she whispered, 'will you marry me?'

*

Maria sat at the window and watched them. She smiled as they embraced and kissed, their shadows stretching across the fresh snow. She watched them walk slowly away. For a moment, she thought she saw Richard glance up. She waved but he didn't see her. Her hand remained suspended in the air as they turned the corner of the neighbouring block. And then they were gone.

She rose to her feet and, using the table for support, hauled herself back into her armchair. She sat down with a sigh. Everything was so much effort. It was six o'clock and she felt exhausted. Reliving those events had drained her. She ought to go through to the kitchen and put Irina's meal into the microwave. But not yet.

How different Richard was from his father; so much kinder, more compassionate. She'd always wanted to tell her son the story of her life but he was part of that Russian generation who didn't want to know. Stalin was history and he, like so many others, was too busy living the present Soviet life without having to confront the previous. She'd feared that Richard would be much the same. But he wasn't. She'd known that within seconds of him stepping into the apartment. Richard, she knew, would listen. Their presence still filled the room, she could smell them, almost touch them. It seemed strange to think they were still within walking distance of her apartment, but they were walking away. And each step would take them further away from her. She was alone again.

For sixty years she'd waited to tell someone there once lived two small girls. Two small girls who, occasionally, still greeted her in the mornings as her dreams faded; two smiling faces who still called her *Mama*. The longing never went away and, after all this time, she still thought of them every day. She used to try and imagine how they'd be as the years passed, from little girls to young women. But now, she preferred simply to remember them as they were, forever caught in that whisker of time when the name Stalin was as unreal and ethereal as God Himself. God, she missed them, still.

And she missed him, too. Dmitry's painting stared at her. It no longer gave her pleasure; it was all too long ago. Perhaps, she'd get Irina to post it to Richard in London. It could be a wedding present. Poor Dmitry, she often wondered how much he'd really loved her. How much easier life would have been for him had they never met. She reached out to the table and picked up the wooden bear. She ran her fingers along the carved contours of its body and pressed her finger gently against the sharpness of the teeth. She flipped open the lid. The empty bottle was still inside, and within the bottle, there was still a slight hint of the perfume that had, for so many years, remained trapped inside. She smiled as the faint smell brought back the memory:

'What a funny little bear.'

'Funny? Looks quite vicious to me. Grrl!'

'That sounds more like a lion.'

'Either way, the perfume is to remind you how much I love you.'

'And the bear…?'

'The bear? Well, he's there to protect you, of course – forever.'

The perfume had long since gone but the bear… Well, it was still there; still protecting her.

THE END

Novels by **R.P.G. Colley:**

Love and War Series:
The Lost Daughter
The White Venus
Song of Sorrow
The Woman on the Train
The Black Maria
My Brother the Enemy
Anastasia
Elena
The Mist Before Our Eyes
The Darkness We Leave Behind

The Searight Saga:
This Time Tomorrow
The Unforgiving Sea
The Red Oak

The Tales of Little Leaf
Eleven Days in June
Winter in July
Departure in September

**The DI Benedict Paige Crime Series
by JOSHUA BLACK**
And Then She Came Back
The Poison in His Veins
Requiem for a Whistleblower
The Forget-Me-Not Killer
The Canal Boat Killer
A Senseless Killing

https://rupertcolley.com